Praise for Vivi Andrews's
Finder's Keeper

"Andrews has produced something truly special with her latest Karmic Consultants novel. Deftly blending humor with heartfelt insight into her unconventional characters, this opposites-attract comedy pairs two characters...whose honesty and compatibility are touching and thoroughly captivating."

~ *RT Book Reviews*

"A fun, fast romance with appealing characters, great dialog, and loads of appeal."

~ *Library Journal*

"*Finder's Keeper* [...] has great characters you can care about. Give it a try. You'll be glad you did."

~ *Literary Nymphs*

Look for these titles by
Vivi Andrews

Now Available:

Finder's Keeper

Vivi Andrews

To Sally,
So great to see you
again! Happy reading!

Vivi Andrews

(you were at my
very 1st conference-
I owe it all to
you)

SAMHAIN
PUBLISHING

Samhain Publishing, Ltd.
11821 Mason Montgomery Road, 4B
Cincinnati, OH 45249
www.samhainpublishing.com

Editing by Christa Desir
Cover by Angela Waters

First Samhain Publishing, Ltd. electronic publication: November 2012
First Samhain Publishing, Ltd. print publication: October 2013

Dedication

For my sister, the scientist.

Author's Note

All the Karmic Consultants books can be read as stand alone stories, but within the timeline of the series *Finder's Keeper* begins one month prior to *The Sexorcist*.

Chapter One

Speed-Dating: It's a Marathon, Not a Sprint

"I have three weeks left to fall in love."

Mia Corregiani, Ph.D, groaned as her date blanched, a look of blind panic entering his eyes. Apparently she wasn't supposed to be honest when the man sliding into the seat opposite her flashed a toothy grin and asked, *So Mia, why speed-dating?*

Her other possible response—explaining the efficiency of testing her pheromone compatibility with twenty potential mates in a single evening, with the assurance that each of those potential mates had been vetted by the agency as educated, of appropriate breeding age and monetary stability, and currently single matrimonial status—had seemed the less romantic choice, but evidently confessing you were on a clock to fall in love was a first date faux pas.

God, why had she let her sister talk her into this?

Mia tightened her grip on her pen and considered the empiric criteria for declaring an evening the Worst First Date since the Big Bang. Did speed-dating count as one date or twenty? Was the effect taken cumulatively or did each five-minute encounter qualify as its own independent assault against humanity?

Or perhaps there was a world record for the fastest dating failure. Mia glanced at her watch. Under sixty seconds. That had to be a personal best.

Bachelor Number Twelve was still sputtering, his face flushing to an alarming purple color. "I... Are you... I mean... Do you have..."

Fabulous. She'd paralyzed his frontal lobe. Mia frowned. "I need more words to understand your meaning."

"Cancer?" Twelve said at a near-yelp.

"Oh no. I'm in perfect health. Excellent condition to breed."

A choked noise erupted from Twelve's throat and Mia flinched. Crap, why had she said that? She may not be socially savvy—okay, yes, when it came to social interaction she was a human wrecking ball—but she knew better than to bring up reproduction in the first five minutes.

She tried again. "It's my family."

"Oh!" Twelve beamed, visibly relieved, and patted her hand in a way that reminded Mia of her mother's priest, Father Bob. "My folks have been on my back too. 'Get back on the horse, Ben. Not every woman is a demented, vampiric bitch determined to take half of everything you own'."

Oooh-kay. Mia mentally dropped Twelve into the My-Ex-Sucked-Out-My-Will-To-Live box along with Bachelors Three, Seven and Eight.

"It isn't that." Well, not *just* that. She toyed with the stem of her wine glass. How to explain the depth of delusion present in her family tree without convincing him the genetic predisposition toward fantasy made her an unacceptable candidate for merging their DNA? She flicked a glance at his nametag. *Hi, my name is Ben. Ask me about Property Zoning!* That was promising. Concrete, logical work. Mia experienced a hopeful spark at the prospect of a kindred analytical spirit.

Please, let him get it. "Ben, do you believe in magic?"

"I... Sure. I guess."

His face twisted with confusion. Like he couldn't quite figure out if she was flirting or accusing him of being a closet magician. Perhaps she shouldn't have flung the question at him like it was weaponized, but this particular topic always made her cool rationality boil into frustration.

"What about soulmates?" she persisted, lifting her glass for a sip of Chardonnay in the hopes that it would soften her unintentionally hard tone.

"Um..." His eyes shuttled rapidly back and forth, the shoulders of his navy blazer lifting toward his ears as he tensed.

"I don't," she informed him flatly and watched his muscles unclench as she handed him the correct answer.

Ben apparently didn't like being quizzed, even about his own opinions. Since interrogation was Mia's primary form of communication, that didn't bode well for his being the loins to spawn her unborn children, but she wouldn't think about that right now. Right now she was determined to salvage this date before the bell rang in three minutes. She could do this. She could conquer speed-dating. Perhaps if she just explained...

"My family is superstitious. They believe in magic, soulmates, signs, horoscopes. The whole shebang."

"That's nice."

"Not really."

Twelve flinched, shrinking into his blazer like a turtle in his shell. Mia sighed.

"We have a family legend."

Ben held his tongue, apparently having learned his lesson about providing color commentary.

"One hundred and forty-odd years ago, my great-great-grandfather bought a gold pocket watch from a gypsy woman. She told him within the next year it would bring him his soulmate and if he gave her the watch, their love would last a lifetime." Her mother told it as *for all eternity*, but Mia didn't like the imprecision of hyperbole. "He met my great-great-grandma the next week. Married her within twenty-four hours of laying eyes on her. Gave her the watch and started popping out kids."

"Mm," Twelve murmured.

She tapped a bitten-down nail against the wine glass. "His brother was also lonely, so Grampa Gianni lent him the watch. He found love and passed it on to a cousin, who passed it back to my great-great-grandma's sister and so on, until the next generation. Each owner had it for one year, found the love of their life and lived happily ever after."

Mia drained her wine to help the story flow. "For four generations, the legend of the pocket watch grew in our family. It was no longer just responsible for finding true love, it was the reason we've never had a single divorce. The reason babies are born healthy. The reason our men came home safely from World War II and Vietnam. For the year each member of my family was custodian of the watch, they were responsible for everyone's happiness. By finding their own love, they ensured the chain continued unbroken and reaffirmed the magic of the watch. It's our goddamn sacred duty to fall in love in that twelve-month period."

Ben was nodding now, caught up in the story, and she realized in a vague, distant way that he *was* a rather attractive man. Pleasant enough to look at. No visible genetic abnormalities he would pass on to their offspring. If he hadn't seemed more than a little afraid of her, she might have checked the little yes box next to his number on her form.

"Obviously, I don't believe in this stuff. I'm a scientist."

Ben kept nodding, his eyes flicking to the *Hi, My name is Dr. Mia. Ask me about Astronomy!* nametag on her blouse. "Astronomy is fascinating."

"It is, but I'm a neurobiologist." The nametag was what she got for letting her little sister sign her up for this event. Gina loved to tell people Mia was a rocket scientist. *Neurobiologist* apparently lacked the same cachet, for all that it had the benefit of accuracy. Gina called them lies of simplification. She said "rocket scientist" was just a brainy nerd and people didn't really care about the finer points of the scientific distinctions.

All Mia saw was the factual sloppiness. "I have a rudimentary understanding of astronomy, but that's not the point."

"I'm a Taurus."

Dear God, not another one. If nothing else, the nametag misprint had convinced her that the number of men who knew the difference between astronomy and astrology was shockingly low. She wept for the state of science education. "Good for you.

The point is I don't believe in magic. Everyone in my family knows I don't believe in this crap, but if I'm the one to break the chain, they'll hold me responsible for everything that goes wrong in my family for the rest of eternity." Sometimes hyperbole was just called for.

"It's still a nice story."

"It isn't just a story. It's a belief system." An unshakable one. And God knew Mia had tried to shake it with logic a thousand times over the years. Now she was running out of time. "Eleven months and six days ago, on the anniversary of the marriage of great-great-grandpa Gianni and great-great-grandma Anna Maria, my parents gave me the watch. In short: I have three weeks left to fall in love."

Twelve's face, which had recovered a nice flesh color, veered toward crimson, the panic in his eyes escalating to abject terror. Mia's frustration peaked.

"Oh, for crying out loud, *relax*. Not with *you*."

Twelve blanched, the bell rang, and he bolted like his chair was wired to blow.

Crap. So much for Gina's assertion that all Mia had to do was show up at speed-dating and the watch would make sure love found her. So far Ethnic-Profiling Eric and the My-Ex-Sucked-Out-My-Will-To-Live Quartet had found her.

Twelve tossed off a rushed "Nice to meet you" and scuttled toward the curvaceous blonde in leopard print who sat fluttering and simpering at the next table. Somehow Mia doubted he would be checking the little "Yes, I'd like to meet again!" box next to her number.

The blonde was popular—Eleven was still hovering, his body bending toward her like a plant trying to absorb the last rays of sunlight, as Twelve crowded in. Mia had caught more than one of her prospective suitors stealing glances at the blonde while they were still talking to her. She should have been insulted, but instead she found herself fascinated at the phenomenon.

What was it that this woman had that made her so irresistible? Mia studied her out of the corner of her eye, trying to scientifically break down the elements of what she was doing to determine how one became a speed-dating success.

The bell rang again, signaling the start of another "date", but the chair opposite Mia stayed vacant. With two more women than men at tonight's event, periodically throughout the evening the women got a five-minute respite. She probably should have been ashamed by the depth of her relief at the reprieve—like a death row inmate receiving a stay of execution.

She was fairly certain dating wasn't supposed to feel like being repeatedly strapped into an electric chair.

Mia glanced at her watch. *God, forty more minutes of this?* Apparently the only speed in speed-dating was how quickly she could repel her potential mates.

She'd never realized how long five minutes could feel until tonight. Time was gloriously, meticulously constant, a second always exactly a second long, but somehow speed-dating could make the minutes seem to stretch into eternities of awkwardness, millennia of boredom. It was an anomaly she'd have loved to study, if it wouldn't have necessitated repeating this experience.

Why couldn't she flirt like a normal person?

Mia's gaze veered to the left, drawn with magnetic force to the leopard-print blonde. She was smiling, leaning forward in her chair, face flushed prettily, nodding slightly, lips damp and parted, maintaining eye contact with her eyes just a bit too wide, lending them an air of naïve wonder. She giggled at something Twelve said, reaching across the table to brush his arm, then returning her hand not to the table, but to her throat, toying with the chain of her necklace, making the pendant bob against her cleavage.

Games. Sexual manipulation. The ploys were obvious, but just as obviously effective. The men all wanted to copulate with the blonde whereas they couldn't get away from Mia fast enough.

She'd rushed to the restaurant straight from her lab, not bothering to change out of her sensible gray skirt suit, late as usual because she'd been sucked into her work and lost track of time, succumbing to the lure of a problem that needed to be solved only to look up and realize an hour and a half had passed in the last five minutes. Yet another example of sensory time anomaly.

Perhaps there was research on time anomalies she could examine, a reputable study she could present to her family the next time she was late to an event—though recently they'd begun lying to her about start times to give her a better shot at being on time. It wasn't like she was late on purpose, but if it was a choice between her research and punctuality, her research always won.

At least tonight no one had been mortally offended. The coordinator had smiled, handed her a form, and slipped her into the line-up between the blonde and a blushing red-head in a sundress. The event had started so quickly, Mia hadn't even had a chance to correct the error in her nametag.

The bell rang again and Mia flinched as the men began their shuffle, saying goodbyes and rotating. *Here we go again.*

No. She wouldn't get negative. Gina would tell her she wasn't giving love a chance and her little sister would be right. *Focus on the positive, Mia. Don't sabotage this.* Beggars couldn't be choosers. And she was rapidly approaching beggar status when it came to her love life. Eleven months of the maybe-if-I-ignore-the-problem-it-will-go-away dating strategy had left her on the verge of desperation with no time left for romantic failure.

Determined to succeed at speed-dating, Mia slapped on a smile and reached for her Chardonnay as lucky number Thirteen plunked down across from her. Emulating the simpering blonde, she leaned forward, widened her eyes until she could feel her IQ points dropping off in protest and faked a smile so brittle it was a miracle pieces didn't chip off. Taking a page from the blonde's overheard script, she cooed, "Kevin, wow, what a great name. Mortgage lending? What a fascinating career. I bet you have lots of stories."

Thirteen instantly flushed with pleasure and began to hold forth about the thrilling world of mortgages.

Really, Bachelor Number Thirteen wasn't that bad. Balding, moderately overweight and directing everything he said to the hands he had folded in his lap—yes. But a thirty-four-year-old workaholic who had suddenly decided she wanted to marry and breed wasn't exactly the pick of the litter either.

As Thirteen droned on, Mia envisioned the day her unborn children would ask how she met their father. *Well, snookums, Auntie Gina blackmailed Mommy into going speed-dating and Daddy, you know, he really wasn't that bad. No, it wasn't love at first sight, but Mommy's uterus wasn't going to last forever. Menopause waits for no woman.*

She cringed internally. Not exactly the fairy tale, but Mia had never been the princess type anyway. That was Gina...and every other female in her family. Mia was the one with her head screwed on straight. The scientist. Analytical.

Somehow that seemed to disqualify her from being swept off her feet. Was that fair? Just because she wanted to know the chemical reactions caused in the brain by the emotion labeled *love* didn't mean she was allergic to romance.

The bell rang, startling her out of her musings, and for once the man across from her didn't launch himself out of the chair like he was spring loaded. Thirteen—*Kevin*—smiled and shook her hand and looked straight into her eyes as he said he hoped she would pick him for a second date.

Mia didn't know which was worse—her guilt that she'd barely listened to a word he'd said, or her mortification that she'd had to pretend to be the blonde for five minutes to get a guy to like her. But it wasn't even *her* he liked.

Thirty more minutes. Did she continue to pretend to be the blonde or just make a break for the door? Why was it so impossible to find a guy who *liked* the fact that she was pathologically direct, socially awkward and scientific to the point of neurosis? Wouldn't the right guy find her faults charming?

Mia gazed longingly across the lounge through the archway to the main dining area of Enzo's. It was a half-assed excuse for an Italian restaurant, but the people on the restaurant side looked so smugly happy—probably because they weren't speed-dating. They most likely already had spouses and children, not having waited to the eleventh hour of fertility to begin the process.

The bell dinged again as Bachelor Number Fourteen settled himself in the chair. Mia flashed a smile that probably looked a little manic and Fourteen returned it, his gaze flicking automatically to her lack of cleavage, then over to where her nametag rested on her lapel.

"Astronomy, huh? So baby, what's your sign? Lemme guess. A Virgo? You look like a Virgo."

Mia surreptitiously glanced at her watch. Fifteen seconds. A new personal worst.

Chapter Two
Stalking for Beginners

Chase stared into the lounge of the crappiest Italian restaurant in a hundred-mile radius and tried to figure out where the hell he'd seen the skinny brunette before. She couldn't have been less his type—he tended to go for voluptuous, laid back and casual, while she was bony and prim and wound so damn tight he could practically feel her tension smacking him in the face from thirty feet away.

So why did she look so damn familiar? And where did this insane urge to kiss her until that pissy expression melted off her face come from?

"*Chase.*" The force with which Brody snapped his name gave Chase a tiny hint that his friend had been trying to snag his attention for a while.

"Hm?" he asked lazily, wrenching his gaze off Miss Prim and tipping his beer for a deliberate swallow.

His college roommate's eyes narrowed sharply. "Have you heard a word I've said for the last ten minutes?"

Not even remotely. Brody's voice had taken on that irritating "this is an intervention" tone and Chase had zoned. People dealt with their shit in different ways. Chase was a master of avoidance, a skill he'd perfected over the last six years.

Instead of answering Brody's question, he grinned and contemplated the label peeling off his beer. "How 'bout them Red Sox?"

Brody flinched, his loyalty to the Yankee pinstripes revolting at the mere mention of the Nation, but he managed not to rise to the bait. "Don't change the subject."

"I thought baseball was always relevant."

"It's pre-season. And this is serious. I'm not just here as your friend, Chase. Your finances—"

"Are in your capable hands. I leave it all to you."

"You're broke, Chase."

Chase laughed at the blunt words. "Maybe your hands aren't as capable as I thought. Now that you mention it, I probably should have considered something beyond your exceptional skill at beer pong when I was picking my financial advisor."

"Your income doesn't even come close to covering your expenses. I'd like to meet the financial advisor who can make a profit under those circumstances."

"How about a Ponzi scheme? I've heard those are pretty profitable."

"If you don't mind going to jail for felony fraud."

The waitress chose that moment to appear at their table with their order and by-the-book Brody, who had lost ninety percent of his sense of humor since his beer pong days, blushed like a middle-school girl at being caught talking about fraud, even jokingly. If he'd been paying attention, he would have noticed the waitress was too preoccupied by her own internal drama to care about Ponzi schemes being hatched in her section. Her eyes were red, hands trembling, and when she'd first come to their table she'd had to ask them to repeat their order three times before she could get it down.

Brody waited until she wandered off to break out his club and start whacking away at Chase's dead horse. "If you would just sell one of the houses—"

"No." The word was more reflex than thought.

Brody pushed on as if he hadn't spoken. "Or rent them. I could hire a property management company to arrange everything. You wouldn't have to lift a finger, the rents would offset the mortgages and taxes, and then at least the properties wouldn't be depreciating due to neglect. You can't just ignore a house for six years and not expect it to fall into disrepair, dude. Being a property owner means maintenance."

Beneath his carefully crafted layers of *I don't give a damn*, Chase felt a faint fluttering of guilt. Whose memory did he think he was honoring by letting the houses fall apart just because he wanted to avoid dealing with them?

Inheritance. It was such a shitty word. The only time it was a good thing was when it came from some old maiden aunt in Kansas no one had ever met. Otherwise it was like being given a bonus for having your life fall apart around you. God had a sick sense of humor. Like He was up in heaven saying, *Sure, I'm gonna yank away everything you've ever cared about in the blink of an eye, but look at the prime real estate you'll inherit! Think of the resale value!*

"I've tried tact," Brody went on. "I've tried to be all sensitive. I know this sucks for you, but it's been six years, Chase. It's time to—"

Chase tuned him out. He didn't want to hear the standard therapy crap. His eyes flicked back over to the skinny brunette. Just like him she looked like she would rather be anywhere but here.

What the hell is she doing speed-dating? Chase didn't examine why it bugged him so much that she was doing the dating version of Russian Roulette. He wasn't big into self-examination these days.

What was it about her? She wasn't even that hot. Okay, yeah, she had a little bit of a naughty librarian thing going on. Her dark hair looked thick and he'd just bet it was silky as hell when she pulled out the pen keeping it in a French twist and shook it down. Her face was narrow, but her thinness made her cheekbones jump out and her eyes look freaking huge behind the wire-framed glasses. Nice bone structure, no makeup. A gray suit that hung off her bony shoulders and flat dress shoes.

Miss Prim had done everything possible to downplay her assets—which should have made her eminently ignorable, but instead Chase found himself picturing her tramped up in sky-high heels and a sex-kitten outfit, like her asexual attire was a challenge his imagination couldn't resist. He shifted in his chair. Christ, he was getting turned on by Miss Prim.

Why sign up for speed-dating if she was going to do everything she could to hide what she had going on? The contradiction tugged at him.

He could crash the event. That wasn't weird, right? There were empty spaces, so clearly they were short guys. If he just—

"Chase!"

Brody's shout was loud enough to make several people at nearby tables shoot him nasty looks, but Miss Prim was too far away to pay them any attention. Chase wasn't sure whether he was relieved or disappointed that she hadn't turned to find him staring at her. Again.

"Do you recognize that woman over there?"

He didn't need to look at Brody to feel the anger vibrating off him. "I don't care if Jessica Alba is doing a striptease on a table over there. I'm not going to let you distract me. You're going to lose both houses if you don't—"

"How much?" he asked without taking his eyes off the brunette.

"What?"

Chase tore his gaze off her and met Brody's. "How much more would I need to make to keep both houses? And hire a maintenance guy," guilt prompted him to add.

Brody frowned, his eyes going distant as he did some mental math. "Property taxes... the mortgages... insurance... maintenance. Six grand a month would be comfortable, but you might be able to squeeze by on fifty-five hundred."

The number was a physical blow, but he didn't show any reaction. "That much?"

"The insurance settlements and retirement accounts helped, and covered you this long, but the equity on your parents' place was pretty much drained with the second mortgage to put you and Marcus through college."

Chase forced his expression to remain careless, refusing to betray the flash of guilt that his parents had put themselves into debt just so he could drop out one semester short of a degree.

Brody cleared his throat, an affectation he'd developed when he was about to say something to which he expected a client to react badly. "You could have avoided getting to this point by getting a job."

"I have a job." *Sort of.*

"A full-time job. And surfing forty hours a week while camping on a beach in Fiji for six months doesn't count."

Chase shrugged, unchastened. "The waves were good."

He wasn't going to apologize for his life. On his board with the waves curling beneath him was the one place where the world seemed to make sense to him anymore, and life was too short to spend being miserable in some cubicle.

"Do you want your parents' house to be repossessed? Or your brother's? Because you aren't far from that."

"I'll pick up some more hours," he conceded. He had a great deal with his boss—taking jobs whenever he felt like it and left to his own devices when he didn't. He'd call Karma. She'd be over the moon he was finally interested in playing psychic detective more than four hours a week—not that she'd ever show it.

Brody's expression clouded. "I don't think that's going to cover it."

Chase didn't either, but he was an expert at ignoring the voice of logic in his head. He shrugged and took another swallow of beer. "I'll work it out." Brody opened his mouth, obviously not done hammering the dead horse and Chase met his eyes, putting an end-of-story iciness into his own gaze that he rarely had occasion to use. "Dude. I get it. It's my problem and I'll deal with it. Let it go."

He looked back over to the brunette and almost swore aloud when he saw that she was rising to leave, gathering her things with quick, jerky moves. He started to stand automatically and forced himself back into his chair when he realized that leaving in the middle of his own meal to follow a stranger out of a restaurant tipped a little too close to stalking for comfort.

She rushed toward the door, head held high, looking neither left nor right. The only thing that kept her from looking like she was fleeing the scene of a crime was her aura of supreme confidence and self-assurance, like nothing in the world could rattle her—and damn if that didn't make him want to try his hand at rattling her.

Why speed-dating if it was her own personal corporal punishment?

And why did Chase care?

"Molly'd love to see you. We were hoping you'd come over on Sunday."

The door closed behind the brunette and Chase swung his attention back to Brody. Sunday. His birthday. Twenty-eight and still kicking.

"I don't think I can make Sunday."

Brody shook his head. "You won't convince me you already have plans. Molly and I would love to have you. We could invite some of the brothers. Relive our frat days."

"Can't. Sorry. Some other time."

Brody looked like he wanted to push it—Molly must be giving him shit about getting Chase to open up and reconnect or some B.S. "Dude," Brody said finally, "it's your birthday. You can't spend it alone."

"I won't," he lied easily.

Chase hated birthdays. And holidays. Every other day of the year, his old friends let him dodge them. They would stop pushing and leave him to his own devices. But on birthdays, on Thanksgiving and Christmas and Fourth of Fucking July he *couldn't* be alone. He *had* to join their perfect domestic bliss— and be reminded of all he'd lost in every goddamn laugh they shared and every mushy, pitying look they shot him when they thought he couldn't see. He'd much rather be by himself, on the water or maybe catching a double feature in a movie theatre if the waves sucked, convincing himself it was just another day.

"Have you heard from Mark lately?" Chase asked to distract Brody from his mission, naming one of their frat brothers who had recently hit it huge with his tech company.

Brody must have felt he'd satisfied Molly's commands because he went with the topic change—even though he was better than just about anyone at seeing through Chase's verbal acrobatics.

The rest of the meal was as pleasant as overcooked pasta could be.

Brody grabbed the check when it came and frowned. "This isn't our bill."

Chase took it from him and pretended to confirm that it was, indeed, the wrong bill before catching the waitress's eye and waving her over. Tammy, as her nametag identified her, was mid-thirties and would have been pretty in a wholesome, vulnerable way if she hadn't looked like she was about to toss her cookies in his lap.

He smiled his most charming, put-the-room-at-ease smile and tipped the black folder in her direction. "We seem to have gotten switched up."

Her face flushed and tears gathered in her eyes. "Oh my gosh, I'm so sorry. Here let me fix it."

Chase made sure his hand brushed hers as he handed the check back to her, opening up the part of his brain where his secret weapon had lived since he was a pimply-faced adolescent. Psychic Detectives R Us.

Through the brush of skin, information crowded into his brain, carrying with it the vague taste of malted milk. The usual murky jumble of intangibles were there—fear, insecurity, self-recrimination, worry—and piercing through that foggy mess, the single sharp desire to find the missing child support check. Something inside Chase jolted, like a steel wire snapping taut and vibrating hard, and he saw the check, folded twice and wedged inside the lining of a black purse.

Then her hand pulled away and the images vanished, leaving only his own thoughts occupying his brain. She darted away from the table, walking with the unhurried speed of a practiced service professional.

Chase pulled out his wallet and yanked at the lining until it tore. When Tammy returned, gushing apologies, he made sure he was bitching loudly to Brody about needing a new one— *everything keeps getting caught in the damn lining and I can never find it. Piece of crap wallet.*

Her expression filled with a sharp hope and she nearly threw the bill at him in her haste to get to the break room where she'd shoved her worn, busted-lining purse in a locker.

Brody watched her hustle away and turned back to Chase with one brow arched. "I don't know why you can't just find a winning lottery ticket and solve all your financial problems."

"First I would have to *lose* a winning lottery ticket. And it doesn't work when I do it on myself. You know that."

Brody grunted the affirmative. "Sucks that you can't do it for yourself. You were the only guy in the frat who could never find his keys after a bender."

"Or his car. Or the Dean's daughter's underwear," Chase commented, remembering some of the more entertaining finds from his college years.

Before he dropped out. Before his life went to shit on one sunny winter afternoon.

"If you don't want to see the guys on Sunday, we could do something different. Molly has a friend she thought you'd like to meet."

Chase's stomach revolted and he nearly spewed mushy pasta all over the plastic tablecloth. He'd dated in the last six years. Or, at least, he'd hooked up. But the thought of Molly— Katie's best friend, sorority sister and would-have-been-maid-of-honor—setting him up with a friend of hers activated his upchuck reflex. It felt so damn *wrong.*

"I'm seeing someone," he lied, rushing the words out. "Cute chick." The brunette flashed in his mind. Miss Prim's prissy mouth and wire-rimmed glasses gave him the inspiration to work the lie. "She's really serious and uh," *prissy...sexy...*"brunette."

Brody's eyebrows flew up. "Serious? That doesn't sound like your type."

"What can I say? She intrigues me."

Brody smiled, his relief so obvious it bordered on patronizing. Sometime in the last six years Chase had crossed the line where reactions to good news changed from be-happy-for-me into be-grateful-you-don't-have-to-feel-quite-so-much-pity-for-me. "I'm glad you've met someone, man. That's awesome. She sounds like just what you need to keep you grounded."

"Yeah," Chase agreed.

Just what he needed. A made-up girlfriend to keep his friends off his back about the way he was wasting his life. The idea had merit. Now he just needed a girl to play the part.

Chapter Three
Houston, We Have a Problem

"Why did I let you talk me into that? How could you have possibly imagined I would be anything but a complete failure at speed-dating?"

Escaping the restaurant, Mia had shut herself in the cozy interior of her car with an immense sense of relief and a driving desire to murder her sister. *When in doubt, blame Gina.* She'd turned the ignition, fired up her Bluetooth and dialed Gina before burning rubber out of the parking lot.

"You liked the idea," Gina reminded her as she sped away from the scene of the crime. "You kept saying how efficient it was."

"Next time I think something is a good idea, remind me of this moment."

"It can't have been that bad."

"The last two hours are ample proof that it can, in fact, be that bad."

She'd wanted to like them. Really she had. And not just because she was on a clock to fall in love.

The problem came down to the dichotomy between theory and practice. In theory, speed-dating had seemed brilliantly efficient, as meeting a man was a necessary step toward her ultimate goal of getting married and procreating. In practice, she'd rather have been at her lab. Or anywhere else.

"There wasn't *anyone* you hit it off with?" Gina coaxed. "Maybe a certain zoning permit guy named Ben?"

The pieces fell solidly into place. "Oh my God. Tell me you didn't talk me into going speed-dating just so you can get a zoning exemption for your addition."

"Do you know how strict they are about handing out those exemptions?"

"Gina! I can't believe you tried to pimp me out for a building permit."

Gina laughed lightly, unoffended. Her kid sister was sunshine and light. Not much dampened her spirits. "Hey, he might have been your true love *and* he could get me an exemption. Two birds, one stone. I was being efficient. You like efficient."

"After tonight, efficiency and I aren't on the best terms anymore." She recalled the way Twelve had tucked his head down like a turtle retreating into his shell whenever she asked him a question. "You seriously thought Ben was my perfect match?"

"He was kind of cute. In a nerdy, Zoning Avenger way. Wielding the Rubber Stamp of Doom. Besides, you're boring. He's boring. To use a math analogy so I know you'll understand, I thought it was like two negatives making a positive."

"I think I'd rather you just told me you were punking me, at least then one of us would have gotten some enjoyment out of the evening."

Gina snorted. "I'm surprised you even know what punking is. That's pretty pop culture for you, sis."

"Hey. I'm not totally out of touch with pop culture."

"Ha."

"The research assistants talk about stuff like that. I pick it up. And could you please stop telling people I'm a rocket scientist? Neurobiology, Gina."

"I think I said astrophysics. The organizer chick seemed really impressed."

"I don't think impressed is the word I would use. She put 'Ask me about Astronomy!' on my nametag and apparently the average male doesn't know that there is a distinction between astronomy and astrology. They kept asking me about my sign."

"Oh, Mia." Gina gave a soft, groaning laugh. "Do you even know your sign?"

It should have been funny, but Mia wasn't laughing. It was hard to find the humor in being a total dating failure. "Apparently I look like a Virgo."

"What does that even mean?"

"How am I supposed to know? I also got two requests to play doctor and was told I'm a total *guidette*—and no, I do not want to know what that means."

"Oh Lord. So...the whole thing was a bust, huh?"

Mia stopped at the light for the turnpike entrance. "I think you can kiss your zoning exemption goodbye."

"Well, crap."

"I'm touched by this continued evidence of your priorities."

"I'm not worried about you finding love. You have the watch. Love is coming for you like a freight train, baby. But the family doesn't have any magic doodads to bypass zoning regulations. Unless Nonna's been holding out on us."

The light changed and Mia's hands tightened on the steering wheel as she took the entrance to the turnpike. "That damn watch."

"Hey, don't damn the watch." She could practically hear Gina making the sign of the cross. "I'm disgustingly happy, thanks to that little piece of gold. Or I will be as soon as we get that permit." A thin mewling cry echoed in the background. "Oh crud, that's Marley. Hang on."

Gina dropped the phone and Mia strained to pick out the sounds of her niece being picked up, cuddled and soothed. Would Gina press her face to the baby's downy head and inhale her sweet baby-powder scent?

An ache of envy throbbed in Mia's chest.

She'd never seen herself as a Mommy type. She was self-centered and impatient with people and their idiosyncrasies. She was also too fixated on her work and spent far too many hours in her lab to be a good parent, and she wasn't going to do it half-assed.

Compounded to that was the fact that she didn't really *like* children. She'd always found them mildly annoying. They were noisy and messy and that was before they hit puberty and became obnoxious hazards to society. She couldn't imagine the rewards of being a parent could possibly compensate for years of headaches and sleep deprivation.

She'd always figured her work would be her legacy and she was fine with that. Happy.

Then, two months ago, Marley Renee Villapiano made her entrance into the world and everything had changed. The first second Mia had laid eyes on her niece, her heart had swallowed that tiny precious bundle whole, swelling up to make room for a love so big and fierce it had dwarfed every other emotion in her experience.

Suddenly patience wasn't a problem. Putting Marley's needs first wasn't an issue. Taking time off work to babysit— even an entire weekend without visiting the lab—wasn't even an irritation. Her sweet girl was one miracle after another, watching her grow and change an endless source of fascination and pride.

Suddenly Mia, who had never thought of biological clocks as something that pertained to her, started hearing a distinct ticking. She wanted one of her own, the intensity of that desire startling. And unnerving.

Her cousins foisting their kids on her had never had the same effect. Her brothers had dodged the marriage watch to date and her older sister Teresa hadn't been able to conceive yet, so it was Gina, the baby of the family, whose baby shattered her preconceived notions about parenthood.

Diapers, sleepless nights, even puberty—in that moment of blinding clarity when she held Marley for the first time, she understood why it was all worth it. And at thirty-four, she was already running short of viable eggs.

She could easily have gone the artificial insemination route—if she didn't mind giving her grandmother a heart attack—but she wanted the husband. The family like the one she'd grown up in. The human experience.

She just didn't want to take the time away from her career to get all those things.

"Okay, I'm back." Gina gave a breathless huff into the phone. "What were we talking about?"

"Who cares? How's my favorite person on the planet?"

"She's getting fat."

"She is not!" Mia protested, indignant on her niece's behalf.

"Well, she eats constantly. Tony calls her Chunky Monkey. Daddy's gonna give you a complex, isn't he, sweet girl? Yes, he is." Gina cooed before returning her voice to a normal octave. "Do you have a date for the Christening?"

"I wasn't aware baptisms were couples-only."

"They are for the woman with the watch."

"Gina," Mia warned.

"I know, I know, you hate talking about it, but hear me out. This is for your own good."

"Of course it is," Mia grumbled. "Have you considered the fact that I *have* found my true love? That it's my work? That maybe not everyone is cut out to be the perfect wife and mommy?" She spoke the words knowing they were a lie. The coward's way. But if she admitted she wanted that life and couldn't get it...

Being misunderstood by her family was one thing, but she refused to be pathetic. Pitied. Better if they thought she rejected their lifestyle than she'd failed to find what they'd all tripped into so easily. Mia didn't accept failure, especially in herself.

"I'm not talking about you finding true love. Like I said, I'm not worried on that front." There was absolute confidence in Gina's tone. Not even a sliver of doubt even though the clock was winding down on Mia's year with the watch. "What I'm talking about is self-preservation. You need a date for the Christening, so it *looks* like you're making progress with the watch. Otherwise Mama and Nonna and all the aunties are going to pester you without mercy—and you'll be double-booked on blind dates every night for the next three weeks before we're halfway through the ceremony."

"God, you're right." She cringed. Why hadn't she checked the yes box next to Thirteen? He'd liked her, even if she had been channeling the blonde when they'd met.

"Do you have any male research assistants you could pass off as a date?"

"Only Rajit. And Mom knows he's married." Her latest batch of bright young scientific minds were predominantly giggly young women—which wasn't terribly surprising, given her research centered on the scientific effects of emotion on the brain. Thank God the girls were also brilliant. She could put up with twittering and simpering as long as it came with competence.

"Could Rajit and his wife be estranged?"

"Gina."

"Just thinking outside the box. You need a warm male body, sis."

Actually, the problem lay more in the fact that she *didn't* need warm male bodies. Mia had never had a very active libido. If she'd needed men more, she would have gone to the effort to acquire one before her thirty-fourth birthday. Sex was pleasant enough, but hardly essential to her physical and emotional well-being.

"What about—"

Mia cut her little sister off before she found herself at the church with another zoning officer. "Gina. The twenty dates you set me up on tonight were more than enough. Thank you."

"Well, did you see any other likely candidates at the restaurant tonight? Even if the Zoning Avenger wasn't The One, the watch should have brought your guy into range. You wore it, didn't you?"

Mia wondered if she could get away with a lie. Gina was annoyingly good at detecting deception, but she might be able to slip one past her over the phone. If she hadn't waited so long... Gina read the pause correctly and screeched.

"Mia! You aren't even wearing it? How is it supposed to work if you don't wear it?"

"There was nothing in the rules about wearing it. Possessing it, protecting it, yes. Wearing, no."

"It's *implied*."

"Well, maybe the crazy gypsy lady should be a little more specific next time she sells a magic thingamabob to our family."

"Mia." Gina's voice dropped, suddenly taking on an uncharacteristic seriousness. "I know you've always thought the watch was a crock. And I'm not going to argue that it works— you already know what I think. But I want you to consider that maybe your willingness to wear the watch isn't just about whether or not *you* believe, but also about whether or not you respect Mama's belief. And Nonna's. And Zia Anna's. You don't have to try to find the love of your life, but could you at least *pretend* to be open to it? For the family? Because we all want you to be happy. And giving you that watch is the only way they know to show you that. So could you maybe not throw that all back in their faces by refusing to even *wear* the thing?"

Mia swallowed past the lump in her throat, her face hot with shame. She knew she could be self-centered and oblivious, but it sucked to have her baby sister read her the riot act— especially when she deserved it as royally as she did. "Damn," she muttered with a thick voice, "only two months in and already you have that Mom Guilt Trip down to a science."

Gina chuckled, easily accepting the apology in her tone. "What can I say? I'm a natural."

"I'll wear it," Mia promised. "I'll go home and put it on right away and wear it straight through until the Christening on Sunday. If it can get me a date so Mama leaves me alone, I will never bitch about how ridiculous a superstition it is...for at least a month."

Gina snorted. "I'll hold you to that." Mia heard the creak of the rocking chair their mother had passed down to Gina when her youngest daughter was the first to have a child. "I bet he's smokin' hot, your guy. And not even remotely scientific."

"You honestly think I would be compatible with someone unscientific?"

"I think you need someone less serious than you to lighten things up. Someone who isn't going to be even more of a workaholic than you are."

"I couldn't be with someone who didn't appreciate how important my work is to me. Men without ambition can't possibly understand a woman whose priorities are larger than him—or even herself. I will allow that many people do seem to thrive with mates who present a polarizing viewpoint from their own, but I am not one of those people. I need someone stable. Educated. Unflappable."

"Someone like Peter."

Mia felt a little jab of guilt—as if she should have thought of him herself and it was disloyal to have forgotten the one long-term relationship she'd ever had. "Yes, someone precisely like Peter."

"If you sounded more passionate than prim when you said his name, I might actually believe you."

"I said someone *like* Peter, not Peter himself. He lives in Edinburgh now and my work is here." And the fact that she hadn't thought of him in almost two years probably didn't bode well for their eternal happiness.

"Well, I for one am glad he didn't immediately get transferred back here as soon as you got a hold of the watch. I'd hate to think the Stodgy Professor was your One and Only."

"He isn't stodgy," Mia defended automatically.

"He sucks all the life out of a room just by entering it. You need someone with energy. Someone who can ignite your inner spark."

"I don't have an inner spark."

"Ha. You have an inner bonfire. I can see it in your eyes whenever you're talking about your work. You need a guy who lights you up like that. Promise me you won't settle for less than a bonfire."

Her heart sank. "Sweetie, I think most of the bonfire-inducing men are looking for someone younger and richer than me, who actually has boobs."

"Your boobs are fine. Proportional. The right guy will love your boobs. And he's coming. Believe it, sis. The watch is a state of mind. Go put it on and open yourself up to falling in love."

The watch was certainly a state of mind. Mia had often theorized that its effectiveness lay only in the zealous belief her family placed on the fact that it *would* work. They made it infallible by being unwilling to accept any other alternative.

But it couldn't hurt to take a page out of their book. It had worked for them.

"I will," she promised her sister. "I'm just pulling into the driveway. I'll have it on in five minutes. Scout's honor."

"Good. You've gotta get your brain out of the equation. Less thinking, more feeling. So here's what you do. Remember that bottle of tequila Jamie and I gave you when your paper thingy was published in that journal? Pop the top on that sucker and do shots until your libido has a chance to catch up with that overactive brain of yours."

"I don't see how drinking by myself at home is going to help me find Mr. Right. Unless I'm supposed to find him at an AA meeting."

"It's not about the tequila. It's about being open. Taking a leap. Just try to be open about this, okay? With or without alcohol enhancement."

"I'll try. Promise."

"Great. Oh, and Mia? Sorry about the speed-dating thing. The zoning dude really seemed kinda nice-ish when I talked to him at the permit office."

"He was nice." *Ish.* "Just wrong."

"Hey, Mister Right is out there. Don't worry."

If only it was as easy to find him as it was to say that. "G'night, Gina."

"'Night, sis."

Mia pulled into her carport. She grabbed her laptop case and trudged across the parking lot and up the steps to her condo. Unless they worked in pharmaceuticals, research scientists weren't the best paid people in the world, but the microscopic two-bedroom townhome was tidy—largely because she spent so little time there. It was only fifteen minutes from the lab, but late at night when her eyes were gritty and aching, she usually just shut them on the couch in her office for a few hours rather than bothering to come home.

The glowing red display on the microwave read nine seventeen as she kicked off her slides. Even after the Night That Would Not End, she was still home earlier than she would have been if she'd just come straight from work.

She padded up the narrow staircase, flipping on lights as she went. She didn't miss having someone waiting at home, all the lamps lit welcomingly when she walked in the door. Guilt flickered again, a reminder that she should have missed Peter more than she did. Not that she didn't miss him at all, but...well, it was more a case of missing what he represented than missing the man himself. She missed the role he had filled in her life.

Someone to go to Christenings and keep her family from shooting her that pitying look they'd all perfected for the Spinster Daughter. But also someone who understood without being told that her work was more important to her than he was, because he felt the same way about his own.

They'd met when they were both in grad school and dated for almost a decade without ever getting serious. She'd expected, in a half-hearted way, that they would someday get married, but neither wanted children at the time and there didn't seem to be a point in rushing into it. When he received the job offer in Scotland, she'd been relieved they weren't married because it meant she wasn't expected to go with him. They parted amicably—though even that word seemed too strong for their emotionless goodbye.

That was when she realized she hadn't loved him. She'd never given the topic much thought before that day.

Mia spun the tumblers on the wall safe in her bedroom closet. She'd dropped the watch in there eleven months ago, annoyed by its existence, but if it could get her a date to the Christening in the next thirty-six hours, she might have to revise her opinion of the damn thing.

She swung open the door and reached inside to flip open the velvet jeweler's case.

The *empty* jeweler's case.

"*No.*" Her heart stopped beating even as blood rushed too loud and fast in her ears. "No-no-no-no-no."

She jerked the case out, flipped it over, and felt around inside the safe with desperation clawing at her brain, but her panic didn't change anything. The safe stayed empty.

She'd lost the watch.

Chapter Four
One Tequila, Two Tequila, Three Tequila, Floor

Mia dragged herself toward consciousness, taking stock of the foreign object where her body should be. There was strong evidence that last night had not ended well.

One—Something small, furry and possibly molding had crawled into her mouth and died.

Two—Every muscle in her body felt like it had been cryogenically frozen and then improperly thawed after a couple decades, leaving her muscles aching and aged twenty years overnight.

Three—Her head pounded as if some industrious soul was using a spike and hammer to chisel away pieces of her skull. Or trying to crack it open like an egg to make an omelet with her brain; she wasn't entirely sure which.

Four—When she opened her eyes, she realized she was lying face down on her living room rug, the short, rough pile mashing into her cheek as light from the front windows assaulted her eyes like the flashlight of God. The light must have woken her.

Five—On the floor in front of her face lay a half-empty tequila bottle, an open telephone book she hadn't even known she owned, and her cell phone.

Mia cringed. Crap. Who had she drunk dialed?

She vaguely remembered a dull date involving small quantities of food and several glasses of white wine entering her system, but not so much that she'd been really tipsy. She'd been clear-headed and steady enough to drive. She remembered talking to Gina, driving home—

The watch.

Mia jolted to a sitting position. Her stomach didn't make the trip with the rest of her body, then decided to catch up by slingshotting its contents toward her throat as the world swooped and dipped around her.

She scrambled toward the bathroom, hunched over like the Cro-Magnon man, and thankfully made it to the Porcelain God of Hangovers before emptying her stomach. She flushed and slumped down next to the toilet, the cool tile feeling disproportionately good against her skin as the room began a slow lateral spin.

Apparently she was in that lovely place where Hungover and Still Drunk overlapped. The Venn Diagram of Drunkard's Remorse.

Mia scaled the sink, using cabinet handles like holds on a climbing wall, and leaned against the basin to stay upright as she rinsed and brushed her teeth—though even minty freshness couldn't entirely banish the fuzzy, dead-animal feeling in her mouth.

The woman in the mirror looked vaguely humanoid. Her hair had come down and been mashed into a rat's nest that stuck out the side of her head. One cheek was red from the carpet abrasion, her glasses slanted precariously, and her eyes refused to open farther than a squint. Something orange and granular was smeared across her forehead and Mia rubbed at it with a wet washcloth, feeling every slimy cool bump on her abnormally sensitive skin.

Staggering back to the living room, Mia caught sight of her cell phone on the floor again, hit like a spotlight with the splash of sunlight streaming through the front windows.

Oh God. Had she drunk dialed her mom and told her the watch was missing? Or any member of the family? Everyone would know. If there was even a hint that she had failed her duties as the watch protector, mass panic would ensue. And the Corregiannis didn't do panic in a small way. They didn't do anything in a small way.

They were probably gathering pitchforks and kindling on their way over. She'd lost the watch. *The* watch. The timepiece responsible for health, happy marriages, job promotions and good parking karma. Her *one job* had been to protect it...and fall in love, but really she couldn't be expected to fall in love on command. Protecting it had actually been a reasonable request. It was a freaking family heirloom. So what if there was superstition surrounding it? It was still valuable as a piece of family history. And she'd lost it.

And they would all think she'd done it on purpose.

Mia's stomach staged another rebellion and she barely made it to the bathroom in time.

She'd never made any secret of the fact that she hated the watch. They all knew how ridiculous she thought it was. No one would buy that she'd lost it by accident. *She* almost didn't buy it.

How could it have vanished from inside her safe? A locked safe inside her bedroom closet. There hadn't been any signs of a break in. Nothing else was missing.

She retched until her stomach was officially empty, then stumbled to the sink for another brushing.

Could she have moved it and then forgotten about it somehow? The case was still in the safe, so maybe she'd taken it out to wear it?

And then completely forgotten about the personality reversal voluntarily wearing the watch would have entailed. Right.

Mia gathered up her cell phone and the phonebook-of-unknown-origin and shuffled toward the kitchen. Only to draw up short in the doorway.

"Whoa."

Apparently she had not only gotten shitfaced last night, she'd also ransacked her own place.

Every cupboard and drawer was open. Pots, pans, utensils and dry goods were strewn around the counters and floors. An economy-size package of Cheetos had burst open and scattered neon cheese curls across the hardwood.

Which at least explained the orange debris on her forehead. Sort of.

Mia slumped to sit on a clear patch of floor, cradling her phone and the phonebook in her lap. She had no urge whatsoever to clean the mess. *One disaster at a time.*

She brought up her call history on the phone. *3:14am: Unknown.* A sense of acute relief let her breathe again when she saw she'd only made one call the night before—after Gina—and it had not been to any of the family numbers. Her caller ID didn't recognize it.

Mia made note of the number and brought up her phone's browser, typing the mystery number into a reverse look-up engine. The result flickered on the screen. *Karmic Consultants.*

Mia frowned. What the hell was a karmic consultant? The name sounded vaguely familiar, but she couldn't place it.

Scrolling down, she found the company's weblink and selected it, flipping over to their official site. The website was clean and professional looking, some kind of private investigators. Mia started to think they might actually be helpful. Until she saw the list of services. *Psychics, Mediums, Exorcisms, Occult Investigations, Aura Consultations.*

Lovely. Apparently in times of drunkenness and extreme stress, Mia called Ghostbusters. How helpful.

At least she hadn't called her mother to confess.

Mia reached above her to set the phone on the cluttered counter and shoved the phonebook aside. It was tempting to curl up on the floor, using the phonebook as a pillow, and sleep until her body stopped throbbing. Disturbingly tempting. The cool hardwood called to her, somehow seeming a thousand times more comfortable than the soft bed that waited upstairs.

She slumped lower. *Maybe just a little nap...*

The doorbell ringing echoed through her skull like an air raid siren. Mia moaned and wondered if she could ignore it. Who dropped by without calling on a Saturday morning? It had to be missionaries. They would take one look at her and see the Save Me written all over her face. *In Cheetos.* And then she'd never get them to leave.

The bell rang again, accompanied by a knock—as if the air raid siren hadn't managed to alert her to the fact that someone was standing on her doorstep.

Mia hauled herself to her feet and staggered toward the door through the flat spin standing caused, absently shoving her shirt tails back into her waistband.

There had to be a rosary around here somewhere. Her mother was always leaving them around the house in the hopes that her second-born daughter would discover the joys of the Church. Maybe if Mia opened the door holding one and muttering Hail Marys, the missionaries would leave her alone.

The bell rang a third time right as she reached the door and Mia flinched at her proximity to the siren. Stunning how something she'd always thought sounded like light sweet chimes sober could sound like the Devil's gym whistle drunk.

She threw open the door, catching her uninvited guest halfway down her front steps. *Damn.* If she'd waited another minute he would have gone away.

At the sound of the door opening, he spun—and his face hit her like a sucker punch. *Sweet mother of God.* Obviously the result of some freakish genetic convergence of all the current standards of male beauty, his double helix should be a national treasure. The man was *gorgeous.*

As an extension of her research into the neurochemistry of love, Mia had studied lust and attraction. She was perfectly aware that the dilation of her pupils and acceleration of her heart rate were just helpless biological reactions—but that awareness didn't stop her insteps from melting.

He was tall and broad shouldered, with the kind of sculpted muscular physique most commonly seen on action stars and professional athletes—which her survival of the fittest animal instincts were telling her body meant he would be a good protector and they would have strong offspring.

While she saw a face of pure, masculine perfection, framec by longish blond hair with a slight curl, her subconscious saw the symmetry of his features that would have earned him an impressive score on the Marquardt Compu-Analytical Beauty Analysis.

It wasn't love at first sight. It was science. And in spite of the potent pheromones he was throwing off and her girly flutters of reaction, he couldn't have been less her type.

The blue jeans that clung to his hips and thighs were worn until the seams were white and frayed, with a narrow hole slashed just above one knee. A threadbare T-shirt completed his surfer-boy sex appeal—featuring a cartoon of a buxom brunette perched on a colorful surfboard and the slogan *Woody's Longboards: Get Lei'd in Hawaii.*

Classy.

"Mia Corregianni?"

He started back toward her up the steps, eyebrows arched inquisitively. Mia's eyes were drawn helplessly to his hips and the lazy, rolling way they moved. *Oh, mercy.* The swooping feeling in her stomach must be tequila-induced. It couldn't have been her girly parts getting hopeful at the sight of Mr. Sexypants. She was attracted to *intellect,* not the physical trappings.

When he reached the top step, recognition flashed across his features and he grinned. "You."

"Do I know you?" she asked, although she already knew the answer would be negative. She would have remembered that abnormally gorgeous face. And the mildly offensive fashion sense.

He shook his head with a smile. "Nope."

Mia narrowed her eyes, which didn't take much effort since she was already squinting against the morning sunlight. "So what are you doing here?" Pretty or not, she didn't have the patience for bullshit this morning. And she'd never really given a damn about social niceties anyway.

His smile broadened, revealing a dimple, as if he found her irritability endearing. "My name's Chase Hunter. Karmic Consultants. I'm a finder."

Oh Good Lord. She'd drunk dialed *him*.

The Ghostbusters were making house calls.

Chapter Five
Librarians Gone Wild

Chase couldn't contain his grin as Miss Prim glowered at him from the doorway. Though now she looked more like Miss Prim after a night of hard partying. Librarians Gone Wild.

Even looking—and smelling—like she'd been run over by a tequila truck, she was pretty damn cute. Grouchy, but cute.

In the bright morning light, without the starched sternness of her suit as camouflage, she looked younger than he'd originally pegged her. Maybe early-to-mid-twenties. He was no closer to figuring out where he knew her from or why he'd been so fixated on her last night, but he couldn't stop grinning like an idiot at the coincidence that had landed him on her doorstep. If he'd known Miss Prim was the client Karma had called him about this morning with an urgent need for his services, he would have hauled ass and gotten here earlier.

Though from the look of her, earlier might not have been appreciated.

As it was, she seemed to be giving serious thought to slamming the door in his face, which would certainly slow down him finishing the job and collecting his finder's fee. Maybe he could arrange a discount for her if she was willing to pose as his girlfriend a few times. That wasn't creepy, right? Seeing her felt like the universe sanctioning his *pretend to have a girlfriend* plan.

But first he had to do his job.

"You lost something, right?" he prompted when she just frowned at him suspiciously from the doorway. "I'm here to find it."

Her suspicious frown coalesced into something harder, icier. "I was impaired last night. Clearly I made a mistake contacting your company. I'm sorry to waste your time."

"Whoa." He closed the distance between them and slapped a palm against the door before she could slam it. She didn't try to wrestle it away from him, but she did prevent him from pushing it open any farther. Strong for such a bony little thing. "Look, sweetheart, you called me. Why don't you let me do my job?" *And earn my paycheck...*

"Your job. Of course." Her smile wasn't a smile at all, more a patronizing parody to humor him. "And how, exactly, do you propose to find my lost item, Mr. Hunter?"

"Chase." He tapped a finger against his temple. "It's a gift."

She snorted. "I'm a scientist."

Her profession was thrown down like a gauntlet. She apparently expected him to stagger back, fatally intimidated by the challenge, but Miss Prim didn't know who she was dealing with. Chase had never met an argument he couldn't talk his way out of—even when he was clearly in the wrong. And this time, he even had the advantage of being right.

He gave her a big easy grin, leaning against the doorjamb. "That's about the prettiest way I've ever been accused of being a con artist."

"I didn't say—"

"Yes, you did."

"I never meant to imply—"

"Don't play dumb, sweetheart. It's beneath you."

Her jaw dropped. He'd bet his best board prissy Miss Scientist had never been called dumb a day in her life.

He pressed the advantage her shock gave him. "You think I'm a phony and a crook, but what if I could prove to you, *scientifically*, that I'm not? I'm not here to bilk you. We've got a satisfaction guarantee policy at Karmic. I don't get paid unless I find your jeegaw. And I sure as hell don't get paid for standing around arguing with you. So how's about you let me look so I can get back to the beach while the waves are still good?"

His little speech had given her time to recoup. Her mouth snapped shut and drew into a tight bow. "I don't let strange men into my house."

"That must eliminate most of the male population. What do you do if you need a plumber?" He added an extra patronizing, let-the-menfolk-handle-this vibe just to watch her eyes darken.

She rolled her eyes. "Why do all men believe a person has to have a Y chromosome to perform basic home maintenance?"

"Have you heard the sounds a woman makes when she tries to snake a drain? It's like mice on helium."

"Of all the chauvinistic—"

"I can see you've never snaked a drain. Lemme guess, your daddy is very handy."

"I—you—" she sputtered. "That is entirely beside the point."

Chase burst out laughing. "That is exactly the point. The Y chromosome can be useful. So why don't you let me help you?"

Her eyes narrowed. He saw the exact moment she realized he'd just run her in a conversational circle until she lost track of her arguments. A flash in her eyes, a pursing of her mouth, the flush of anger high on her cheeks—pissed off was a good look for Mia. "You're worse than a used car salesman."

"Sweetheart, trust me, I'm much better than a used car salesman. Car salesmen can't find shit."

A smile almost twitched her lips, but didn't quite make it. "Charming. Still, I think I'll pass. Have a nice day."

The door started to close again and Chase added a foot to the hand holding it open. Mia glowered. Damn, she was a tough nut to crack. Usually the whole *let me help you* bit combined with a smile and a stack of references was a sure sell. Especially with women. Hell, most days he didn't even have to speak with women. Just stand there and look pretty.

"I have references. Glowing recommendations from pillars of the community."

"Is barging into people's homes part of the service? References can be faked. I've seen *Leverage*. For all I know you stole my…you stole it yourself and now you're trying to get me to pay you to tell me where you stashed it."

"Hey, you called me, honey. I'm an honest psychic." At her snort, he shifted tactics. Just walking away would have been easy, but walking away didn't pay the mortgages—or get him a fake girlfriend to get Brody off his back. This was the new Chase. The determined Chase. Next up: *appeal to the panic.* "How bad is it?"

"Excuse me?"

"Karma said it was an emergency. That you sounded pretty ripped up about this thing you lost. So how bad is it?"

The irritation left her face, leaving in its wake a blank hopelessness that was much worse. "It's bad," she admitted. "But I don't see how you can possibly—"

"You don't have to see. You don't have to believe. All you have to do is let me try."

"Why are you so pushy?" she countered. "Why is it such a big deal to you that I let you find my missing…thing?"

"Why are you so resistant? What does it cost you to let me try?"

He saw the answer she wouldn't admit written all over her face. For a scientist, letting him try was admitting there was a chance he would succeed. It was giving in to the idea of psychics and magic and the supernatural. It shouldn't surprise him that Mia wouldn't surrender her skepticism easily.

"What kind of science do you study?" He was willing to bet a bucket of board wax it wasn't parapsychology.

Her mouth puckered and her chin tipped up, giving her an air of such arrogant self-assurance he was obviously meant to feel like an uneducated peasant regarding an intellectual queen. "I have Ph.Ds in molecular physics and neurobiology, but the primary focus of my research at present is the study of the physiological impacts of emotion on brain chemistry. Specifically the way love chemically alters our neural pathways."

Chase should not have gotten solid wood listening to a conceited brainiac brag about her work—but there was something in her voice when she talked about it. Sure, she was the arrogant queen, but there was fire rather than ice behind her words, and he wanted to tap into that reservoir of heat. Especially in the face of her stand-still-so-I-can-scrape-you-off-the-bottom-of-my-shoe attitude. He could never resist a challenge in a short skirt.

"That's so..." *Hot. Sexy. Fuck-me-now.* Somehow he didn't think Mia would go for that. So he blurted the first safe word that popped into his head: "Cute."

Mia went stiff and Chase saw his life flash before his eyes as her face morphed into something from *Children of the Corn.*

"Cute?" she asked in a low voice the Grim Reaper would have run from screaming.

Shit. So much for safe.

Cute. He'd just called her research cute.

Her blood began to boil, a nice steady simmer.

Mia had heard a lot of reactions to her work. Some people were intimidated or awed by her intellect, others just zoned out on that boring science stuff, while still others pretended to understand and nodded along before asking a question that made it patently obvious they had no idea what she'd been talking about—but *cute*, that was new.

He got bonus points for originality, if nothing else.

"Cute was the wrong word," Chase said, back-pedaling frantically.

"No, no, science is *adorable.* I don't know why I've never described it that way before," she snapped.

The idiot man smiled at her. Why couldn't he just react like a normal person? He was impossible to argue with properly. None of her scathing comments seemed to land on him. They just slid right off the easy slickness of his bullshit.

"Look, you're a scientist, I get it. You aren't going to be taken in by smoke and mirrors. But as a scientist, aren't you even a little curious to see if I can actually do what I say I can do? And how? Don't you want to know the science behind it?"

She was curious. Dammit. She wanted to know how his con worked. *If* his con worked, there was a chance it could work for her.

Her best hypothesis involved hypnosis—accessing her subconscious mind's memory of an item's location. Hypnosis wasn't magic. It was simply a method of bypassing the parts of the brain that function to suppress extraneous memory or maintain impulse control—so the subject clucks like a chicken in front of an audience of strangers.

But she wasn't going to give this stranger open access to her subconscious—no matter how smooth he could talk. Or how good he looked.

She might have been more likely to trust an ugly, awkward man. This one was too slick. Not polished, but naturally slippery.

"I think you should go." What else did people say in situations like this? *It's not you, it's me?* Something about doors hitting asses on the way out?

"Suit yourself," he said, making no move down the steps. "You don't want my help, that's fine, but I'm afraid I'll have to invoke the Prank Clause."

"Excuse me?"

"With as many crank calls as an office like Karmic gets, we have to have a policy in place for people who schedule appointments just to jerk us around. Now, we wouldn't normally charge just for a consultation—unless the appointment was a fake. Then we have the prank fee. One hundred dollars. No out-of-state checks, please. Just make it out to Karmic Consultants."

"That's extortion."

"You'd pay a plumber for making a house call—oh, that's right, your daddy's your plumber." He pulled a crisp white business card from one pocket of his ragged jeans. "You got a problem, take it up with Karma. She's the boss."

"People lie on the phone."

"People lie in person too, but not Karma. Go see her, if that's what it takes to convince you we're for real."

It was oddly tempting. Part of her was curious to see for herself what sort of woman ran a paranormal investigating agency, but... "It's Saturday."

"And the office is technically closed, but Karma will be there. She's always there."

Dammit. Mia still felt like she was being taken for a ride, but she had called them, not the other way around. Maybe she had just identified herself as a mark by doing so, but maybe, just maybe, they could actually help. Was she desperate enough to resort to supposedly supernatural measures?

From the kitchen, her cell phone began playing her mother's personalized ring tone. Mia flinched. She could *not* talk to her mother. And if she sent this lunatic away, she didn't have the first idea how to find the watch. "Okay. I'll go talk to this Karma person." She snatched the card from his fingers.

"I'll just pretend you were convinced by my winning charm rather than that phone call," Chase said with a lazy grin.

Mia glared up at him. She hated assumptions and she wanted to hate his, but the damn man kept jumping to the right conclusions. It was kind of...*nice* not having to guide him through the conversation with a roadmap to get him to what she meant. He could skip ahead in the conversation and actually keep up with her.

Not just keep up, she realized. Get ahead. *She* had to struggle to keep up with *him*, conversationally. He was verbally cagey. Clearly upfront, almost obvious about it, just using a heavy dose of charm to smooth over his verbal manipulations. It was an unfamiliar challenge.

"You can go now," she snapped, sending a pointed look at the foot he'd wedged against her door.

He pulled back his foot and began backing down the steps. "I'll call ahead to let Karma know you're coming, but if the front door is locked, just ring the bell. You'll probably beat me there."

He was coming too? "You don't have to—"

"Oh, I have to. I wouldn't miss this for the world." He reached the bottom of the stairs and grabbed a bicycle she hadn't noticed leaning against the railing. Maybe the alcohol was still slowing her brain down, but it took him throwing his leg over the seat before she realized it was his.

"You came here on a *bike*?"

Chase shrugged, the muscles of his shoulders doing interesting things beneath the almost see-through thinness of his shirt. "I don't like cars."

"Oh God. You're one of those techno-phobe tree huggers, aren't you?"

It was not the most tactful thing to say. Mia could have blamed her lack of verbal filter on the alcohol still working its way out of her system, but the truth was her social filters were pretty much permanently busted. But Chase just laughed. An easy, open burst of sound that made her want to smile with him. The man was impossible to offend.

"Nope," he said. "I'd just rather get around this way when I can." He tipped an imaginary cap at her. "See you soon, sweetheart."

He kicked off and pedaled smoothly out of her neighborhood, Mia watching his every move until he turned the corner and glided out of sight. He biked everywhere. *Bet you can bounce a quarter off that ass.*

Mia flushed, slamming the door and putting her back to it. Riding a bike wasn't hot. It wasn't. He was like a middle schooler. A grown man who looked like a Calvin Klein model and rode a bike. That was *not attractive.*

It was eco-friendly though. Mia wasn't against the environment. She just disliked the rabid environmentalists who were anti-science. Anti-progress.

Chase Hunter just seemed... God, she didn't know what he seemed. He confused her. Something she could safely say no man had ever done.

But could he help her?

From the kitchen, her mother's ringtone sounded again. She couldn't answer. Not yet. Not until she had the watch so her mother wouldn't hear the lack of it in her voice and drive over here to murder her.

My fate is in the hands of a beach bum on a bicycle. Mia groaned and sank to the floor. She'd give herself five minutes to wallow. Then five minutes to put herself in order, and twenty to research the hell out of Karmic Consultants. Thirty minutes to regain her sanity; then she had to go meet the Ghostbusters.

Right after she called the cops.

"And here's a copy for your insurance adjuster."

Mia's brows pinched together as she accepted the police report being extended to her by the one-foot-in-retirement officer who had taken her complaint. "Why would my insurance adjuster need one?"

Officer Grant shrugged. "Standard policy for reimbursement." When she blinked at him blankly, he went on. "So you can replace the watch."

Mia frowned. "I don't want to replace the watch. It's irreplaceable. I want you to find it. Won't there be an investigation?"

"No sign of forced entry. Nothing else taken. A time frame of a year when the item could have been taken. *If* it was taken." Officer Grant shook his head. "Look, lady, we do what we can, but petty theft isn't enough to mobilize the force, okay? My advice? Go home and take another look. Odds are you put it in some drawer and forgot about it. Happens all the time."

"Not to me. I'm organized."

"And that's commendable. But everybody makes mistakes."

Losing the watch wasn't a mistake. It was a catastrophe. "There isn't anything you can do?"

Officer Grant reached into his desk and pulled out a card— a very familiar-looking card. "It's out there, but you could try this private consulting firm. They've worked on missing items cases with us in the past. I don't put much stock in it, but damned if they don't get results."

Mia accepted the card, her scientific heart sinking at the sight of the name emblazoned boldly across the front. Karmic Consultants.

Chapter Six
Neurotic & Neurotic-er

Karma studied the fervent young woman seated in her office. Mia Corregianni leaned forward in the straight-backed chair, so tense the air molecules around her seemed to vibrate with suppressed energy.

Her skirt suit was conservative and wrinkle-free despite the humidity, as if the fabric itself knew better than to threaten the ordered perfection of her appearance. Even her glasses didn't dare slip out of place. Her name and coloring betrayed Italian descent, but there was nothing effusive or unrestrained about her. She was bony enough to make any Italian mama tie her down and force-feed her a platter of lasagna, and she'd yanked her dark hair back in a bun so tight it had to be painful.

At first glance Miss Corregianni seemed perfectly composed, back straight, hands neatly folded. Poised. Calm. Until you heard the barely-holding-it-together edge to her voice and looked closer to see the white-knuckled clench of her fingers and the glassy panic in her eyes.

And until one recalled the slurred hysteria that had caught Karma's attention on her call last night.

Karma found her utterly fascinating—rigid control was something of a hobby of hers and Mia was an intriguing case. Not just in the restrained fervor of her need for *it*, as she had repeatedly blathered on the phone last night though she had carefully avoided explaining what *it* was, but also in the way she seemed to deeply resent her need for *it*, and correspondingly her presence in Karma's office.

Karma laced her fingers together on her desk and revealed none of her fascination in the coolly professional tone with which she said, "Miss Corregianni, I assure you, in spite of his somewhat less-than-professional appearance, Chase is one of our best."

Every instinct Karma possessed demanded it had to be Chase who handled Mia's case. If only to pit the finder's lazy, surfer-boy attitude against Mia's unrelenting control. Karma'd pay good money to watch *that* show.

"How does this work exactly?"

"I see no need to invoke the Prank Clause in your case. Should you elect to use our services, the consultant will work with you to locate your missing item. In cases involving our finders we do not charge any fees unless we deliver, and we use a sliding pay scale. The longer it takes us, the less it will cost you." Karma indicated the pricing brochure in Mia's hands.

"No, I mean I want to know how this finding, this...magic supposedly works." She lowered her voice. "I'm a scientist," she confessed as if she half expected to be thrown out for the admission.

Professional skepticism explained part of her reluctance to be there, but Karma had a feeling there was more to it than that. And her gut was rarely wrong.

"All this is quite a lot for a student of scientific skepticism to swallow." Mia unclenched her fingers long enough to flick them around the office, as though there were three-card monty hucksters dripping from the walls and bearded ladies dangling from the ceiling instead of the clean, classic lines and subtle Asian influences Karma chose to surround herself with at work.

She couldn't entirely fault skeptics like Dr. Corregianni. She'd fielded job applications from far too many fakes and con artists over the years to still have any naiveté intact on that subject.

"I don't actually know the science of how my finders' abilities work," Karma admitted. "I simply know that they do. Seeing is believing."

Mia grimaced—just a slight twitch of her oh-so-restrained facial muscles—and rocked back in her chair, though her back still stayed a strict two inches from the chair back. "I see. I'm on a tight time frame," Dr. Corregianni said with the same crisp precision she'd stated all the other facts of her case. *It* had been stolen out of her condo safe sometime in the last eleven months. She had no idea who had taken *it* or why. *It* was a family heirloom of particular significance but no great monetary value. She needed to hand *it* off at a family event in three weeks' time.

"I appreciate the urgency of the situation. That is why I sent Chase first thing this morning." At which point Mia had refused to let Chase do his job. One of her best finders was cooling his heels in her reception area when he could have already completed the find and moved on. Karma tried to remind herself the customer was always right. Even when they were working against their own interests. "I'll just call him in and we can begin, shall I? Hopefully we'll have your item back to you within the hour."

Mia blinked once, the only indication that Karma had startled her with that declaration. She'd evidently expected vague promises and sleight of hand, not an air of confident guarantee. "How can you be so positive you can help me?"

"We specialize in the impossible, Dr. Corregianni. Isn't that why you came to us?"

The words were meant to be comforting, but Mia's lips pursed with icy disapprobation. "Ms. Cox, that which we believe to be impossible or inexplicable is just that which we do not yet have the scientific maturity to understand."

Karma smiled, unruffled by the scold. "True enough. I, for one, would love to see more serious scientific studies into paranormal phenomenon." She lifted the telephone from her desk and pressed the intercom to reach the outer office where her surfer finder waited.

Mia became even more still and Karma got the sense that was her version of squirming in her chair. She was not comfortable with Chase, but why? Was it just scientific skepticism or something more personal?

"Chase," Karma spoke into the phone, a shadow of a smile curving her lips. "Why don't you join us?"

Karma, the proprietress of the unconventional investigation firm Mia had turned to in her hour of drunken desperation, was everything she could have hoped for. Tidy, controlled and professional. Anal. Mia respected those qualities—all of which could be used to describe Mia herself quite accurately. She didn't deal well with messy, emotional, impulsive people. Chase Hunter seemed inclined to be all of those.

Karma set the phone back into the cradle and folded her hands on the desk. Her deep red manicure was as perfect as her makeup. Her hair was smoothed back in a French twist with a blue-on-black silk sheen and the subtle Asian configuration to her features made her even more striking.

Karma couldn't have been much older than Mia was, but Mia couldn't imagine anyone gasping with shock when they learned her age. Her maturity was there in the regal way she held herself. Mia on the other hand...

Somehow no matter how maturely Mia dressed, no matter how many uncomfortable suits and toe-pinching heels she bought for the express purpose of demonstrating she was not a twenty-five-year-old grad student anymore, people still assumed she was a child playing dress up. And then she was supposed to be flattered that she looked so young. As if being treated like an inexperienced apprentice was ever flattering.

Mia kept her own bitten-down-to-the-nub nails hidden in her lap, feeling distinctly outclassed by the poised and elegant proprietress of Karmic Consultants in a way she rarely felt anymore. She'd built confidence in herself through her career accomplishments, thriving with the knowledge of her own competence, but five minutes in a room with Karma Cox and she was back to being the awkward, nerdy girl with impossible hair and inch-thick glasses. It just went to show you never completely escaped the psychological conditioning of your youth.

She was already uncomfortable enough just being at Karmic Consultants. A *paranormal* investigating and consulting firm. Specializing in the *supernatural*. Every synapse in Mia's scientific brain rebelled against the very idea.

But the references were beyond impeccable. She flipped open the brochure. Federal Agents, CEOs of Fortune 500 companies. It was an impressive list.

It had taken her exactly one Google search to remember where she'd tripped across the name Karmic Consultants before. Her ghost-fanatic brother Joe had left an article at her apartment about the newest Haines Hideaway Hotel, The Haunted Hideaway. Ghost hunters were eagerly reserving rooms for the grand opening at outrageous rates, but what caught Mia's attention was not the gullibility of the masses, but the single-line mention of Karmic Consultants, the paranormal solutions firm which supplied ghost-wranglers for the Inn.

Gazillionaire hotel magnate Wyatt Haines didn't seem the type to throw money at a bunch of charlatans. Of course, he hadn't seemed like the type to open up a Ghost Inn either.

Then again, Mia wasn't "the type", but here she was. In the tasteful, upscale offices of a consulting firm unlike any other.

Desperate times and all that.

Just not quite *that* desperate. "If I were to move forward with this, I would be more comfortable with another consultant," Mia said, matching Karma's precision with her own.

Chase snorted out a laugh from behind her. "Don't be shy, honey. Tell me how you really feel."

Mia felt her face heat, but firmed her chin, holding her ground. "I don't mean to offend, Mr. Hunter, but this is not a trivial matter to me, no matter how insignificant it may appear to you. I'm sure you're quite capable, but I would feel more comfortable with someone a bit more..." *Mature. Professional. Unattractive. Boring. Old.* "Experienced."

She was rather pleased with herself for pulling that excuse out of her ass. Chase couldn't be more than twenty-six or twenty-seven. He couldn't have been doing this for long.

"Oh, I'm experienced, sugar."

Mia felt herself blushing again. What was wrong with her? Flirtation and innuendo usually rolled right off her back.

Karma shot her finder a quelling look as he strolled past Mia's chair and propped himself against the edge of his boss's desk. A white stick thrust out between his lips and Mia realized he was rolling a lollipop around in his mouth. *The man is a child.*

"Dr. Corregianni," Karma said in her low, soothing tones. "Appearance aside, Chase is excellent and quite experienced. If another finder is better suited to your case, I assure you I will assign one. Why don't we start with a description of the lost item?"

Mia studied the surfer dude who was supposedly going to save her ass and keep her from being disowned by her entire family. He did not inspire confidence.

Chase sprawled against Karma's massive desk—too boneless to actually be considered leaning on it—with a Tootsie Pop rolling around in his mouth and an I-know-exactly-how-hot-I-am twinkle in his eye.

She needed Hercule Poirot and here she was faced with Matthew McConaughey's younger, buffer and even less-responsible brother. He had that I-can't-even-hold-a-minimum-wage-job-when-the-waves-are-good look. Or maybe that was just the god-awful T-shirt talking.

Her future depended on this man-child?

Mia swallowed past the lump of desperation clogging her throat and forced herself to respond to Karma's question. It was the first time she'd actually said aloud (and sober) that she'd lost it, but she ensured her voice betrayed none of her hesitation, keeping the words simple and precise. She valued precision. "It's a pocket watch. Gold, about the size of a silver dollar and probably worth about as much."

"Is there anything distinctive about it? Anything that will help our finders distinguish it from the millions of other small gold watches in the world? A mark of some kind?"

Other than the fact that my entire family thinks that stupid charm safeguards the romantic fate of five generations of Corregiannis?

Mia sealed her lips together. She may be sitting in Kooks and Charlatans Central, but that didn't mean she had to join the insanity. She refused to tell them that the watch still ran and supposedly had never stopped ticking in the last hundred-odd years it had been in her family's possession. She didn't believe that myth herself anyway. "No. Nothing distinctive."

Karma nodded once, a comfortingly exact gesture. "Since the uniqueness of the item lies primarily in its significance to you, Chase really is the most suited to this task. I encourage you to let him try."

He grinned around the candy obstruction in his mouth. "I promise to be gentle the first time."

Mia pushed up her glasses—the better to glare at the blond surfer camped out on Karma's gorgeous Asian-influenced desk. Honestly, who over the age of ten sucked on lollipops? Food on a stick was for crass state fairs and elementary school lunches.

Evidently sensing her animosity, Chase leaned back and said conspiratorially to his boss, "She's seen *Leverage*, you know."

"Ah." Karma's lips twitched. "Perhaps you would like to check up on us before we proceed?"

"No. That won't be necessary." She refrained from mentioning that she'd already done a thorough Google search and an Angie's List check before driving over here. Karmic Consultants was a legitimate, if unorthodox business. And they might be able to save her ass, if she let them.

Mia took a breath. When one exhausted logical options, the illogical was all that remained, and you couldn't get much more illogical than hiring a company specializing in occult solutions.

The magical lost-stuff-finder-guy in the sleazy T-shirt was about as far from rational as she could go.

God, what was she doing here?

The phone on the desk bleeped cheerfully. Karma glanced at it and gave Mia an apologetic smile, professional and reserved. "If you don't have any other questions for me, I'll leave you in Mr. Hunter's capable hands."

Mia smothered the urge to ask more questions, just to avoid putting herself in those hands. She wasn't afraid of being alone with Chase. *Certainly not.* He didn't make her nervous. Not one little bit.

Even if his face and form did have such perfect symmetry and proportions even researchers using mathematics to dissect attractiveness with the Marquardt Beauty Analysis would struggle to find fault with them.

Mia could acknowledge, empirically, that he was the single most attractive man she had ever laid eyes on, but that did not mean she herself was attracted to him. Michelangelo probably wished he had a model like Chase for the David, but a pretty face did not necessarily equal an agile mind. Intellectual stimulus was Mia's only erogenous zone and so far Chase Hunter had shown himself to be a woeful underachiever in that category.

He can talk circles around you, a sly little voice reminded her. Mia ruthlessly silenced it.

His baby blues could sparkle all they wanted. Sun-bleached hair could flop boyishly over his brow. The warm, beachy scent of him could wrap all around her in an intoxicating cloud. But she wouldn't be even the slightest bit affected by him.

"Dr. Corregianni?"

Mia started, realizing with a jolt that Karma had been waiting for a response. "Ah, no. No, thank you. No other questions."

She stood, smoothed the wrinkles from her tailored gray suit with a sharp tug, and moved quickly to the door before the flush rising to her cheeks could expose her embarrassment. She was *never* caught wool-gathering. Mia was on top of things at all times. Controlled. Cerebral. She did not fantasize about immature frat boys in sexist T-shirts.

Chase held the outer door to the office for her and Mia swanned through, pulling up short in the parking lot outside when she realized she had no idea what came next. She turned to face Chase, focusing intently on the oversized cartoon breasts on his shirt rather than the pheromone-enticing body beneath it. Lust was a chemical reaction, nothing more.

She didn't actually *like* him.

"You ready to play nice?" He flashed pearly white teeth that would have long since decayed from sugar-shock and rotted right out of his mouth if there were any justice in the world. Mia resisted the urge to yank the lollipop out of his mouth and smack him with it until his oh-so-pretty face was bruised with sugary smudges.

She'd give him five minutes. Then she was going home to ransack her house again. There had to be a better way to find the watch.

Chapter Seven
Captain Jack's Surfer Punk

"What happens now? Do you need the last known location to begin your search?"

Chase rolled the sucker from one cheek to the other, clacking it against his teeth along the way—just because he knew it would annoy her. "I'm not a bloodhound, sugar. I'm a finder."

Her prissy mouth pursed into a tight knot. "That doesn't mean anything to me."

"It means you think real hard about what you want and why you want it, and I find it." He snapped his fingers. "Poof."

"Poof," she repeated dismally, rubbing a hand across her flat stomach. "Do you have any Tums?"

Chase snorted back a laugh. "I'm sensing a certain lack of faith in my methods."

"Can we just get this over with?"

"No problem. We'll skip the foreplay and just get nasty."

"Oh, good Lord," she groaned.

Chase grinned. He knew he should be playing it straight, pretending he had even a passing relationship with professionalism, but she was just so much fun to wind up. He extended a hand, palm up. She looked at it as if he was offering her the plague. "You have to take my hand," he prompted.

With a visible display of reluctance, she slid her small, soft palm across his. His hands were smooth, polished by salt water and sand, and her skin was just as smooth. Long, slim fingers rested tentatively against the pad of his thumb. He'd never really thought of himself as a hand man, but hers were gorgeous. And freezing.

"Christ, your hands are like ice."

"Poor circulation. Now what?"

He was an idiot. Waxing poetic on her hands instead of doing his damn job. Chase sighed. "Just think about why you want the watch. There might be some thought transference, but I won't pry any more than absolutely necessary." He tightened his grip on her fingers so she wouldn't pull back and opened up the part of him where his gift lived.

Instantly, a fog of intangibles swamped him, pouring from her into him, a cloying tangle of unsatisfied longings flavored with Mia's unique taste, the fizzy acidic tang of a mimosa. *Conclusive neural scan results...a halfway decent date for the Christening...sweet, soft baby cuddled into her shoulder...acceptance from her mother...*

Chase jerked back, snapping the link. He rubbed one hand in a circle over his sternum as if he could rub out the uncomfortable intimacy of feeling her deepest desires. The intangibles were the things people wanted that he couldn't find—because they couldn't be found. They were the background noise he tried to ignore as he searched for the connection to the missing object, but the intangibles weren't usually so loud. Or so clear. *Fuck.*

He needed to apologize for invading her most private thoughts—that should *not* have happened—but she was glaring at him, arms folded tightly, skepticism radiating off her. "Well?"

Chase swallowed thickly, for once struggling for words. "I couldn't get a lock on it."

Mia rolled her eyes so hard she nearly fell over. "Of course you couldn't."

Her accusation snapped him out of the strange place her most private thoughts had thrown him. He frowned down at her. "Don't blame me, sweetheart. You were the one who wasn't even bothering to think of it."

"Yes, I was!"

"Stop it. You aren't even a good liar."

The death glare was back. "I don't see what difference it makes *what* I think about."

"I *told* you it made a difference. You have to focus. You have to want it badly. More than you want anything else in that moment."

"I *do* want it."

"Not badly enough."

"I can't believe you're trying to make your failure my fault. Is this how you people do business?"

"Did you see *Pirates of the Caribbean*?"

"What? How does that—"

"Did you see the movie or not?"

"I saw it," she snapped, turning to stalk toward her car.

Chase followed, almost stepping on the back of her sensible pumps. "Do you remember Captain Jack's compass? How it couldn't find shit unless it was what you truly wanted?"

"Yes. So?"

"Think of me as the human version of that compass. I can find any object, as long as it is what you want the most in the moment you touch me."

She spun to face him, stopping so abruptly he nearly plowed into her. He caught her arms to steady her and she nearly fell again smacking away his hands. "That is the most ridiculous thing I've ever heard."

"*That's* the most ridiculous thing? You should get out more."

"I think we're done here."

Chase rocked back on his heels. "You sure give up easy."

"I have better things to do with my time than stand here indulging your fantasies. Like pursuing *legitimate* means of reacquiring my watch, rather than wasting my money on mumbo jumbo."

"Shit, Mia, would it kill you to visualize the thing for five minutes? Think of it as an experiment. Controlled variables and all that shit."

"Visualization isn't scientific. I'll draw you a picture."

"Won't help. Finding it isn't about the item. It's about *you*. Your connection to it. Your imprint on it."

"My imprint," she repeated, her tone so dubious it bordered on disgust.

"The things we value, the things we *need*, we tend to leave our psychic fingerprints all over them, creating a link with them. Sometimes even without ever coming into physical contact with them. That's why I need you to want it. It tells me what kind of fingerprint I'm looking for and that lets me find your link."

"This is ridiculous."

"It ain't science."

"No, it most certainly is not."

She turned away from him, stomping a few feet before stopping and riffling through her purse with a frenzy that was all too familiar. She cursed under her breath and a big ole grin spread across Chase's face.

Dr. Mia Corregianni couldn't find her car keys.

For a moment, he hesitated. He didn't want to crawl around in her innermost thoughts again. His little parlor trick was supposed to be a surface thing. He wasn't supposed to see inside her soul like that and he was pretty sure he didn't want to. *Don't be a pussy, Hunter.*

Chase reached out and brushed the bare skin at the back of her hand. A mimosa rush. *Get away from the goddamn surfer punk...find the damn KEYS.* That internal metal wire snapped taut with a twang, an image smacking hard into his brain. *That's* what it was supposed to feel like. He pulled back his hand, dropping the connection.

"You put them in your coat pocket. And you left your coat inside."

"I didn't bring a coat," Mia snapped, fiercely satisfied to prove him wrong. Then memory asserted itself and her spine jerked straight. "Shit. I did bring a coat."

"Would you like me to get it for you?"

She glared at him, pivoting to stalk back inside. He couldn't have *found* the keys. It was impossible. "You saw it earlier."

"Nope. You just really wanted those keys."

She grabbed the dark gray wool coat off the rack in the foyer and shrugged into it. He wasn't psychic. He *wasn't*.

"Left inner pocket," he prompted cheerfully, earning another icy look.

She stalked back out the door, brushing past him. He trailed her into the parking lot.

"You're something when you're upset. You know that, Mia?"

"I'm not upset."

"Oh, you're livid. What I can't figure is why. What's so terrible about me having a little psychic gift? Why not let me try to find your watch?"

"Because I don't *want* you to be able to find it!" She spun to confront him, flinging the words at him, and only when his eyebrows rose in surprise did she even become aware of what she'd said. *Shit.* Her anger sucked back in on itself like a supernova in reverse.

She didn't want him to find the watch because then she would have to believe him. She would have to face the fact that he could. Mia leaned against her car door, trying to find her mental center.

She *loved* science. She loved knowing the why behind things, figuring out how all the pieces came together. Science was order and logic. It was everything good and solid in her world. It was the foundation upon which she'd built her life and she hated the idea of superstition threatening it. She'd spent her entire life defending science against the superstition that ran rampant in her family. She'd gotten to the point where she *needed* magic to be ridiculous. On an emotional level.

And that wasn't scientific, that emotional need. When had she become so irrational?

"You're right." The words tasted sour coming out of her mouth, but she forced herself to say them anyway. "I can't discount a hypothesis without testing it simply because I don't like it and I don't want it to work. That goes against every scientific precept I know." Mia sighed, studying the grooves in the asphalt at her feet.

Fifteen minutes ago she'd told Karma that magic was just that which humanity did not yet have the scientific maturity to understand, but here she was being just as willfully ignorant as all those people whose beliefs seemed so foolish to her.

"True science doesn't make allowances for what I want the results to be. I have to take my emotions out of this. Treat it like a proper experiment." She had to really jump in with both feet. Yes, it was ludicrous and unbelievable to think he could psychically conjure her pocket watch, but maybe that was fitting, since the reason she needed it back so badly was pretty ludicrous and unbelievable.

She lifted her face, tipping back her chin and bracing for the worst. "I want to try again."

Chase made a face. "I feel like the firing squad of your beliefs."

"I don't have beliefs. I have theories."

He shook his head. "I don't buy that. Science is a religion to you. It's a belief system and you hold it just as sacred as most people do their God."

She gritted her teeth, hating how true that statement felt. She didn't want it to be true. Any more than she wanted him to be a real psychic. "Let's do this."

Chase hesitated. "Focus, okay?" he instructed. "Really think about the watch. Block everything else from your mind and just think about how badly you want that watch back in your hands, okay?"

"I can do that."

"You got it? All focused?"

"I'm ready." She extended her hand, the fingers held stiff.

Chase didn't take her hand this time, just rested his lightly on top of hers.

Mia closed her eyes, pushing aside every thought but the watch. She pictured it in her mind, the damn thing that was causing all this trouble. If only her family didn't put so much faith in a stupid collection of gears. If only they would ever forgive her for losing it. It hadn't worked for her anyway. She didn't know how long ago it had vanished from the safe, but she'd never had a time in the last year when she felt like her romantic prospects were looking up. She just wished her parents had never forced her to take a turn with the damn thing in the first place. She would so much rather have been left alone. Why couldn't they just let her be happy alone? Not that she wanted to be alone. She wanted what Gina had, without having to be Gina to get it, but none of this would have happened—

Chase jerked back and swore. "You aren't focusing."

"I am!" Mia protested—though her focus had kind of deteriorated. He wasn't listening, anyway. He was too busy pacing and rubbing his hands like Lady Macbeth.

"I've had tough finds before," he muttered and she wasn't sure whether the pep talk was for her or him. "I broke through them and I'll break this one. We can do this. We just need to shake it up. Change…" Chase stopped pacing and spun to face her. "Tell you what. Let's return to the scene of the crime. Sometimes reliving the experience of discovering something is lost will help trigger a stronger desire to find it."

Mia hesitated. Instinct still demanded she just say *Sorry it didn't work, have a nice life*, but Gina's comments from the night before came back to her. She hadn't meant to mock her family's beliefs. She certainly hadn't *intentionally* lost the watch. Giving this superstition a chance seemed only fair. A real chance. She'd follow it through to the end. If only to prove to herself that she wasn't irrationally discounting a scientific possibility.

"Let's go back to my place," she said, hitting the button to unlock her car. "The safe is there. Will your bike fit in the trunk?"

This time it was Chase who hesitated, his eyes shadowed, but only for a moment. "Yeah. Yeah, let's go."

Chase jerked his hand away from Mia and slammed the door in his mind, trying to shake off the murky swell of her intangible desires—and the disturbing intimacy they caused. "Ooookay," he muttered, slumping against the wall beside the safe, the acidic bite of her mimosa taste still lingering in his mouth. "That didn't work."

He'd had clients who had mixed motivations and had a hard time focusing on the item they wanted, but this was the first time it was as if she resented both the item and the method of retrieving it. He couldn't break through the walls she'd constructed within herself against magic—though she didn't seem to be consciously resisting anymore. At least that was a step in the right direction.

"What am I doing wrong?" Mia grumbled.

"You don't actually want to find the watch," he told her.

"Yes, I do!"

He held up his hands in surrender. "Easy on the death glare, honey. I come in peace, remember?"

"I *do*," she insisted, a little less violently. "I need it."

"You might need it, but you don't want it. And your mixed feelings about the damn thing are making me dizzy."

"I'm *trying*." Mia slumped to her closet floor. "It's just hard to turn off thirty-four years of hating the damn thing long enough to actually want it back."

Thirty-four. Wow. He would have pegged her a decade younger than that. Though he guessed multiple Ph.Ds didn't come much younger.

He crouched next to her. "You wanna talk about why you hate it? Purge a little before we try again? Maybe tell me why you need it if you'd just as soon drop it over Niagara Falls?"

"A hundred and fifty years," she groaned. "It's been passed around my family for a century and a half and no one has ever lost it. How can I face my parents after I tell them I lost the single most important piece of our family history? They all know I think the legend behind it is idiotic. They all know how hard

71

I've tried to avoid being its caretaker, even for a day, and now this? They'll think I've done it on purpose. They'll think I *wanted* it to be lost forever just so they would stop talking about it."

"Well, didn't you?"

"Of course I did, but I didn't do it intentionally!"

Chase took her hand, just for comfort, keeping his gift firmly locked down. "Look, I know this is probably the last thing you want to hear, but maybe you aren't the best person for me to be using as a guide. There's something different about the read I get from you. The intangibles...the emotional static of what you want... It's louder with you and I'm picking up on more of your thoughts."

"You're reading my mind?" she asked, her skepticism clear.

"In a manner of speaking. I don't want to invade your privacy." Or experience the jarring intimacy of the connection any more than absolutely necessary. "Is there someone else in your family who might have a more pure relationship with the watch who would be willing to—"

"Oh God, no! They can't know it's missing. *No one* can know."

"Just one person. Someone who can keep a secret."

Mia snorted out a humorless laugh. "You clearly haven't met my family. Secrets aren't a concept they understand."

"Are you sure? No one trustworthy? "

"Let's keep that as a last resort. Or maybe right *after* the last resort on our list of options. Okay?"

"Deal. So we have to find a way to make you actually want it back."

"I told you I'm trying. I don't know what else I can do."

"Maybe we should visit your family. When you're around them, you'll probably want it more than you do right now. Use your guilty conscience against you."

Mia moaned. "I can't. I'm terrified that they'll know as soon as they see me. Like I have *I lost your precious family heirloom* tattooed on my face."

"Sounds painful. I was thinking of getting a tribal tattoo on my face, but I don't like needles."

She shot him an incredulous look before being distracted by her pocket ringing. Mia flinched. "That's my mother. I've been ignoring her all day. She'll just keep calling until I pick up."

"So answer it. Maybe she'll make you want the watch back really badly. Just grab my hand if you're feeling particularly desperate and I'll try to get a read."

"I don't—"

"Do you want it back or don't you?"

Mia shot him another of her patented death glares and jerked out the phone. It was one of those cutting-edge, one-upped-every-six-weeks by the *next* next-gen techno-phones. A far cry from his eight-year-old flip phone with the numbers worn to invisibility.

She tapped something on the screen to connect the call.

"Hi, Ma."

Chapter Eight
Prophecies, Beards & Devil's Bargains

"Mia Rochelle Corregianni, where have you been all day? I've been calling and calling."

Her mother had jumped straight to her full name. Never a good sign. "I had some errands to—"

"Never mind that now. Zia Verna had one of her prophecy dreams."

Mia cringed. Her grandmother's youngest sister had been declared the family seer and every time she ate spicy food before bed, they were treated to a *prophecy.* "Ma—"

"This is serious, Mia. She had a vision. A vision of such disaster I had to call you right away to confirm it wasn't true. Did you *break* Great-grandmother Anna Maria's watch?"

Her stomach made a leap for her throat. She swallowed it back down to its natural position. "No, Mama, I didn't break it." *I lost it.*

"Oh, praise Mary, Mother of God. I haven't been able to breathe right all day, worrying that something really had happened to it and that was why you weren't answering your phone."

"No, I promise. The watch's in one piece." *Wherever it is.* "It's probably just a false alarm. Like when Zia Verna predicted the Royals would go to the World Series three years in a row."

Chase smothered a laugh.

"She should stay away from the sports," her mother agreed. "Gina told me you had a date last night. Did you wear the watch? Are you bringing him to the Christening tomorrow? Is he handsome?"

"Why do I have to have a date to a baptism?"

"Don't you want to bring your new friend to meet your family?"

Mia glanced at Chase, hunkered down on her closet floor beside her, then reminded herself that her mother was asking about Speed-dating From Hell, not Chase the Mega Hunk. "It was speed-dating technically, and just because I spend five minutes with a guy doesn't mean I'm going to inflict the whole family on him."

"Inflicting! Mia, really. As if we would be rude to your guest."

"You would mob him and force him to propose to me before dinner."

One of Chase's eyebrows slid upward and his lips twitched.

Her mother tsked. "I don't know where you get these fanciful ideas about our family, Mia."

"Then how would you describe Nicky knocking cousin Jamie's boyfriend's knees out from under him last Easter and telling him he might as well propose while he was down there?"

"Your brother was just teasing..."

"Or two years ago when Zia Anna locked Mario and his girlfriend in the bathroom for three hours and then told everyone Laura was compromised and they'd have to marry quickly because of the baby?"

"A little joke. You always take things so seriously."

"I'm not bringing a date, Mama." She was too busy trying to locate the cursed watch to try to find one.

"Well," her mother sniffed. "If that's how you want to be."

Chase shifted beside her and Mia looked at him. He arched an eyebrow questioningly and she remembered she was supposed to be longing for the watch—which was a challenge at the moment since she was busy wishing the thing to the deepest darkest circle of hell.

"Mama, I'm busy. Can I call you later?"

"You're working, aren't you?" her mother said in an aggrieved tone that made it sound like she was hooking for spare cash.

Mia's shoulders knotted with all-too-familiar defensive tension. She forced herself to take a deep breath. "My work is very important to me."

"Would it kill you to take a weekend off? That watch can work miracles for you, *mia bella*, but it's running out of time. It has *never failed*. You must trust the magic. Your soulmate—"

"Maybe I don't have a soulmate. I like being on my own. Have you considered that?"

Her mother gave a theatrically loud gasp of horror. "Mia!"

She'd known her mother would react that way. Mia didn't know why she'd said it, daring to oppose the idea that True Love was the be all end all of the universe. Must have been the stress of the day.

She felt Chase's eyes on her, but refused to look at him.

"I'm sorry, Ma. I've gotta go. See you tomorrow." She disconnected before her mother could work up a guilt trip to keep her on the phone. Dropping the phone to the carpet, Mia thunked her head back against the wall, the muscles in her neck going limp. "I'm going to Hell for misleading my mother."

Chase settled down beside her, stretching his legs alongside hers, their shoulders just brushing. "You weren't even remotely uncomfortable with me eavesdropping on your half of that conversation, were you?"

Mia rolled her head to the side to meet his bright blue gaze. "Should I have been?"

"No, no. It's just...there's no awkwardness in you. You're so much yourself. It's...unusual to see someone so comfortable in her own skin."

Mia gave a soft huff that would have been a disbelieving snort if she had more energy. *No awkwardness?* Please. She was all thumbs and elbows. She didn't know who he was seeing when he looked at her, but it wasn't the real Mia. She wasn't comfortable in her skin, she was defensive of it. Protective against everyone who seemed to want to stretch it into a different shape.

"So you need a date for a baptism, huh?"

"Mmm," she hummed vaguely in the affirmative.

"Is this a Sadie Hawkins thing or should I take the hint and ask you?"

"What?"

"Would you do me the honor of accompanying me to—" Chase flashed a knee-melting smile. "Where are we going?"

"It's my niece's Christening."

"What time should I pick you up?"

"On your bike?"

"Don't knock riding on the handlebars until you've tried it. What time?" His face was close, his blue eyes impossible to look away from.

"The Christening is at two with a command performance at family dinner afterward with the cast of thousands." A slow flush crept up her neck. Was he really asking her out? This smooth-talking demi-god? "Trust me, you don't want anything to do with it."

"And neither do you. Which makes it perfect."

"Perfect?"

"You'll be surrounded by your family, wracked by guilt. What better time to find the watch? What do you bet I'll have a read on it inside five minutes?"

Of course. Finding the watch. She must be more tired than she thought if she was imagining this genetic anomaly of physical perfection would be asking her out. "Do you ask all your clients out?"

"Special circumstances."

Mia told the obnoxious part of her that turned to mush at the warm look in his eyes that he wasn't saying she was special. Just defective when it came to finding the watch. "So I'm wracked with guilt. Then what? You take off to find it?"

"Actually, I have a proposal for you."

Mia's suspicious nature tried to rise up at the glint in his baby blues, but she was too exhausted to work up much skepticism. "What kind of proposal?"

"You need someone to run interference with your family at this Christening, right? Well, it just so happens, I could use a...let's call it a romantic beard of my own."

"You're gay?"

"Sweetheart, I have *all* the hetero tendencies."

"So this beard...?"

"A fake girlfriend. For reasons I won't go into, I need to convince a few friends that I'm seeing someone more seriously than I usually do."

The idea that he went through women like Kleenex wasn't a stretch for her imagination. "Why me? I'm not one of those cool nerds."

Chase's eyes lit with merriment. "There are cool nerds?"

"You know, the Comic-Con nerds who know all that pop-culture sci-fi stuff. That whole nerd chic thing. I don't own a television and I've never played a video game. Lots of people think science nerds are all really techy, but I'm not. I'm just awkward. I don't know that I'd be a good fake girlfriend."

"You'll be perfect."

"Why?"

"You're available and you're breathing. Besides, you're a genius right? How hard can being my fake girlfriend be?"

"I'm a terrible liar. Awful. Appalling. Horrendous."

"You missed your calling as a thesaurus. But it'll be easy. Trust me. And you can't tell me it isn't efficient."

God, that word again. It was going to kill her. "So you'll pretend to be my boyfriend for the Christening if I'll pretend to be your girlfriend...."

"...at an event in the near future. It'll be painless, I promise. Probably a backyard barbeque or something similar that reeks of suburban bliss."

Mia hesitated, feeling inexplicably queasy at the idea of faking a relationship with the man beside her. Logically, it was an excellent idea. So elegant in its simplicity she should have been jealous of him for thinking of it first. Using Chase as her fake boyfriend would get her family off her back and put him in touching range during the time when she was most likely to actually want the watch back.

So why this uneasiness? Why was she almost disappointed by his suggestion? It wasn't like she'd had her heart set on dating him for real. He was all wrong for her. All slick surface and smooth talking. Mia preferred substance and depth. She would have said no if he'd asked her for real. Wouldn't she?

But this wasn't a real date. It was a handy ruse. And it just might work.

"Deal."

Chapter Nine
The Morning After Symphony

It had seemed like such a good idea at the time.

Mia paced in front of the bay window, waiting for Chase to arrive for their first "date" and wallowing in regret. She'd agreed to Chase's plan in a moment of weakness, but during a long night of tossing and turning, she'd had plenty of time to itemize, rank and color code all the ways in which introducing Chase to her family was a Very Bad Idea.

Her family would notice the lie. They would never believe she would go for Chase, or that he would go for her. And even if they did, she wouldn't be able to pull it off. The lies. God, her heart turned to stone just thinking of it. Falsifying a relationship. One of them would slip up and reveal something about how they met and then her entire family would know she'd lost their magic trinket.

And if they did believe her... That was almost worse.

Her relatives were like baby ducks. They would imprint on him as The One and harass her for the rest of her life with *whatever happened to that lovely Chase boy, Mia?* She wasn't sure their hope that she had finally found someone, when she so obviously hadn't, was going to be any less painful than their constant disappointment over her solitary state.

She would just tell him thanks, but no thanks. She would have canceled already—she had a speech prepared and everything—but she realized this morning she didn't have his phone number and calling Karmic Consultants and asking Karma to break her date was a level of embarrassment she wasn't ready for yet.

So she paced, and waited, and mentally rehearsed her brush off. She'd have to keep her wits about her. The man was slippery. If she wasn't on her toes, he had an alarming way of getting her to agree to things.

Mia tugged at the collar of her stretchy charcoal gray dress. It was a turtleneck style that covered her from wrists to knees, but she hadn't been thinking of modesty when she put it on. Her only priority was covering her throat and chest so her family wouldn't notice she wasn't wearing the watch on the chain her mother had strung for her to dangle it between her boobs like a fishing lure.

She fidgeted with her clutch, frowning out the front window into the gray, rainy afternoon. Was he biking here? In this weather? Maybe that was a good thing. If he was drenched, she could tell him she simply couldn't bring him to the church like that. No need for pretty speeches that could get garbled on their way out of her mouth.

Or better yet, maybe he wasn't coming anymore. He wasn't late, but he *felt* late because she'd been agonizing over this afternoon all morning and had been ready for twenty minutes.

This was a terrible idea. What did she really know about this guy? She'd met him twenty-seven hours ago and she hadn't exactly been at her best during those hours. He could be the world's hottest serial killer for all she knew, hypnotizing his victims with his easy charm and abnormally symmetrical features.

Okay, that might be a touch extreme. The most likely scenario painted him as a con artist, not a murderer. But should she really be bringing possible con artists into her family home? Introducing him to a collection of the most gullible people ever put on the earth? They believed in a magic watch, for Christ's sake. There was no telling what damage he could do over cannelloni.

An old rust-pocked Subaru station wagon pulled into the visitor parking and Mia snapped to attention, forgetting to breathe for a moment as she stared out the front window. Was that him?

Chase straightened out of the driver's side and Mia nearly moaned. Yep, he was just as freakishly attractive as she'd remembered. His crisp white dress shirt was untucked and open at the collar, framing the richly tanned column of his throat. A dark blazer hugged his muscular shoulders, falling open as he shoved back one side to tuck his hand into a front pocket as he strolled toward her door. Strutted, more like. A peacock in wolf's clothing. His jeans were dark blue and looked brand new—not a ragged edge in sight.

The man cleaned up *nice*. Dammit. It would have been so much easier to send him packing if he'd shown up to take her to the Christening in an obnoxious shirt and holey faded denim.

Not that she would let his appropriate attire faze her. She had a plan. A speech.

Mia crossed to the door and flung it open, catching Chase with his hand hovering halfway to the doorbell. His bright white teeth flashed out from his tanned face in a lightning-strike smile. "You ready?"

"I've changed my mind," she announced. "I'm sorry you came all the way out here, but I didn't have your number or I would have called to cancel."

Chase arched an eyebrow. "Hm."

"Excuse me?"

"You surprised me, Mia. I hadn't taken you for a girl who reneged on her bargains."

"I'm not reneging. I'm reevaluating. I'll still do your barbeque thing, since I did agree to that, but I don't think your presence at my niece's Christening is appropriate or wise." She would never be able to fake easy intimacy with this man. He made her feel too unsteady. Too precarious.

"I thought you needed a date."

"I do, but the risks involved with bringing you outweigh the potential benefits. Too many things could go wrong."

Chase grinned. "I bet you're a blast on a Vegas weekend. Man, I'd love to see you play roulette."

Mia pursed her lips. "You're implying that risk-taking is a pleasurable activity, but the adrenaline high associated with gambling has never appealed to me."

"Because you've never tried it."

"I don't need to jump off a bridge to know it would hurt."

"But what a rush all the way down. I'll add bungee jumping to the list."

"The list?" she asked, knowing even as she spoke that she should have ended the conversation already.

"Roulette, bungee jumping... I'm going to teach you to love risk. There's a wild child in you, Mia Corregianni. I'm sure of it."

"Which just goes to show how little you know me." Her definition of risk was moving forward with an experiment before the funding was approved. "My family would never believe we're a couple."

"I thought opposites attracting was a scientific principle."

"In electrons and protons, maybe. The science that governs human attraction is a bit more complicated."

Chase groaned, pressing a hand over his heart. "I love when you go all scientific on me. Tell me about your degrees again?"

His eyes twinkled and there was nothing derisive in his expression, but Mia couldn't escape the fear that he was mocking her. She swallowed down a sudden lump in her throat. "We don't suit. This farce wouldn't last five minutes, but thank you for being willing to try. I appreciate your dedication to your job."

"Honey, I never work this hard for a job."

Mia felt her face flushing. Was he implying he was working this hard because of her? Why? How did he benefit from it? People were motivated by self-interest, but she couldn't seem to figure his out. "What are you getting out of this?" she blurted.

A laugh burst out of him. "The pleasure of your company? I like you, Mia."

She narrowed her eyes. "Stop trying to charm me."

"You're going to like me too."

"I doubt it."

"Everyone does eventually."

"I'm not everyone. You and I aren't going to get along, Chase. You can't charm me and I can't cut through your layers of protective bullshit, no matter how direct I am."

Something sober and real flickered in his eyes. "So we're at an impasse."

"Precisely."

His teeth gleamed in another quick, flashing smile. Just like that, any trace of sobriety was gone. "Are you sure I can't charm you?"

"Positive."

"But you have to admit, I'm charming. Your family would love me."

They would. Too much, no doubt. "I can't risk—"

"What's the worst that can happen? They find out the watch is missing? They're just as likely to discover that with you alone. This way, at least you have someone to take the attention off the watch. I'll be like the magician's assistant, standing there looking sexy so no one notices you rigging the tricks behind the curtain."

"Just think. If you weren't so aware of your own attractiveness, you'd be even sexier."

"Like if you didn't know you were so damn smart, you'd be even smarter?"

Her hands fisted. "That's hardly the same thing."

"Confucius say *The wise man knows only that he knows nothing.* Or something."

"I don't think that was Confucius."

"Einstein? Machiavelli? I get all those dead smart guys mixed up."

Mia's jaw dropped. "Did you just compare Albert Einstein to Machiavelli?"

"Yep. Or maybe I was thinking of da Vinci and Oppenheimer. Which one invented the clock?"

"Neither. Unless by clock you mean atomic bomb."

"Well, whoever it was, we're gonna be late if we stand here debating it. You look great, by the way. That dress is hot on you. Ready to go?"

Mia had collected her clutch before she collected her wits enough to realize Chase had somehow evaded all her attempts to break their date. His charm was totally in her face, so much so that she was focused on the fact of it, rather than the realization that it was working and he was getting his way. It was a smoke screen to conceal his constant evasions and manipulations.

Maybe, just maybe, he could handle her family.

"Relax, Mia," he said from the doorway when he saw her hesitate. "What could possibly go wrong?"

What could go wrong? She was only going to a church with the hottest man she'd ever met in order to pretend he was her boyfriend in front of her entire family so they wouldn't suspect that she'd lost the single most important object in their world.

What indeed?

Chapter Ten
Prepping for the Executioner

"Just promise me one thing." Mia locked her door and descended the steps at Chase's side. "Whatever happens, if anyone in my family suggests doing a Christening-slash-wedding since we already have the church for the afternoon, promise me you'll run like hell."

He laughed. "I'll keep the getaway car running. Just try not to slow us down in those heels."

"I'll drive." She hit the button on her key fob and he changed course across the parking lot as her tail lights flashed.

Chase's grin was intended to tease her, but she couldn't figure out why. He was always laughing, always teasing, but half the time she felt like she couldn't keep up with the witty commentary that must be running quickly though his thoughts. The internal thoughts of most people didn't interest her, but with him she felt like she was missing out on some fabulous joke by not being inside his head.

This time he let her in on it. "Don't want your parents to see I drive a beater, eh?"

She stopped in her tracks, frowning between Chase, his car and her own. "I hadn't taken into account the status differential between your car and mine. I assure you, my reasoning was purely logical. I know the way to the church and my parents' house where the party will be held after the Christening. My car is more fuel efficient and since the family obligation is mine, it seems fair that I be the one to provide transportation. I would have suggested picking you up previously if I had been thinking clearly yesterday." And if she hadn't been trying desperately to think of any way to avoid bringing him.

The logic and practicality of her choice were clear, but she tended to forget how few people made decisions based on reason. Of course Chase would be the kind of person who made decisions based on emotion. Of course he would see her choice as a slight against his car, and by extension against his very masculinity.

Yet another example of how much Mia sucked at social nonsense. If he was anything like the other men she'd dated in the last few years, he would pout for the remainder of the day or make snide comments about her rampant penis envy—which was exactly what she didn't need at Marley's Christening.

Mia sighed. She hated making concessions for social ridiculousness, but she needed today to go smoothly. "Are you going to feel like I'm symbolically chopping off your penis if I drive?"

Chase burst out laughing. "I think my penis can take it. I was just teasing you, Mia." He nudged her into motion toward her car again. "I thought maybe you were planning to pass me off as some doctor or lawyer and my car was screwing with your agenda."

"I don't have an agenda."

The unfamiliar heels caught on the uneven pavement and Mia wobbled. Chase's firm grip was instantly at her elbow, steadying her—but Mia started at his touch, nearly tripping herself all over again.

God, this was never going to work. She could say all the right words, but her body was going to be screaming the lie if she jumped every time he brushed against her.

He was hitting all the right notes—the secret, just-between-us smile, the hand on her arm. If their deception relied only on him, it would have gone off beautifully. No. She was the problem.

"I can't do this." Mia dug in her heels. "They'll see through me immediately. I'll never be able to fake the necessary intimacy to convince them we're a couple."

"So we aren't a couple." He coaxed her into motion again. "Why can't it be our first date?"

"You're only the second guy I've ever introduced to my family. My parents would never believe I chose throwing them at you as our first date."

"So we met yesterday, love at first sight, and—"

"I don't believe in love at first sight."

"Which makes it even more romantic."

"I don't do romance." Her definition of romance was a man who didn't mind being ignored in favor of a stack of scientific journals.

"Maybe you do with me."

She narrowed her eyes at him. "Maybe I had a lobotomy last night. It's the only way I could have believed this was going to work."

"We just have to stay close to the truth. We're less likely to get tripped up or contradict one another that way. Trust me, effective lying is all about circling around to check out the truth from a different angle."

"But *yesterday*? That makes me sound so..."

"Impulsive? Romantic?" He drew her to a stop next to her car and brushed a finger across her cheek, just a feather-light caress.

Mia released a shuddering breath. He angled his head close to hers. *Oh my. Oh my oh my oh my.* Was he going to kiss her? Now? Like this? *Why?*

"Just keep looking at me like that, sweetheart, and your family will buy everything we're selling them." He reached out and opened her door for her. "Your chariot, m'lady."

Mia glowered at the door, jolted out of the spell he'd woven around her. "You don't need to do that. No one is here to see you."

"What if I'm just a gentleman? Did you consider that?"

"I think it's best if we keep things on as professional a footing as possible, all things considered. Kindly save your chivalry."

He grinned cheekily. "Maybe the chivalry makes me feel manly. After the vehicular emasculation, the least you can do is put up with a little door opening."

"Fine." She slid into the driver's seat and buckled in, then fidgeted with her clutch where she'd tucked it against her hip as Chase rounded the hood. When he opened the passenger door she pointedly ignored the intensely masculine way he folded himself into the car.

"Telling my family as little as possible about you will make it less likely they will discover the real nature of our relationship," she announced as she started the engine and pulled out of the lot. "We'll be vague, implying a relationship of substantial duration."

"You went out speed-dating on Friday. I don't think they're going to buy that we've been secretly seeing one another for months."

"How did you know about that? Never mind—the call with my mom. We'll say that we'd had a fight and broken up and that was why I went speed-dating. None of this love-at-first-sight stuff."

"How did I get back in your good graces?"

"Shouldn't we be focused on how we met?"

"This is important. How did I win you back? I might need to know this stuff."

"You... I don't know. You showed up on my doorstep with flowers."

"Flowers? You're that easy?"

"Fine. Forget the flowers. You showed up on my doorstep and talked and talked and talked until I agreed to go out with you just to shut you up."

Chase grinned. "That sounds like us."

"There is no us."

"Aw, snookums, don't talk like that. There will always be an us. Ever since I first laid eyes on you at Bubba's Shrimp Shack, I knew you were my one and only."

"Bubba's Shrimp Shack?"

"I thought it gave the story some color. What do you think?"

"I think color is less important than credibility." She frowned, trying to think how she could possibly have met a guy like Chase. "Maybe you came in as a volunteer test subject for my last experiment."

"Kinky. I like it."

"There is nothing kinky about my work." She scowled at a red light. "How long have we been together? Not too long. We don't want them to think we're too serious. Maybe three or four weeks?"

"Have we had sex yet?"

Mia's face went up like a torch—a series of wholly delicious images flashing *very inappropriately* through her brain. "Jesus, Mary and Joseph."

"I should know, in case your father gives me the evil eye, should I look guilty or virtuous?"

"Virtuous. Very, very virtuous. But he won't give you the evil eye. He'll be too busy hiding in his den. And even if you meet him, they aren't puritanical like that. My family..." Mia sighed. "Picture the exact opposite of me in every way. Loud, overbearing, fun."

"Hey, you're fun. And funny too."

"No, I'm not. Every last one of them is the life of the party, except me. If I didn't look so much like my dad, I'd be convinced I was switched at birth." She rubbed at the bridge of her nose. "I'm the second of five kids. Three girls, two boys. My parents are both from big families—my mom has four sisters and my dad has three brothers and two sisters. All of them married. All of them with a pack of kids of their own. And every single one of them will be there today. I'll try to help you navigate who's who, but it's pretty much hopeless the first time, unless we can get everyone to wear nametags like we did at my cousin Mario's wedding. Except my other cousins made a game out of switching their nametags every fifteen minutes, so even that system wasn't perfect."

"Sounds like an adventure."

"It is what it is. I love my family, but there are days when I secretly wish I'd been born an only child to a pair of yuppy WASPs." She forced herself to take a breath. "What about you? What's your family like?"

For a fraction of a second, Mia saw Chase go still out of the corner of her eye. Then his bright easy smile flashed out and she decided she must have imagined his momentary tension. "Not much to tell. Typical yuppy WASPs. When did your family come over from Italy?"

"Late eighteen hundreds. My great-great-grandfather was called Gianni Correa, but at Ellis Island they got his name mixed up and we've all been Corregiannis ever since." Mia didn't miss the fact that Chase had dodged her question. He really didn't like to talk about himself. Who was this man with the slippery charm? "What should I know about you, Chase Hunter?"

"I love to surf."

"Um, okay." Not exactly what she'd been driving at. Clearly a faulty question. Imprecise. "How long have you been a psychic finder?"

"I could always do it, but I've only been doing it for cash for the last five years."

"Maybe we shouldn't mention that part. Just in case my family gets suspicious." She mentally tracked through the standard get-to-know-you small talk she'd always thought was such a waste of time. "Have you always lived around here?"

"More or less. You?"

"Except for college. Cal Tech. Did you—?" Mia broke off. Was it rude to ask if he'd gone to college? Or worse to assume he hadn't?

"Penn," Chase said, anticipating the question.

She blinked. "Wow. That's a good school."

"I dropped out."

He said it without a trace of defensiveness or resentment. Just stating a fact, so comfortable with himself it didn't even faze him, but Mia felt her inner intellectual snob deflate at the admission. "I see."

"I can lie about it if you don't want your parents to think you're slumming."

A blush seared her cheekbones. "No. Of course not. I would never ask you to... Lots of people don't finish college." Just no one she would ever consider dating. She swallowed around a sudden clog in her throat, inexplicably nervous. Awkwardness filled the car's interior like sulfuric gas—noxious and cloying. Icebreaker. She needed an icebreaker. Didn't people tell jokes to break the ice? "Do you want to hear my favorite joke?"

Chase gave a short coughing laugh at her abrupt question. "Sure. That'd be great."

"It's not a very good joke."

He laughed again. "Then why is it your favorite?"

"Well, *I* think it's funny, but no one else ever does. It's a science joke."

"I didn't even know there were science jokes. Now I'm dying of curiosity. Lay it on me."

"I just didn't want you to have unrealistic expectations. I'm not a good joke teller and—"

"Mia."

"Yes?"

"Just tell the damn joke already."

"Right." Mia pressed each of her fingers in turn against the steering wheel, concentrating intently on getting the words in the right order. Jokes were a serious business. "An atom walks into a bar—"

Chase snorted.

"That isn't the funny part!" she protested.

"I'm sorry. I'll try to only laugh at the funny parts. Carry on."

She shot him a quick quelling glare and began again. "An atom walks into a bar. He's visibly depressed. He slumps up onto a stool and the bartender says to him, 'You look terrible. Are you all right?'"

A soft wheezing, panting sound came from the passenger's side. Mia snuck a look at Chase and found him biting his lower lip to keep from laughing.

"Chase!"

A bark of laughter exploded from his mouth. "I'm sorry. See? It's a great joke. I can't even keep a straight face."

"We aren't to the funny part yet!"

"Quite right. A depressed molecule is talking to a bartender."

"Atom."

"Sorry. A depressed atom. Go on."

"So the atom says…"

Chase snorted.

"Do you want to hear this joke or not?"

"The atom says, 'Do you want to hear this joke or not?'"

"Of course not! God, you are so infuriating. Just shut up and let me finish." She cleared her throat. "The atom says, 'The most horrible thing happened today. I lost an electron.' And the bartender says, 'Oh no! Are you sure?' And the atom sighs and says, 'Yes.'" She smiled to herself, gearing up for the punchline. "'I'm *positive.*'" Mia giggled. "Get it? *Positive?*"

She laughed again until she realized the car was eerily quiet. *Crap.* He didn't think it was funny at all. She pulled into the church parking lot and threw the car into park. "You hate it," she grumbled.

Then she looked at him and her heart developed a worrying arrhythmia. He was smiling. More than smiling. His eyes were twinkling, shoulders shaking, dimples flashing. He laughed silently, his grin broad and easy. "Mia," he shook his head, wiping away a tear from the corner of one eye, "I think that might have been the best joke I've ever heard."

She frowned. "You're making fun of me."

"*No.*" His blue eyes flashed. "No, I'm not. That joke was perfect because it's so perfectly *you.*"

"It's nerdy. I told you I wasn't funny. You were laughing at me the whole time."

"I wasn't laughing at you. Christ, Mia, do you have any idea how adorable you are when you tell that joke?" He reached up, gently brushing the pads of his calloused fingers along her jaw.

"Adorable?" People didn't call her that. She wasn't cute. She wasn't sexy. She was all cutting, androgynous intellect.

"It's a fabulous joke," Chase murmured. His face was suddenly oh-so-close. His tan made his eyes jump out like sapphires, but it was his lips Mia couldn't take her eyes off of. His lower lip was invitingly full. She wanted to lick it, suck it, bite it. Her breath was coming too fast and she knew if anyone looked at her in that moment they would see dilated pupils and flushed cheeks. Chemistry in action. But for once Mia was more concerned with sensation than science. He was inches away, then centimeters. Leaning in, tantalizing. Her lashes fluttered down.

A harsh knocking next to her ear had her yelping and jerking back.

She twisted and saw the twin wrinkled faces of Nonna and Zia Anna peering through the driver's-side window, eyes wide, identical dentured grins beaming at her.

"Am I seeing double?" Chase asked.

The realization that he hadn't been about to kiss her shattered her illusions with a crash. He'd been performing. *Of course.* Just as they'd agreed to. A guy like Chase wouldn't be interested in a girl like her. To hide her mortification, Mia spoke rapidly. "They're twins. My grandmother—call her Nonna, everyone does—and on the right is her twin Zia Anna. But if you can't tell them apart, just call them both Nonna. They're both grandmothers a dozen times over."

"Who's your young fella, Mia Rochelle?" Zia Anna bellowed through the glass.

"He looks like a stud," her grandmother proclaimed at a similarly ear-splitting decibel, giving her an enthusiastic double thumbs up.

"Sweet Mary, Mother of God," Mia groaned. "We're here."

Chase grinned. "And so it begins."

Chapter Eleven
Christenings a la Corregianni

It took her family approximately seven seconds to separate Mia from Chase. Like lions separating a wounded gazelle from the herd for easy slaughter.

As Chase stepped out of the car, her male relatives swarmed him, smiling and back-patting in a deceptively genial manner. Meanwhile, Mia was flanked by her grandmother and Zia Anna as the eighty-three-year-old pair speculated gleefully about whether Chase had taken The Steroids to enhance his manly physique and whether The Steroids had adversely affected the size of his package.

Then Nonna's hawk-like gaze zoomed in on her chest. "Mia Rochelle! Why aren't you wearing the watch?"

"It doesn't go with this outfit."

Zia Anna gasped and Nonna crossed herself, both of them gawping at her like suggesting the watch didn't match every outfit in the known universe was akin to calling the Virgin Mary a dirty slut.

She was almost relieved to see her mother sailing across the parking lot, her substantial bosom thrust out in front of her like the prow of a ship—no doubt drawn in by her standard issue one-of-my-children-is-embarrassing-me Italian mother tractor beam.

"Mia, why are you upsetting Nonna?" Her eyes locked on Mia's cleavage—or what would have been Mia's cleavage if she'd had breasts and a low-cut top. A frown puckered her mother's brows and mouth in unison, accentuating the little lines that spiked out from her lips like the *Enterprise* going warp speed. "Where's the watch?"

Mia resisted the urge to shoot Chase an I-told-you-so look. "I can't wear it every second of every day."

Zia Anna and Nonna gasped as one and swayed against one another, emitting little moans. Her mother took a more direct approach—pinching the skin of her upper arm and twisting it.

"Ma! *Ow.*"

"How can the watch work if you don't wear it?" Angelina Marconi Corregianni flung her hands in frustration, her Italian-by-way-of-Jersey accent thickening as she bemoaned the stubbornness of her second-born daughter. "Your sister needs you in the sacristy."

Her mother's face was tense—much more stressed than it should have been on such a joyful occasion and Mia's heart tumbled hard against her ribcage. "Is everything okay? Is it Marley?"

Her mother waved away the question with an eloquent flap of one hand. "Go."

Mia met Chase's gaze over the roof of the car. "Chase..."

He grinned and shooed her off. "Go on. I'm fine."

Her brother Joey threw one All-State linebacker arm around Chase's shoulders, his the-devil-made-me-do-it smile anything but comforting. "Yeah, go on, Mia. We'll take care of your friend here."

"He has immunity. Nobody touches him." She took a moment to fix a quelling stare on each of her brothers and cousins in turn, knowing that her efforts were largely useless. Chase was on his own. "I'll be back in two minutes," she told him before taking off toward the side entrance to the sacristy as quickly as her uncomfortable heels could carry her.

Mia wasn't a believer, but Catholicism wasn't so much about belief as ritual in her family. This was their church, where every marriage, baptism and confirmation took place. She knew it better than her own condo. Letting herself into the sacristy, she found Gina pacing, bouncing a fussy Marley in her arms. Their older sister Teresa, the godmother-to-be, was nowhere in sight.

"What's wrong?" Mia said as she crossed to Gina's side, reaching out automatically to take Marley for a quick cuddle.

Gina passed her over. The baby, like any Corregianni offspring, was accustomed to being passed from family member to family member. She curled willingly into Mia's arms, knotting one tiny fist in the small hairs against Mia's neck and tipping her small, red face up to her aunt to better display her indignation. Mia breathed in her soft, clean baby smell and gently patted her back, taking up the time-honored baby sway to soothe her niece.

Gina gave a wry smile when Marley continued her hiccupping wail. "Am I a bad person that I'm happy she didn't immediately quiet down for you? She was up a million times last night and she's been a pain all day. If she was suddenly perfect for you, I think I would have had to kill you."

"You're human," Mia said in a crooning voice designed to calm Marley, though it had no effect. "What's the emergency? Mama looked freaked."

"Mama's going to herniate something." Gina sank down onto a stack of kneelers. She'd always been round where Mia was angular and the baby had added extra padding to her curves, but she wore the weight well, looking fresh and bountiful, warm and soft and maternal. Now she laced her hands over the gentle swell of her belly.

"I need you to stand as godmother."

Mia ignored the quick flash of pleasure the idea of being godmother to sweet, perfect, fussy, cranky Marley inspired. "Where's Teresa?"

"Sitting in the front pew. She just said that she and Martin couldn't become godparents. 'Not now.' Whatever that means. I thought Mama was going to have a seizure."

"So the godfather...?"

"Tony's asking his brother." Gina turned dewy brown eyes on her. "Please say you'll do it, Mia. I wanted to ask you in the first place but I thought Teresa would be mortally offended if I didn't ask her and Martin because they're the portrait of domestic bliss and you're..."

"And I'm me. I get it. And I'd be honored."

"Thank God. And just think, all the drama about Teresa backing out will take any attention off the fact that you didn't bring a date."

"Actually, I did bring a date."

"You're kidding." Gina straightened abruptly, nearly falling off the stack of kneelers as it listed precariously beneath her. "The zoning guy?"

"Don't sound so hopeful. You aren't getting that exemption."

"Then who?"

Mia felt her face flush. This was her first test. She wasn't sure whether it would be her easiest or her hardest. Gina was closest to her, so would that make her easy to fool or impossible?

"His name is Chase."

God, she was a terrible liar. She hadn't even said anything untrue yet and already her cheeks were Bunsen-burner hot and her eyelids were starting to twitch. Mia hid her face against Marley's dark, peach-fuzz hair.

"'His name is Chase'?" Gina mimicked. "That's all I get?"

"He..."

Salvation arrived in the form of Gina's husband Tony and his nineteen-year-old pizza-delivery-boy brother who would be Marley's other spiritual guide.

"The church is packed," Tony boomed. He had two volumes—loud and louder. He'd never make it as a librarian, but he was a total teddy bear, and he loved her baby sister more than life itself. Gina had picked a winner. Or, as she put it, the watch had picked one. Tony gave a sharp clap and hunkered down like he was inviting them all to huddle up. "We ready to get this party started?"

"Absolutely!" Mia said, rushing toward the door to the sanctuary before Gina could stall. If they were up at the altar, her sister couldn't interrogate her about Chase.

Or so she thought.

The holy father intoned in Latin, Marley kept up a constant keening complaint, and, on this sacred occasion, as Mama and Nonna and all the aunties dabbed at their eyes, Gina stood, with her baby dripping holy water, and gossiped.

"Which one is he?" she hissed in Mia's ear during the Lord's Prayer.

"Shut up. I'm praying."

"Oh please. You barely know the words."

"Then I'd better learn them if I'm going to be your daughter's religious compass. Be quiet and concentrate on Marley's immortal soul."

"I'd rather concentrate on the guy who might be able to help my sister get laid some time in the next decade."

The priest slanted them a look, but didn't even lose his rhythm. You had to respect that in a clergyman.

"Which one is he?"

"Oh for Chri—crying out loud." Mia pretended to search the congregation. As if she hadn't locked eyes on Chase the second she walked in the room. "There in front. Between Nonna and Zia Anna."

A combination which inspired no small amount of dread. The pair of them had long since used up their lifetime allotment of shame, achieving the age when they could do or say just about anything with impunity. Nonna caught Mia looking their direction and gave a hearty thumbs up, which quickly turned into a suggestive hand gesture she would have preferred not to know her grandmother even knew, let alone could perform with such enthusiasm.

"*That's* your date?" Gina yelped—thankfully at a whisper. "Is he a gigolo?"

"*Gina.*" Insulting as it was, she couldn't really blame her sister for the question. She'd known from the start that no one in her family would believe she could land a guy like Chase. "He's a friend doing me a favor. That's all," she said, giving up the idea of conning Gina. She could never have pulled it off.

"Since when do you have friends like *that*?"

"I didn't pay him, Gina."

Silence. Then, "Nonna looks like she's in love. Are you sure it was smart to bring a prize stallion for Show and Tell?"

"I know it was stupid, but he wanted to come and..." Mia gave an exasperated huff. "He can talk me into things, Gina. One second I'm making a rational argument and the next thing I know he's getting his way. It's uncanny." Chase flashed her a grin from the first pew. "And annoying."

"You're kidding." Her sister's gaze pinged back and forth between Chase and Mia. "Can he really talk you out of reason?"

"Don't get too excited. He's a friend. Just a friend." She elbowed her sister. "Focus on the baptism. Enjoy the moment. This is a crucial day for your daughter's immortal soul and all that crap."

"Huh," Gina muttered, continuing to stare at Chase.

Mia held out as long as she could before curiosity overrode good sense. "What *huh*?"

"Does he know he's just a friend? Cuz the way he's looking at you..."

"He isn't looking at me. He's watching the ceremony. Something you might want to consider participating in."

"He's looking at you," Gina said with absolute conviction. "Are you wearing the watch?"

Mia ignored the question, grateful it was her turn to step forward and hold Marley over the basin of holy water.

Just a couple more hours. They'd slip out immediately after dinner with the family. Chase would have a read on the watch because she had *never* wanted the damn thing as much as she did right now. She'd have it back by this evening and everything could go back to normal. She just had to maintain damage control for a few more hours.

As she watched, Nonna slipped her own engagement ring off one gnarled finger and pressed it into Chase's palm, launching into what could only be explicit instructions on how to properly execute a proposal.

Mia cringed, wondering what a girl had to do to get struck down by lightning.

Chapter Twelve
Commando Courtship

Chase couldn't remember the last time he'd had this much fun in church. Of course, he couldn't remember the last time he'd been in a church so that might have something to do with it, but his dim memory of religious experiences wasn't nearly this entertaining.

Mia's family members were all cheerfully insane.

The octogenarian sybarites seated on either side of him had pinched his ass so many times before they sat down it probably looked polka-dotted. Mia's brothers and cousins had alternated between laughing suggestions that he make an honest woman of her and if-you-lay-one-finger-on-her death threats that made contract killers look warm and cuddly. And adding to the entertainment factor was Mia, standing at the front of the church, arguing in whispers with her sister during the ceremony and shooting him desperate looks.

Chase's finely honed sense of the ridiculous was lapping up every second of it.

The ceremony ended abruptly. Mia handed off the baby and descended to his side at light speed. She helped her grandmother and great-aunt to their feet, foisted them off on a loitering relative and marched him toward the door before he could do more than wink at the sweet biddies. Her arm wrapped tight around his, dragging him along. She nodded at family members who called out to her or just ogled the pair of them, never breaking stride as she hauled him up the aisle.

"Change of plans," she muttered hurriedly. "We're friends. Just friends. Did you say anything to anyone to contradict that?"

"No one asked, actually. They were all too busy issuing death threats and coaching me on the best way to propose."

She groaned. "What we lack in subtlety, we make up for in enthusiasm."

Chase laughed. "So what happened? Why have I been relegated to the Friend Zone?"

"You have to ask? Did you not notice my grandmother slipping you her engagement ring?"

"I gave it back to her. She just thought it would look great on your finger."

"Mary, Mother of God."

"For someone who isn't religious, you sure swear like a Catholic."

"It's environmental. You try growing up Corregianni and not appealing to the holy mother for mercy."

"How did your ex-boyfriends escape unscathed? Or are they buried in a basement somewhere for breaking your heart?"

"They aren't usually this aggressive. It's the wa—" She grabbed the bare skin of his wrist, latching on with surprising strength. "Here, try to find the watch now. I'm motivated."

There was a wealth of meaning in that last word, but Chase didn't bother trying to pick through it. Instead, he opened the door to his gift—and was nearly knocked on his ass by the flood of intangibles that pushed through on a fizzy mimosa tide.

Get them to back off, accept me, stop trying to force Chase, let him want me on his own terms, if he could ever want me...

He jerked back, rubbing a hand across his face. "Sorry." His voice sounded choked, raw. It felt like the worst kind of violation, being inside her desires—especially when he had somehow become a part of them. She was so restrained, so reserved—more inclined to lean away from him than into his touch. From the outside he would never suspect her interest or the powerful vulnerability attached to it.

He couldn't keep invading her wishes. He felt dirty for sneaking inside her thoughts, even as an inescapable satisfaction churned in his gut at the knowledge that she was attracted to him.

Mia cursed. "What am I doing wrong?"

"You—" He broke off, not sure he could answer that question. "It's too tied up in your emotions, I think."

She shook her head. "That doesn't make any sense. I'm the least emotional person you'll ever meet."

"Not about this, you aren't."

She swore again, yanking him toward the car as the parking lot filled with chattering Corregiannis. "When we get to my parents' house, we stick together. Got it? Don't let them separate us. And no proposals. Just friends."

"If I had a nickel for every time a girl had to give me that speech…"

"I'm sorry about all this." Her face screwed up in a remarkably expressive picture of contrition for a woman who believed she was unemotional. "Bet you're wishing you'd made a different bargain right about now."

"Are you kidding? I can't remember the last time an eighty-year-old woman groped me. And now two in one day? Classic."

"I hope you still feel that way after you've been stuffed with cannelloni."

Chase snorted. "I think that's one of the threats your brothers gave me. No, I think it was *skin you, stuff you and serve you as cannelloni if you hurt her.*"

"Oh God. They're really very sweet. I swear."

"The big one—Joey?—looks like he can bench press a truck. I'm pretty sure he can take me."

"He's a pussy cat. Cries like a baby at chick flicks."

"I think in the interest of not being beaten to a bloody pulp, I will pretend I don't know that."

"The ones to watch out for are the women. Sure, they look all sweet and innocent, but don't let that fool you. The women wear the pants."

Chase seriously considered making a crack about letting Mia wear the pants as long as he could get into them whenever he wanted, but the rigid line of her spine shut him up. She didn't look like she could handle a joke right now without snapping in two.

They reached her car and he opened the door for her just as someone called out her name from the church steps. Mia waved once and dove into the car, escaping from the loving bosom of her family with an air of desperation. By the time he slipped into the passenger seat, she had the engine running and in gear. He barely had the door closed before the car started rolling. And he thought he'd been joking about the getaway car...

Mia was tense in the driver's seat, gripping the wheel firmly at ten and two, her spine so straight it didn't brush the seatback. She looked ruthlessly composed—as long as he didn't notice the way her mouth pressed in on itself in an unrelenting line.

"You seemed to enjoy yourself," she grumbled.

"I did," he admitted, surprising himself with the depth of truth in that statement.

He hadn't known he had expectations, but now, looking back, he realized he had almost planned on being uncomfortable. Miserable, but hiding it behind his usual obfuscations. It wasn't until the reality of his enjoyment startled him that he realized he'd scheduled awkward discomfort into his emotional palate for the day.

Family gatherings, they were supposed to be painful, right? He was supposed to be unable to see anyone happy and in love without remembering the day a senseless accident had taken everything he loved—his parents, his brother, his brother's pregnant wife and his own fiancé in one fell swoop.

But Mia's family was a force of nature. He couldn't compare them to his own—and the fact that they didn't know about his tragedy made all the difference. They didn't look at him as if they were checking to see if he was all right. And so he was all right.

Their ignorance was his bliss.

Mia slowed and pointed to a house as they passed. "That's it. My folks' place."

"Nice." A sprawling two-story stucco, it looked like an Italian villa that had been picked up and dropped into an American suburb. At least from what he managed to see before Mia zipped around the corner. "We aren't going in?"

"If we park in the driveway, we'll be blocked in until midnight." She pulled the car to the curb directly in front of a Craftsman cottage with a prominently displayed *No Parking* sign. "The Shumakers have known me since I was five. They never have us towed," Mia said when he arched a brow at the signage. She turned off the engine, but showed no inclination to exit the vehicle.

"Mia?"

"They're going to try something. I don't know what, but there will be some trick when we're least expecting it."

"Mia honey. It's dinner. I think we'll survive."

"Just try not to commit to anything." She opened the car door.

He followed her out to the sidewalk. "Sweetheart, I've been avoiding commitment for six years. I'm a pro."

Mia looked dubious, but didn't have a chance to vocalize her doubt before a late-model Mercedes pulled up to the curb behind her car. "Crap. That's Teresa, my older sister, and her husband Martin."

"Ah, the one who was supposed to be godmother instead of you. Tell me, did you feel slighted?"

"One hour and you already know all the family gossip."

"Your grandmother is a font of information."

"My grandmother is a menace."

"Sweet little Nonna?"

Her sister climbing out of the Mercedes forestalled whatever she would have said. According to the family gossip, Teresa was only two years older than Mia, but she looked at least a decade older. She was curvy—Mia was the only rail-thin one he'd seen so far on her family tree. They had the same eyes, but Teresa had a rounded sweetness like the younger sister Gina, rather than Mia's sharp angles and lines.

"Teresa! Have you met my *friend* Chase?"

And so it began.

Over the next half hour, they ran the gauntlet of formalities there hadn't been a chance for at the church. Chase met aunts, uncles, cousins and siblings—and with each introduction, Mia grew more emphatic in her *just friends* disclaimer, until she was practically composing odes to their sexual incompatibility.

After his tenth "Oh, God, no, I'd never date *Chase*," it was starting to get annoying.

He'd never been in the Friend Zone before. Not that he was a bad friend, but most women took one look at him and saw an irresponsible good time, not a bosom buddy. As Mia tugged him from room to room, fielding more family members than most people had in five generations, he was discovering he didn't like the Friend Zone. It was galling to hear Mia professing that she would never think of him *that way*. Especially when he knew for a fact she was lying and he was damn glad she was since he'd been thinking of her *that way* since the second he laid eyes on her.

But he'd agreed to be friendly today, so he just smiled as she waxed eloquent on their lack of chemistry until she finally ran out of relatives to introduce him to and he managed to corner her for a semi-quiet moment in the kitchen.

The room wasn't empty—he doubted any room in the house was with the masses of family members swarming—but with the elder Corregianni ladies crowded around the stove, arguing loudly over the marinara, he and Mia had about as much privacy as they were going to get.

"Do you have to be so gleeful about our incompatibility?"

Mia flicked a glance at the women huddled around the stove and turned her back on them, lowering her voice. "If we give them even a spark of hope, they'll never let it go."

"Don't you worry about the lady protesting too much?"

He saw his words sink in and the color leech from her face. "Crap. You're right. So should I just ignore you? Be completely uninterested?"

"I don't think changing strategies at this point is going to do any good. Maybe keep the *we're just friends* monologues to a minimum."

She studied his face and a tiny smile slowly tugged at her stern lips. "Is it denting your fragile male ego, Chase?"

He laughed, always ready to have one at his own expense. "I don't think anything as massive as my ego counts as fragile."

She shook her head, a smile playing in the air between them. "I—"

"Seven Minutes in Heaven!"

"Nonna!" Mia yelped, a fraction of a second before a surprisingly hard shove hit him between the shoulder blades and knocked him through a darkened doorway. He caught Mia as she was thrown in after him, setting her on her feet as the door snapped shut behind her and darkness closed around them. A scraping that sounded alarmingly like a heavy chair being dragged in front of the door followed. Then only the sound of the two of them breathing filled the small space.

"Did your sweet little Italian grandmother just lock us in a closet to make out?"

He heard Mia's exasperated little huff in the darkness. "Technically it's the pantry."

"The pantry," he repeated, still trying to wrap his head around the commando matchmaking that reigned in Mia's family.

"And I'm not entirely sure she wants us to make out. She's always going on about the way to a man's heart being through his stomach. She probably wants me to whip up some homemade pasta and a nice marinara for you."

Chase snorted at her dry tone. Mia may not see herself as the life of the party, but her little muttered comments were funny as hell. And all the more appealing because she didn't say them loud enough for everyone to hear—like her humor was a secret she only shared with him.

A suspicious thumping sounded outside the door, followed by the unmistakable opening notes to "Let's Get It On".

Mia groaned. "Oh sweet Jesus."

Chapter Thirteen
The Pantry o' Love

Mia thumped her head back against the pantry door. "On second thought, she'd probably be ecstatic if you knocked me up in here. There's a long Corregianni tradition of getting a head start on the wedding night—though they'll scratch your eyes out if you imply that Uncle Tommy was anything other than the world's first ten-pound three-ounce preemie."

"A wedding night, huh? Was that a proposal?"

"Not funny, Chase."

His chuckle was low and far too delicious in the dark. An invitation to things she had no place hungering for. "So, now that you have me in the pantry, what are you going to do with me?"

What indeed? Mia's heart had been doing double time ever since Nonna shoved her in here. The inky blackness inside the pantry seemed to amplify all her other senses—and give her permission to indulge them. She could hear the rustle of his shirt, the slightest shift in his breathing. And, Lord almighty, he smelled amazing. Like summers at the beach with lowered inhibitions—not that she'd had any of those.

"I say we go with it," Chase said, his body suddenly so close she could feel the warmth of him.

"Go with it," she repeated, defensively trying to sound quelling and disdainful rather than like a trembling pile of hormonal mush.

She must have succeeded, because Chase made a low scoffing noise, the puff of breath stirring against her skin in the darkness. "Stop trying to plan everything, Mia. Sometimes you've gotta go with the moment. Have you ever done that? I bet you have a boyfriend checklist. Itemized and ranked."

And color coded. Mia cringed, glad he couldn't read on her face how right he was. So she liked to plan. And, yes, she knew what she required in a mate. Was that a crime?

Outside Marvin Gaye's crooning segued from "Let's Get It On" into "Sexual Healing". Nonna was nothing if not subtle.

"This isn't a moment. It's a hostage situation," she protested, but the words wavered as a calloused hand brushed across her throat and around to cup her nape.

"I say we pay the ransom," he murmured, his voice so throaty and low...and close. The words practically touched her lips. And then his lips did.

The kiss was a jolt to her system. She'd heard of toes curling and always thought it was a metaphor, more for poets than scientists, but with the warm, gentle press of his mouth against hers, synapses she'd never known she had started firing and, sure enough, her toes curled in her impractical shoes.

Mia held herself still, observing the kiss more than participating in it. Until his tongue traced the seam of her lips and then slipped between them, and Mia remembered she was supposed to be kissing him back.

She flicked her tongue against his and leaned into his chest, fisting her hands on the lapels of his blazer and hanging on for dear life. As soon as she relaxed against him, Chase's arms came around her and suddenly he was all she could feel, swamping her senses. He was warm and hot and smelled deliciously of sunblock and citrus. Damn if the man couldn't kiss. She was swooning—actually swooning!—in his arms, clinging to his lapels to keep from careening into the dry goods.

He murmured something indistinct and utterly intoxicating against her lips, some mumbled exclamation of surprise or pleasure, and angled his head to take the kiss deeper, sucking her under until all she felt was his mouth and all she heard the rushing of her blood, the pounding of her heart...

And the creak of the pantry door opening.

Light splashed across the tangle of their embrace and a high, young voice sing-songed, "I *fooound* them!" The words echoed throughout the house as Mia jerked away from Chase, knocking several cans of soup off a nearby shelf.

Mia ignored the fallen cans and Chase and everything except her cousin's six-year-old daughter Imogen, standing in the doorway, staring at them without blinking, her arms folded disapprovingly. "Nonna says you hafta come to dinner 'fore we can eat."

"Of course! We were just on our way," Mia yelped, grabbing Imogen's shoulders and spinning her to face the dining room where half the family would be gathered, the rest spilling out onto tables in the side yard.

Imogen took off toward the dining room as Chase stepped out of the pantry behind her. "They were *kissing,* Nonna!" she shouted, her high, clear voice carrying back to them and echoing throughout the house as she ran. Chase covered his mouth—either to conceal the evidence or his laughter, she couldn't tell which. A cheer rang out from the dining room. Mia flinched.

So much for just friends.

Suddenly it all felt like too much. The missing watch, Chase, her family crowding around her pushing so hard for her inevitable, fated happiness. It all weighed on her chest, brick after brick after brick. She couldn't get a full breath.

"I just...one second. Be right back. It's... I forgot my...in the car."

Mia bolted for the back door, panting and trying to remember what to do in the case of hyperventilation. Something about paper bags. How was that logical? How was a paper bag supposed to help her breathe? An O2 tank. That's what she really needed. Or a chest tube and a breathing machine, since her body had clearly forgotten how.

On the back step, she pressed her spine against the door and closed her eyes, trying to remember the mechanics of getting oxygen into her lungs. She could do this. She'd been doing it for thirty-four years. In and out. Easy. In...out...

Her breathing finally eased and Mia closed her eyes, relieved to be thinking of something outside her lungs. The clouds had cleared off, but a cool wind still rustled the leaves. Around the corner of the house she could hear the Corregianni hordes gathered for the traditional feeding frenzy—and beneath that medley of voices, two more arguing just around the corner, hidden from sight. Two familiar voices.

"This isn't the time, Martin," her sister Teresa snapped, her voice sharper than Mia'd ever heard it—and growing up as the sister most likely to dissect Teresa's Barbie dolls, she'd heard some pretty sharp tones.

"Putting it off won't make it any easier." Martin's ever-reasonable voice was aggravated, impatient. "Maybe they'll understand. They all know how hard it's been for us lately—"

"I said no, Martin. This is Gina's day. I'm not going to ruin it for everyone. We'll tell them next week at Nonna's..."

Teresa's voice drifted off, retreating back to the party, and Mia realized she was leaning half over her mother's back porch rocker, shamelessly eavesdropping.

Sweet Jesus. Were Teresa and Martin getting a divorce? No Corregianni ever had, but it was more than that which shocked Mia. They'd seemed so happy. So perfect for each other—whether ordained by an idiotic bit of gold and gears or not, she'd thought they of all couples would go the distance.

But what else could it be? What else would so upset the family that it would totally ruin the day? And why else would Teresa have suddenly declared that she and Martin couldn't be godparents?

A horrifying—and completely unscientific—thought tracked across her brain, leaving numbness in its path. Was this somehow her fault? Had she *caused* the divorce by losing the watch?

She couldn't have. She knew it was impossible. A superstition. But if she admitted she'd lost it now, of all times...

Mary, Mother of God. She had to get it back. Chase had to find it.

Chase...

He'd kissed her. That couldn't be standard professional conduct. And she'd let him. She'd more than let him, she'd practically mounted him in the pantry. Given a few more minutes, she may well have.

And now her entire family knew she'd kissed him...and he was in there talking to them. Alone. Unsupervised.

Nonononono. Mia jerked open the door and rushed inside.

She found him in the dining room. As she watched, he pulled something from behind the china cabinet with a magician's flourish and the entire room burst into applause.

Zia Verna leapt up from the table as soon as she spotted Mia in the doorway, rushing toward her with her hands flapping. "Mia *bella*! How could you not have introduced us to this wonderful boy sooner? He has The Sight!"

Chase held up his hands in obviously false humility and flopped into the chair between Nonna and Zia Anna, both of whom immediately fell to cooing over him. He was the belle of the ball. The prize stallion, all right. She'd brought him home and her family, who had always looked at her as if she was a changeling, instantly fawned over him and beamed at her, delighted that she had finally done *something* to prove she was, in fact, a Corregianni.

"*This* one is a keeper, Mia!" her grandmother gushed. "Not like that Peter."

A chorus of agreement met that proclamation and Mia bit back her protest that Peter was a lovely man and there was absolutely nothing wrong with a relationship based on common interests and intellectual compatibility.

Instead, she smiled and let herself be pulled into the boisterous bosom of her family, shoved right alongside Chase as Nonna scooted down to make room for the happy couple. But she couldn't help the low boil of resentment in her blood at how easily this stranger had become one of them, how instantly he had been embraced. How she had needed someone like him as her entre into the group when she should have been accepted from birth.

She wanted to kick him when he winked at her and all the women at the table swooned a little. He did *not* need to be feeding the flames, even if they'd officially burned the just-friends bridge to cinders in the pantry.

She could still salvage this evening. And next week when Teresa dropped her bomb, everyone would forget all about Chase's winks and smiles.

If only she could be certain she would forget his kisses so easily.

Chapter Fourteen
They Say It's Your Birthday

Chase's phone rang while he was helping clear the table—amid Zia Anna and Nonna's play-by-play commentary on his candidacy for sainthood, interspersed with tips on how to word his wedding proposal. Mia was shooting him the same glare she'd been giving him since their escape from the pantry. If she hadn't kissed him like he was the second coming of Casanova, he might have been concerned.

Until he looked at the caller ID and saw Brody's name, he'd forgotten he was supposed to be hovering awkwardly around Brody's barbeque grill this afternoon, while all his old frat buddies grimaced at him sympathetically over their brewskies.

He ignored the call, knowing that would just make Brody even more of a pain in his ass the next time they talked, but not ready to interrupt his afternoon of domestic bliss.

Zia Anna beamed at him, visibly pleased that he'd silenced the call even though she patted his arm and cooed, "You go ahead and answer it, sweetie. We're not formal here."

Mia rolled her eyes. "Says the woman who flushed Mario's new iPhone down the toilet last Thanksgiving because it rang during grace."

"It interrupted *God*," Nonna gasped.

"The Devil's cell phone," Zia Anna agreed, and they crossed themselves in unison as Chase's phone began to ring again.

"I'll turn it off," he offered apologetically, barely glancing at the screen where Brody's name had flashed again.

"You can take it in the living room," Mia suggested, her gaze scuttling to the pantry like she was afraid her grandmother would find a way to get them back in there. "I'll say my goodbyes and meet you there in a few minutes and we can take off."

Chase studied the I-will-kill-you-if-you-say-you-want-to-stay-longer wildness in Mia's eyes and nodded meekly, retreating to the living room, which was surprisingly empty, most of the party having moved outside.

The third time Brody called, Chase flipped open his phone with a casual, "Yo."

"Dude, I'm on my way over to pick you up. You aren't spending your birthday alone. Molly and I won't stand for it."

Chase had been idly pacing, but he stopped in his tracks. He'd forgotten his own birthday. And it was the best one he'd had in six years.

"My best friend doesn't turn twenty-eight moping by himself in his apartment," Brody continued. "Be ready to go in fifteen minutes."

"Sorry, man. Can't do it."

"Molly said you'd say that. But we're not taking no for an answer—"

"I'm not at home."

"You're coming with—what?"

"And I'm not alone."

Brody's planned monologue sputtered to a stop. "You aren't?"

"Actually I'm at my girlfriend's place. Big family thing. We couldn't get out of it."

"You're shitting me."

Chase grinned, enjoying this far more than he should be. "I shit you not. In fact, things are kinda busy here. I've gotta call you back later."

"I don't believe you. Put her on the phone."

"Who, Mia?"

"Oh, so the imaginary girlfriend has a name now, does she?"

"What makes you think she's imaginary?" Other than the fact that as far as Chase was concerned she had been until yesterday.

"Molly thought you might've made her up."

Smart Molly. "Have I ever lied to you?"

"Constantly."

Smart Brody. Chase laughed. "I swear to you Mia Corregianni exists. And I was making out with her in a pantry earlier today because it was the only private place we could find in her parents' house."

"Now I know you're lying."

Mia chose that moment to march into the living room, a woman on a mission to get him the hell away from her family before he could flirt her into submission again. "There she is," he said loudly, beckoning her over. "Come on over here, honey, and talk to Brody for a minute. He's convinced I made you up."

She shot him a death glare, but came to his side and extended her hand palm up for the phone, still glaring.

"Be nice," he commanded, unsure whether he was telling Brody or Mia, as he passed the phone over.

Mia stuck out her tongue, then cooed, "Brody, it's so good to finally talk to you" in the warmest, most welcoming tone he'd ever heard from her, for all the world like she'd been hearing about him for months.

Chase listened, trying to glean the gist of the conversation from her "Mm-hms" and exclamations of "He did, did he?"

Until one of her brothers rushed into the room. "Chase. Bro. Tyler hid Marley's binky thingy and she's freaking out. Can you do your finder thing on her?"

"On an infant?" He laughed. "Sure. I love a challenge."

He brushed Mia's arm and nodded toward the side yard, then headed out after her linebacker brother to save Marley from a fate worse than death—at least as far as the baby was concerned.

Mia was vaguely aware of Chase leaving the room, her attention focused on trying to sound suitably fake-girlfriend-like on the phone.

"You'll have to meet Molly," Brody gushed. "You'll love each other," he declared, and Mia bit her tongue on the urge to tell him he had no basis for his hypothesis since he didn't even know her.

"Chase talks about you guys all the time," she lied.

"I'm just so glad he's not alone on his birthday. Wait till I tell Molly. After everything that happened with Katie and his folks... You're a godsend, Mia."

"Um..." Mia's brain had shut off with the word *birthday*. It was Chase's birthday. And he hadn't told her. He'd let her drag him to her family thing and never once mentioned that he might have other plans. What kind of man did that? And who the hell was Katie? Some bitch of a maneater ex who ripped out his heart and stomped on it?

"Hey, no pressure!" Brody said with a laugh. "I don't want you to think we're pushing you guys into anything."

"Don't worry. My family has the pushing covered."

Brody's laugh was even more booming, almost hysterically overjoyed. "You've got to come have drinks with us this week. How's Thursday? We'll get a sitter. Do you like O'Flannigans? That pub on Second?"

"Oh, well, I, um, I should really check with Chase. He's been working a lot..." He was certainly working this weekend with her.

"Chase?" Brody gave a disbelieving bark of laughter. "He'll be free. Thursday. Don't let him back out, Mia. He needs a good woman to ride herd on his lazy ass and you're just the girl to do it."

Again, how could he know that? Was Chase really so hard up that *any* woman was a great sign? He seemed so sexy. So sexually confident. Hardly the kind of guy who would be talked about like he was a romantic charity case. Though Brody seemed pretty macho. Maybe it was a sexuality thing. If Chase was gay...

The kiss in the pantry came back to her. Vividly.

Chase wasn't gay. Either that or he could fake heterosexuality with the best of them.

"See you Thursday, Mia!"

"Oh! Brody—about Thursday..." But the phone was already dead. "Crap."

Flipping Chase's phone closed, she stepped out the side door and froze at the top of the steps leading down to the yard.

He was standing in the center of her family like the nucleus of an atom, all of them orbiting him like excited electrons. Marley cuddled in his arms, contentedly slurping at her pacifier.

Mia waited to feel that same flare of irritation she'd felt at dinner over how at home he was with them, but it just didn't come. Instead, her stomach tightened and something warm and wanting unfurled in her chest. Something she refused to acknowledge. He wasn't here for real. She needed to keep reminding herself of that. The kiss was an act, best to just forget it happened, wipe the slate clean and act accordingly.

She strode down the steps and cut through the crowd around Chase, keeping her expression businesslike. "Ready to go?" she asked briskly.

A cacophony of protests rose up around them. Mia snatched her niece for a few extra cuddles before handing her back to Gina while Chase bid farewell to his fan club.

"You have to come to Nonna's marinara competition next week," Joey insisted as he slapped Chase on the back. "It's a family tradition. Everyone competes and everyone eats."

"I wouldn't miss it."

Mia shot Chase a horrified look, but he just winked, crowding close to her to whisper, "I guess I'm just not very good at staying in the Friend Zone."

He took her hand and guided her around the house. She glanced back to see her entire family lined up to watch them walk away, arms around one another, heads resting on shoulders. She could almost feel the wind of their collective sigh as Mia and their new favorite person disappeared from sight.

"That went well," Chase commented as they wandered down the sidewalk—probably still watched from every front-facing window on her parents' house.

Mia did not want to discuss the subtle train wreck that was the last three hours of her family congratulating themselves for giving her the magic watch. Instead, she went on the attack. "I hear it's your birthday."

"Brody was feeling chatty, was he?"

"He expects me to drag you to O'Flannigans on Thursday so I can meet Molly and become her best friend."

They reached her car—Teresa and Martin must have snuck out already because the Mercedes was missing from the space behind them. Mia thumbed the lock and rounded the hood to climb in. Chase didn't bother with the holding-the-door nonsense this time, thank goodness. He was already seated by the time she slid behind the wheel.

"Are you free Thursday?" he asked. "That would square us."

"It would have squared us. If you hadn't promised to come to Nonna's marinara competition next week."

"I promised that on my own. It's not part of the deal."

"*Why* did you promise that?" Mia threw the car into gear with more force than necessary. "I was trying to keep them from getting attached to you. They're back there engraving wedding invitations, Chase. That wasn't the plan."

"You still don't have the watch. I wasn't sure if we'd need to try to find it again next week. You didn't ask me to try tonight..."

"I never wanted the damn watch tonight. This was not the right approach. We need to think of another way."

"We could still use someone else as the anchor. Your entire family will want that watch back. Your sister Gina, maybe. She seemed pretty trustworthy."

"She isn't rational about that stupid watch. She won't be trustworthy about that."

"So we're back to relying on you. And you hate it."

"I don't hate it."

"Is it because of the love spell?"

Mia's knuckles tightened on the wheel. "Nonna told you."

"That the watch is supposed to find your true love for you? Half your family found some way to tell me. So what do you have against love, Mia?"

She stared straight ahead out the windshield. "I'm not having this conversation with you."

"Who's Peter?"

"None of your business."

"Aw, come on, Mia. As your pseudo-boyfriend, don't I deserve to know—"

"Who's Katie?"

Silence hit the car hard.

"Chase?"

"Do you want to try to find the watch again tonight?"

Apparently Katie, whoever she was, was off the table. Fine. "No. We'll try again when I pick you up on Thursday. Or would you rather meet me there? He didn't say what time."

"Seven thirty. We always meet at seven thirty. And I'll pick you up."

"I'll be working."

"So I'll pick you up at work."

She wanted to argue, then realized she would only be arguing for argument's sake and she was *tired* of trying to get her way today, exhausted by three hours in the loving bosom of her family and her restless night last night.

She'd never been more relieved to see her townhome than she was as she pulled into the parking lot alongside Chase's beat-up station wagon. She climbed out quickly, needing to avoid the intimacy of having a conversation with him in the darkened interior of the car—like a teenager at a drive-in.

The cool air in the parking lot hit her skin. It was a deliciously crisp night, one on which she might have enjoyed taking a long walk, holding hands, pretending she was sappily romantic, but all she wanted tonight was to crawl into bed and try to forget the day.

"Thank you," she said, not entirely sure he deserved her thanks for making her family adore him. "I'll see you Thursday."

"Don't I get a kiss good night?" He grinned at her, too gorgeous and too cocky.

"Good night, Chase," she said at her most repressive. She began to march across the parking lot, every joint stiff and rigid.

"I programmed my number into your phone," he called after her. "Call me if you want to find anything."

Of course he'd stolen her phone at some point to infiltrate her life even further. Why was she even surprised? Mia kept marching toward the door, refusing to turn back. Then his voice sing-songed across the parking lot.

"G'night, sweet lips."

Mia practically growled. So much for pretending the kiss hadn't happened.

Chapter Fifteen
Romantic Experimentation

Forty hours. Chase managed to stay away that long, but by noon on Tuesday he found himself standing outside the Lathrop Research Institute, jonesing for another Mia fix.

He hadn't realized until he'd watched her stomp away on Sunday night, spine rigid and head held high, how different he felt when he was with her. More alert somehow.

It wasn't at all like what he felt when he was on the waves, the water clearing his head and only the whims of the surf dictating his next thought. No, this was different. This wasn't that smooth, even calm. This was active. A spark inside him. She woke the devil in his nature, making him want to bait her and prod her until Miss Prim rolled her eyes or gave him an exasperated smack.

But then she'd walked off and taken the spark with her.

He'd worked a full day Monday—finding a missing engagement ring for a freaked-out newlywed, locating the sole remaining copy of a grandfather's will for an overworked estate lawyer whose office had burned down the month before, and tracking down the secret hiding place of a client's great-great-uncle's secret stash—rumored to be filled with carpetbagger riches which had turned out to be nothing but an antique version of *Playboy* and a case of rotted cigars.

None of it had made him feel the way five minutes with Mia did. He'd been back in his fog.

He *needed* to see her. And he needed to come clean about his past before Brody told her any more about Katie and his family than he already had. It was the perfect excuse.

The Lathrop Research Institute was housed in a modern, six-story structure composed of odd angles, blue glass and geometric slabs of concrete. Somewhere inside that blocky mass was Mia's lab.

He figured she'd refuse to see him if he called ahead and he figured she'd chase him out of her lab with a Bunsen burner if he tried to get her to leave for lunch, but even Mia had to eat—and from the look of her she worked through lunch more often than she should. An overflowing take-out bag from Zorba's, his favorite Greek restaurant, was his peace offering of choice. Surely she wouldn't turn him away if he came bearing calories to fuel her genius.

Provided he could get past the front desk security...

Ten minutes and a lot of fast-talking later, Chase knocked on a door on the fourth floor with *Dr. M. Corregianni* etched into the frosted glass. He was about to knock a second time when the door flew open and two girls who were definitely not Mia gaped at him.

"Well, *hello.*"

Behind them, the lab wasn't at all what he expected. No beakers, no bubbling test tubes, just cubicles with computers and a series of closed doors. It could have been any office in America.

The girls barring the door both wore lab coats and identical, rapt expressions, though physically they could not have been more different. One was a curvy girl of Middle-Eastern descent in a gray blouse and slacks, the other a gangly Scandinavian blonde who wore an explosion of neon colors beneath the white coat.

"We didn't order delivery," the black-haired one said, earning an elbow in her side from the colorful blonde who'd initially greeted him.

"Yes, we did!" the blonde gushed. "Lots of delivery."

"Steph, someone will complain when their lunch doesn't arrive—"

"Who *cares?*"

"I'm not a delivery man," Chase cut in.

"Are you a volunteer? Please tell me you haven't fallen in love yet," the blonde, Steph, said.

Chase blinked, startled by the unusual thought sequence.

"We don't scan volunteers on Tuesday," the dark one insisted.

"We do now." Steph beamed at him. "Ignore her. You can totally volunteer."

"Is Mia here?" Chase interrupted again, before they could come to blows over whether or not he could volunteer.

"Mia?" they asked in unison. There was a long moment of silence as they both studied him.

At length, the dark one frowned. "Mia never orders delivery."

They knew Mia. So at least he was at the right lab. "Can you tell her Chase is here?"

Both jaws dropped. "Mia knows *you?*" Steph gasped.

"How does Mia know you?" the dark one asked suspiciously.

Chase whipped out his most endearing smile and lifted the Zorba's bag, determined to get these two on his side. "She never remembers to eat so I thought I'd bring her lunch. Is she in?"

Steph craned her neck without moving from her spot blocking the door and yelled, "Dr. C!" over her shoulder.

The dark one rolled her eyes. "Since when does that ever work?"

Steph tried again. "Dr. C! Chase, the Super Hottie, is here!"

There was a thud from the depths of the lab and then a door opened at the end of the hall and Mia emerged. Glowering.

"What are you doing here? How did you get past security?"

"Einstein's ass," Steph gasped, "she does know him."

Chase slipped past the gaping girls and transferred his most endearing smile to Mia.

She rolled her eyes. "Of course. God forbid anyone should ever say no to you. This is *supposed* to be a secure building."

"I'm charming."

"So you keep telling me."

"I come bearing food." He lifted the Zorba's bag again.

Mia looked at the bag, at the women he could only assume were her assistants—both of whom were tracking the conversation with avid eyes—and back at his face where he was still wearing his trust-me-love-me-give-me-my-way smile.

"Oh for the love of... Fine." She waved him back toward the door she'd come through. "You might as well feed me since you've already hopelessly disrupted my lab. Come on."

She led the way back down the hall as the pair of lab-coated girls called, "*Very* nice meeting you, Chase!" after him.

Mia rolled her eyes and opened the door to a snug little office, barely big enough to turn around in, but the view was killer. Floor-to-ceiling windows looked out over a man-made pond.

"I see you've hit it off with Tweedle Dee and Tweedle Dum." She slipped around the edge of the desk and flipped her laptop closed as she sat.

"They're smart girls. Clearly they have excellent taste." Chase began setting out the take-out, noting the way Mia eyed the Greek feast hungrily. He'd have to make a point to bring her lunch again. "Why aren't you wearing a lab coat?"

"We don't wear lab coats here except on volunteer days—so the subjects know to whom they can direct questions. They were just showing off for you. They probably looked through the hallway's security feed and got a good look at you before they opened the door and wanted to look scientific."

The words were caustic, but there was an underlying softness when she talked about them. "You love them. Don't try to deny it."

She shrugged, reaching for the dolmades and heaping several onto her plate. "They're two of the best research assistants I've ever had, but they do get a little overly preoccupied with the romantic aspects of our science."

He handed her the moussaka, taking some dolmades for himself. "What exactly is your science, Mia?"

"I told you."

"Something about love and the brain?"

She dug into her food, shaking her head to dismiss his question. "You aren't here to talk about my work."

"But I'm interested, and you're eating my food, so you should be nice to me and answer my questions." And he was stalling. He'd come here to talk about his history, but now that she was sitting there across from him, gulping down moussaka, now that the spark was back, he didn't want to talk about anything dark and heavy and real. "Is it about dopamine and why chocolate is like an orgasm and all that?"

"Not quite." Mia gave a put-upon sigh and obliged him. "We're doing neural mapping on a range of subjects to determine how the emotion we like to term *love* actually alters our neural pathways and decision-making processes, at times even circumventing the logical or instinctive responses that are in our personal best interest."

"So why people are stupid for love."

A smile flickered in the vicinity of her lips. "Essentially, yes. We're taking it beyond the chemistry of pleasure because love is not always pleasurable."

He took a bite of moussaka, the smooth flavors of eggplant and lamb blending on his tongue. "I could help you," he offered.

Mia didn't even glance up from her food. "I sincerely doubt that."

"Finding doesn't have to be something tactile. I could help you find your best results."

"Results aren't about good or bad." She was using her uptight professor voice. The one that made him want to be the bad student so she would make him stay after class. "Just because a result isn't the one we expect or perhaps even desire does not meant the data is not valuable. Even disappointing experiments have merit."

"But don't you ever want to find the missing variable?"

"There is no substitute for hard work and brainpower."

"Sure there is. There's me."

"Look, no offense," she said, a classic gear-up to a majorly offense-giving statement, "but your magical skills haven't exactly been foolproof."

"Because you're conflicted about whether or not you really want the watch."

She glared at him. "For whatever reason. But even if you can find missing keys and lost pacifiers, so can anyone who disengages their panic over having lost something long enough to think calmly and rationally about where they would have left the lost item."

"You're forgetting that you called me."

"This situation is unique. I didn't lose the watch. I've already done several thorough searches of my home, car and office to confirm that I did not, in fact, move it without remembering. It was taken from me—which is a unique variable. But under any other circumstances, cool heads and clear thinking would prevail where magic is unreliable at best."

"Wanna bet?"

She puckered her lips in that prissy little frown. "I told you, I don't gamble."

"Just think of it as a challenge with stakes attached. A friendly wager. Magic versus science. My instinct against your logic."

"What stakes?"

Chase thought fast. He had to have something she wanted. "Wanna scan my brain?"

"Yes." She said the word before he even finished speaking.

He laughed. "That isn't how you negotiate, Mia. You're tipping your hand too early."

"But I *do* want to scan your brain."

"Yeah, but if you get me to think that letting you scan my brain is doing me a favor, I'll give you what you want for free. Now you'll have to win it."

"Not that I'll lose, but what do you get if you win?"

He wouldn't. The challenge would be set up for her to win because people liked winning and she would associate that endorphin high with him. And he got to spend more time with her while she scanned his brain, keep that spark. "Gotta love that confidence. How about if I win, you play my fake date at this belated birthday thing Brody's throwing for me in a couple weeks?" There was no party, but it was plausible and that's all that mattered when he was spinning shit to get his way.

Mia pursed her lips and tapped them with her fork. "I would want to run a full series of scans, testing both the accuracy of your ability and the neural network that enables it. It could take several days."

Perfect. "Sounds like a prize worth winning. Now we just need a challenge."

"This is ludicrous. I'm not betting on this, Chase."

"Then you must not really want those brain scans. Pity."

"Can't we just do another bargain? My scans for your fake date?"

"Nope."

She scowled. "Why not?"

Because deals could be broken but she would never walk away from a debt, whichever of them won. "I only do one deal a week. Today the offer is a bet or nothing."

"Has anyone ever told you you're evil?"

"Charming. Similar to evil, but more insidious."

She snorted, then looked at him between her lashes. "Are you sure you don't just want to give me the scans?"

"Seduction! Well done, young padawan. I'll make a master manipulator out of you yet. But nope. No dice. It's a friendly wager or nothing."

She glared at him. It was a testament to how much she wanted to run tests on him that she hadn't already told him to take a hike. "Fine." He thrust out his hand and she shook it firmly. "What's the challenge?"

She started packing up the leftover Zorba's and Chase rose to help.

"How about we use your lab assistants? One of them hides something that belongs to the other one and we both try to find it—me using my magic, you using your logic. The first one to recover it, wins. Sound good?"

"I would say that I don't want to disturb their work, but they're probably lurking outside the door waiting for another glimpse of you rather than getting anything productive done anyway." Then she frowned. "Did you rig this with them?"

"I'd be offended if it wasn't something I would have done, but no. In this case there was no cheating. Scout's honor."

"I'm pretty sure you weren't a scout and I *know* you don't know the meaning of honor."

"It's just a chance you're going to have to take. Don't you think your clean, virtuous science can beat my dirty, cheating magic anyway?"

Her eyes narrowed as she considered it. "You do realize they've worked with me in this office for two years. I know them and I know the building. I know everywhere they're likely to stash things. You're at a distinct disadvantage."

Which was exactly where he wanted to be. "Magic doesn't need any foreknowledge. Does that make it better than science? Are you scared to test it?"

"Not scared. Just wondering when I'll manage to fit your brain scans into my schedule."

Chase laughed. "Trash talk. I love it. All right, Dr. C. Let's do this."

She led the way out of her office and down the hall to the open office area where her assistants were oh-so-casually typing away at the computers.

"Nasrin, Stephanie, this is Chase Hunter. You are not required to do anything this man tells you. Ever," Mia announced before he could say a word. She launched into a quick explanation of the challenge, Stephanie's eyes widening with excitement at each word while Nasrin's narrowed suspiciously. When she was finished, both girls consented to participate in the experiment and Mia and Chase retreated back to her office so Nasrin could steal something of Stephanie's and stash it.

Mia paced in her office, clenching and releasing her fists.

"Nervous?"

"Of course not. I have absolute faith in the powers of logic."

"It doesn't have to be one or the other, you know. Magic and science can coexist."

She shot him a Look. "They do coexist—in that they are the same thing. What you call *magic* is science interpreted by someone who sees the wonder and doesn't look beyond it to the facts."

"The wonder is pretty awesome. Why ask for more?"

"It never ceases to baffle me how many people in the world would rather be blind than see."

"So seeing wonder rather than jaded science is blindness?"

"Seeing magic rather than reason. Seeing fate rather than choice. Seeing things just *happening* rather than cause and effect. How can you live like that?"

"You'd be surprised how easy it is to go through life without questioning every little thing. Relaxing. You should try it."

"No, thank you."

Chase leaned back against the door, folding his arms. "You know why I love to surf?"

"You like to be surrounded by women in bikinis?"

He grinned. "Not a bad guess, but no. It's because it's unpredictable. You can't plan a wave. Oh, you can try—pick the best beach, the best set, the best wave—but you're wrong more than you're right, and then you're just reacting. Trying to stay up, trying to get inside the barrel, moving, shifting, *being*. You don't think. You just are. It's all instinct."

"That sounds horrible."

"God, I'd love to see you surf."

"I'll pass."

"Could be fun. You might learn something."

"I'll stick to learning in environments where I can control the variables."

"You can't control life. Fate will just bitch-slap you if you try."

"Fate." She snorted. "Figures you would believe in pre-destination."

"What's wrong with the idea that there's some kind of plan to the universe? I bet you'd believe in fate if I told you your fate was to win the Nobel Prize."

"If that was my fate, that would be fine, but if I lived my life with the *belief* that it was my fate and my own actions had no bearing on the realization of my fate, then I would never be able to win the Nobel Prize because I wouldn't bother studying—I would just wait for life to hand me my acclaim on a silver platter. *That's* what's wrong with fate."

"So it's not fate you have a problem with, it's the fact that people believe in it? Is that your issue with magic too? Not that I can do it, but that people believe I can?"

"They *rely* on the fact of magic," she said. "They don't look for their own keys because they know you can find them. They don't make their own choices because magic will take care of everything."

"This is about the watch, isn't it?"

She shoved her hand toward him. "Here. Search for it."

Chase gripped her hand. A mimosa blast of frustration. He jerked his hand back. "You don't want the watch. You want your family to stop planning their lives around it. That's not going to help us find it."

"Dr. C?"

Mia spun toward the door, yanking it open. Nasrin shifted nervously on the other side. "Did you want to do that challenge thing now?"

Mia gave a stiff nod. "Yes. Absolutely. Thank you." After Nasrin retreated back to the front office, Mia threw a glare over her shoulder. "How do you always distract me from the matter at hand?"

He grinned. "It's a skill. You ready to be spanked by magic?"

She stumbled a step, shooting him a startled glance.

"Trash talk," he explained. "I promise not to spank you unless you ask me nicely."

"You are a strange man."

They entered the main office area and Stephanie's wide eyes convinced him perhaps he shouldn't have mentioned spanking quite so loudly.

"You ready for this?" he asked Mia. "Science versus Magic, Round One?"

"I was born ready."

He snorted out a laugh. "All right. Challenge on."

"I won!" Mia twirled in a circle, holding Stephanie's misplaced cell phone above her head like a trophy as she shook her booty in a victory dance. "I won, I won, I won, I won, I won."

Chase couldn't hold back a grin, leaning toward Stephanie to stage-whisper, "I think she might have won."

He should've known she'd be a competitive little thing.

She was still smiling when she turned to him. "I'll go with you to your belated birthday thing, too. It's only fair."

"The loser isn't supposed to get what he wants, Mia."

"I want to. Think of it as a consolation prize after the way Science whooped Magic's ass." She beamed at him, smug with victory. "Besides, I owe you for bringing me lunch. Oh! I have something for you."

She darted back into her office. Stephanie and Nasrin instantly closed in, leveling identical glares at him.

"I don't understand," Stephanie began.

"Science won. Congratulations, your careers are vindicated."

Nasrin frowned. "But we cheated so Dr. C would have to go on another date with you. You were supposed to win."

"And yet Science emerged victorious."

"I *told* you where I hid it," Nasrin growled.

"I thought of it as hard as I could," Stephanie protested.

"And you were both very helpful."

"So you threw it?" Nasrin asked indignantly. *"Why?"*

Mia emerged from her office, all but walking on air, her smile beyond radiant. Chase felt his own lips curving in response. "Wouldn't you do just about anything to make her smile like that?"

Mia bounded over to them before her assistants could reply. She thrust a Tupperware at him. "Nonna said you wanted to try her cannoli. I almost forgot I had it in the fridge here. I planned to drop it off on my way to work, but then I realized I don't know where you live."

"I don't remember any discussions about cannoli."

"Okay, technically, she shoved this on me and told me I should tell you that I baked it for you, but it's Nonna's special recipe. You'll love it."

Chase accepted the chilled Tupperware with a grin. "I should probably get going. Let you get back to work."

She tipped her head to the side. "Was there some other reason you came by?"

The accident...his crappy past...

She was smiling. Her eyes were bright. Everything felt easy and light and wonderful. Sparky.

He couldn't tell her. Not now.

"Nothing that can't wait. You probably have a lot of work to do."

"I am behind. I've wasted half the morning trying to figure out why the—well, let's just say there's a test anomaly that's bugging me."

He caught her arm, rubbing his thumb across the smooth skin at the crook of her elbow. He was braced for the intangibles that always hit him when he touched Mia, but this time there was only a single, sharp, focused and unwavering thought. *I want to know why the dopamine levels are high in the test results out of Birmingham.* The internal chord snapped taut and Chase saw the answer.

"They're lying about sex."

"How did you...? Oh. *Oh.*" Mia frowned and her eyes went distant, her brain obviously moving at warp speed. After a moment, she cursed under her breath. "We asked about recent intercourse, but the results were from a strongly religious area... If the screeners skipped the questions about sexual activity... Crap. That could explain the elevated dopamine levels. I have to..." She was gone. She might still be standing right in front of him, but her thoughts were a million miles away.

Chase caught her hand and gave her fingers a squeeze. "I'll see you Thursday." He slipped out of the office without even a blink of reaction from Mia, her RAs staring after him—Nasrin with a puzzled frown and Stephanie with gooey adoration.

As he trotted down the stairs to the parking lot where he'd chained his bike, he pulled out his cell phone and dialed Brody, leaving a message telling his buddy he'd see him on Thursday...and that he'd better start planning a belated birthday bash.

Chapter Sixteen
High Hopes, Heartbreaks & Houses

If possible, Mia was even more nervous on Thursday afternoon than she had been on Sunday.

She'd known what to expect on Sunday. Her family's insanity was predictable, at least, but she was out of her element tonight. She'd always sucked at social situations. All those pretty, useless social lies. Pretending she gave a damn about the weather and traffic and other idiotic surface topics which existed only so people could feign agreement with one another and avoid conversing with any depth. Mia liked to slice through to the heart of the matter. No nonsense, no bullshit. If there was nothing of substance to say, she would much rather sit quietly and mull over the results of her latest experiment. Thoughtful silence over thoughtless chitchat. Which made meeting new people excruciatingly awkward.

She'd never before felt such a need to make a good impression on a date's friends. Even when she'd been dating Peter, there hadn't been this nervousness. They'd known all the same people, run in all the same circles, so there were no awkward introductions. No nervousness about the fact that she sucked at small talk. If she was perfectly honest, she'd never really cared if Peter's friends liked her because Peter was more an accessory than an attachment.

Chase was different. Even if they weren't really dating.

She wanted to be perfect for him tonight.

Nasrin and Steph had helped her pick out her outfit, arguing the entire time about whether she was a summer or an autumn—with a Skype-conference consultation from Gina to settle the matter.

Mia studied her reflection in the windows of her office as she waited for Chase to arrive. The burgundy wrap dress gave the illusion of cleavage where she had none and flowed around her knees when she walked. She looked feminine and she felt weird. Like a girl. From the nervous knot in her stomach to the urge to fuss with her loosely flowing hair.

She *never* felt like a girl. And she wasn't sure if this change was a good thing, or a very, very bad one.

The door to her office flew open as Stephanie rushed in, flapping her hands in excitement. "He's *here*," she gushed. Nasrin stood behind her, her hands clasped at her bosom and her black eyes gleaming wetly like a proud mama seeing her baby off to the prom. The pair of them had declared they would be working late as soon as they heard Chase was picking her up at seven.

Mia smoothed suddenly icy hands down over her hips and grabbed her clutch. Her research assistants parted like the Red Sea as she approached the doorway. She stepped into the hallway and saw Chase waiting in the outer office, once again looking like he'd stepped right out of a Calvin Klein ad. Mia reminded herself this wasn't a real date, but it was hard to remember when her heart started to race at the sight of him, when Chase told her she looked lovely and Nasrin and Steph sighed in unison. Harder still when he winked at the pair of them and opened the door for her. Then opened the car door of his station wagon downstairs. Chivalry. It was...kind of nice.

The car was in better condition than she'd expected. Cleaner. A palm tree-shaped air-freshener hung from the rearview mirror and the back was cluttered with colorful hockey puck-shaped containers she thought were surfboard wax, but there were no old fast food bags littering the floorboards and not even a speck of sand.

The engine started smoothly as Chase turned the key and steered them toward O'Flannigans. The car cut through the night and Mia watched the passing lights blur. Preoccupied by her own nerves, she barely noticed how silent Chase was until he suddenly spoke.

"There's something you need to know. Before we get there."

Mia looked over at him, noting for the first time his clenched jaw and rigid posture. Strain marked the lines that framed his baby blues. It was like all his charm had been sucked inside him and the doors barred to keep the world out. "Are you okay?"

"I'm fine," he said, the sharpness of the words marking them as a lie. He didn't look at her, staring straight ahead. "I just don't talk about this if I can avoid it."

"You don't have to—"

"No. Brody will mention it and if we were a couple, it would be weird that you didn't know."

Know what? Was he terminally ill? About to go on trial for a felony? Mia was suddenly very sure she *didn't* want to know whatever he was about to tell her. Good, bad or ugly, it would make him real in a way she wasn't sure she was ready for him to be.

"Six years ago, I was studying architecture at Penn..."

Crap. Already her perceptions of him were shifting. Penn was a damn good school and architecture was a real profession, none of that useless Eighteenth Century Russian Literature crap.

Chase's voice took on the sing-song lilt of a well-told story, even though Mia was certain this was a story he never told. "I was a semester away from graduation when I asked the cutest, sweetest sorority girl on campus to marry me..."

Her stomach clenched. He'd been engaged?

"My parents had come up for a weekend to celebrate the engagement, along with my brother and his wife, who was expecting their first child. Katie...my fiancée...went out to dinner with them to talk wedding plans with my mother, but I'd had to study. I had a big project due on Monday and promised to meet them at the restaurant when I was done, but I lost track of time. I never made it to dinner. All work and no play..."

The sing-song words choked off and Chase coughed. The harsh sound seemed unnaturally loud in the hush of the car.

Mia sank deeper into her seat, cringing against what she could feel was coming.

"There was a storm that night, rain falling sideways it was coming down so hard. An instant. That's how quickly it happens. They died instantly—people kept telling me that. What they managed to scrape up of the other driver showed a blood alcohol level of twice the legal limit. But whether I blamed God or the poor ass who died with them, it didn't bring them back."

Mia wasn't a crier, but Chase said it so matter of factly, she felt her throat tighten on the threat of tears. She pushed them back. She wouldn't do him any favors by blubbering all over him. "All of them?" she asked, when she could be sure her voice wouldn't break.

"One fell swoop," he said without inflection. "I dropped out of school, starting surfing a lot, and the rest is history. Seemed like you should know."

It obviously pained him to talk about it.

"Thank you," Mia said softly, swallowing down the bubbling tide of her shock. Her chest hurt, the pain that of her heart cracking open.

The knowledge didn't change who he was so it shouldn't change her opinion of him, but she couldn't dismiss him as a too-hot-for-his-own-good charmer anymore. He wasn't just a caricature of his own attractiveness—which admittedly, he hadn't been for days, but he wasn't just an antagonist who liked to push her buttons either. He was real now and she ached for him.

"Here we are," Chase announced as they pulled into the parking lot. He cleared his throat, still pointedly not looking at her. "Sorry to lay all that on you right before you meet Brody and Molly, but...well, they were going to be the best man and maid of honor at my wedding so it might come up."

"No, I'm glad you told me."

"They're great though, Brody and Molly. You'll love them." He was making an effort to change the subject so Mia went along.

"Will they...will they like me? I mean, am I what they had in mind for you?" She wanted to ask if she was anything like Katie—not sure whether she was hoping to be similar or different—but stopped the words.

"They'll love you. They both think I need to grow up so the fact that I'm dating an adult will delight them."

Mia squirmed in her seat, suddenly hyper-conscious of the fact that she was older than Chase. And not by just a month or two. Six years was a daunting margin. Wanting maturity wasn't the same as welcoming a woman who was already past her best child-bearing years.

He flashed her a smile, and for the first time she saw layers in it. The twinkle in his eye was wry, the quirk of his lips amused. There was intellect in his charm, and a carefully constructed wall. "Come on, beautiful. You'll be great."

O'Flannigan's Pub was crowded for a Thursday—at least to Mia's socially ignorant eyes—but Chase knew exactly where he was going. He navigated them through the tables with a hand on the small of her back, guiding her to a booth in the back corner whose high seatbacks formed walls to block out the noisy pub. They were five minutes early, but the booth was already occupied by a professional-looking, dark-haired man and a trophy-wife-perfect brunette, both about Chase's age.

The dark-haired man, Brody apparently, launched himself out of the booth as soon as he saw them coming. "Mia!" he shouted. "You exist!"

Molly followed him out of the booth, smacking him playfully on the arm. "Ignore him," she said to Mia dryly. "He thinks he's funny."

She shook hands with them, her nervous awkwardness multiplying by the second, and they all slid into the booth, Mia and Molly first, Chase and Brody taking up positions beside their respective dates. The pair across the table had the easy physical familiarity of a couple who've been together long enough that they don't need to touch to be aware of one another. They sat close, elbows brushing, but it was a cozy, comfortable distance.

Chase, on the other hand, scooted right up to Mia's side and dropped his arm across her shoulders. She stiffened, unable to check the reaction, and hoped his friends would just attribute her reaction to a discomfort with public displays of affection rather than a defensive reaction to her hypersensitivity to his pheromones.

"So Mia!" Brody leaned across the table eagerly. "Tell us all about yourself."

"Well... I'm a scientist."

"See?" Brody turned to Molly triumphantly. "I told you she was different."

Molly rolled her eyes and shared a conspiratorial *Men* look with Mia. "What kind of science do you study?"

Mia opened her mouth, nervous about how much to say, how to say it. She was so used to the glazed look when she talked about her work, but Chase had been genuinely interested and his friends looked equally intrigued. So she just...talked. She didn't filter and for once there were nods and smiles and intelligent questions. The knots in her shoulders slowly unraveled and she relaxed against Chase's side.

Chase teased her, Brody laughed, Molly made wry cracks under her breath and the evening flew by, easy, light and *fun*. Mia couldn't remember the last time she'd enjoyed herself so much. Suddenly all the emphasis psychologists placed on social rituals made much more sense.

The only wrinkle in an otherwise seamless evening was the moment when Brody brought up real estate. It took Mia a moment to realize the houses in question belonged to Chase. It was the stiffness of his body against her side that tipped her off.

"Help me out, Mia," Brody pleaded over his fourth beer. "Maybe you can convince him where I've failed."

"I don't know..." Mia hedged, when Brody clearly expected a response.

"I'm not selling them, Brody. Let it go."

"The financial burden alone—"

"Brody," Molly intervened as Chase's expression darkened. "Maybe now isn't the time to discuss it."

Brody leaned close to his wife and the couple whispered to one another. Mia took advantage of their distraction to lean into Chase and mumble, "Am I supposed to know what's going on?"

"My parents' and my brother's houses," Chase said tersely. "I inherited them and Brody thinks it's time I unloaded them."

"You don't live in them," Brody protested, once again paying attention to their side of the table and pleading his case. "They're just a financial and emotional burden..."

"Which it is my choice to bear."

"I just think—"

"How about them Yankees?" Molly interrupted her husband and Chase took up the blatant attempt at a change of subject eagerly.

Mia, knowing nothing about baseball, just sat quietly, cuddled into Chase's side, and thought about the revelations of the night. She was surprised by how much she wanted to be in a position to help Chase deal with his emotional and financial burdens, but she was still the fake date. No matter how real tonight felt. No matter how real he was to her now.

She couldn't dismiss him anymore.

She didn't realize exactly how badly she wanted their relationship to be real as well until they were back at her office, where he was dropping her off so she could collect her car. He opened the door for her and walked her the five feet to her car, waiting until she had unlocked it and opened the driver's side door—all in an anticipatory silence.

She felt certain they were building up to something, to a good-night kiss, almost like a real date, but when she turned to face him, he'd already taken a step away from her and jammed his hands into his pockets, rocking back on his heels.

"So, your Nonna's marinara thing is Sunday?"

"Two o'clock. Come prepared to be stuffed with pasta till you can barely stand. Shall I pick you up at your place?"

"No, we can meet at yours again. That worked well." He wasn't looking at her. He certainly wasn't leaning in to score a kiss. Before she could work up the courage to try for one herself, Chase gave a businesslike nod and said, "Thank you for tonight, Mia. I appreciate it."

Then he was walking away, back toward his car, without a backward glance or a good-night kiss. Tonight, Mia wanted one.

She started after him, her feet moving almost without direction, then stopped, hovering in the middle of the parking lot, reminded that she had no right to ask for kisses. She was the fake girlfriend.

Fake. The word felt so wrong. This, whatever it was between them, was very real. Sexual attraction, companionship, a strange understanding—she wasn't sure what they had, but they had a relationship. A real one. A very unconventional real one.

She couldn't wrap her head around what they were and what they weren't. Not quite a friend, certainly not someone just hired to do a job and nothing more, but a boyfriend? No, not that either. Chase was a gray area. An incomplete data set. And she hated not knowing how to fit him into her life. There was no easy compartment for a man like Chase Hunter.

But she wanted him to have a place in her life. She just had no idea how to go about assigning him one.

Mia lingered in the parking lot long after he'd driven off into the night, wondering how one went about keeping a finder.

Chapter Seventeen
Marinara Mercenaries

"Marry her now, Chase. I'm begging you. If her matrimonial future depends on her marinara, we all might as well give up hope, so please tie the knot before you taste that sauce."

Mia glowered at her cousin Mario and elbowed him away from her pot. Trash talking was a time-honored part of the Corregianni Family Marinara Competition. As was trying to sneak unwanted ingredients into the pots of other competitors, so Mia knew better than to let Mario anywhere near her burner.

Not that she had any expectation of winning. Everyone knew Teresa's sauce would reign undefeated until someone pried the recipe from her sister's cold dead hands, but second place was still bragging rights and Mia wanted to show off for Chase.

She glanced across the few feet to where her date was chatting and back-slapping with the other manly men. Nonna's competition meant Nonna's rules and that meant only the ladies were allowed to touch the tomato sauce.

While she mixed and stirred, Chase was laughing easily with her family, showing none of the odd, guarded silence he'd had with her on the drive over this morning. Things between them had been strained since Thursday—she had no idea what to say, puzzled by her own muddled feelings and he seemed even less inclined to fill the silence—but at least her family hadn't noticed.

Or so she thought, until her mother leaned across her own pot to hiss at Mia, "Something is off between you two, isn't it? Did you do something? Whatever it is, you can tell your mama."

Mia wasn't sure what her mother expected her to have done, but she found herself protesting, "No, of course not, Mama. Everything's great. Better than great, really," before she remembered she was supposed to be laying the groundwork for a break-up, easing her family into the idea that Chase might not be their newest in-law. Just because she wanted something non-fake with Chase didn't mean he was going to stick around.

He was suddenly at her side, reinforcing her lie with an arm looped around her waist. "Do I get to taste this sauce?"

"No!" all the women shouted at him in unison.

Mia smiled as he held up a hand to pacify the rabid females. "The women cook, the men judge, and tasting a sauce before the blind taste-test at dinner is sacrilege. And grounds for disqualification."

"Damn. Mario said—"

"Just on general principle, don't listen to anything Mario tells you. He's trying to get me booted since I beat his wife last year."

Chase rested his chin on her shoulder, taking a deep breath of the steam rising off her sauce. "Smells good." He gave her waist a squeeze. "All this and she cooks too."

"Don't sound so surprised."

"I'm not. I just hadn't pegged you for the domestic type."

"Just because I rarely take the time to cook doesn't mean I'm not good at it. Cooking is a science too."

"I thought it was an art."

"Science can be art."

"Says the woman who will be scanning my brain with a massive scary machine tomorrow."

She smiled just thinking about the scans. "It's totally painless. You'll barely even notice it."

"That's what they always say." He leaned closer until his lips were brushing her earlobe, defying even her mother's ability to eavesdrop. "Do you want me to try to find it again now?"

Mia went still, as much from the brush of his breath against her ear as the question. "That would probably be wise..." At that moment, she would have agreed to just about anything as long as he didn't move.

"Concentrate," he reminded her.

Mia tried. Oh Lord, did she ever try. But as his fingers circled her bare wrist, the thoughts racing through her head were not of watches. He pulled away quickly, shaking his hand as if she'd given him a static shock.

"How can you be so clear about what you want at work and so confused here?" he asked softly.

"Easy. My work is the one place where I know what I'm doing, and I know what I need."

Chase inhaled against her neck and goose bumps broke out across Mia's arms, but whatever he was taking a breath to say was lost when Nonna bellowed, "Time's up!" and began ushering them to the judging table.

Fifteen minutes later all the contestants and their significant-other judges were crammed elbow-to-elbow around the banquet table in Nonna's formal dining room, meant to hold twelve, not twenty-two. Ten bowls of mystery marinara lined the table, each marked with an identifying number and nothing else. Nonna reigned at the head of the table and went over the rules, for tradition's sake and for Chase's benefit as the only new face at this ritual.

"We're going to have a fair fight, people, so let's keep it clean," Nonna said, cracking her knuckles and sounding eerily like a WWF ringmaster. "Bowls will be selected at random. Each dish is passed around once and only once. There will be no cheating and telling your fella which one is yours, ladies. Absolutely no signals allowed and any winking, coughing, nudging or ear-tugging will result in immediate disqualification. If he's living with you and he can't identify your marinara by taste, you might as well start divorce proceedings since he's clearly stuffing his cannoli elsewhere."

Mario snorted and Nonna reached over to smack him upside

the head without losing her place in her speech.

"Notepads are by your napkins to make notes about your favorites, but ballots will not be passed out until all ten have been tasted. Good luck to all our competitors." She nodded to the ladies around the table, giving Mia a little wink. "And now...let the games begin!"

Chase gave a whoop and the whole table laughed. Mia grinned at him as the first bowl began to make the rounds. Somehow this year the marinara competition felt less like an obligation and more like the game everyone else had always treated it as.

The first bowl elicited thoughtful murmurs and fierce scribbling as eyes darted around the table, speculating on who had gone in such an oregano-rich direction this year.

Bowl number two had Gina screeching and everyone reaching for their water glasses and dinner rolls in a desperate attempt to cleanse their palates after the overpowering, competing tastes of dill pickles and cayenne pepper.

"Dammit, Mario!" Gina complained as she chucked a roll at his head. "This was going to be my year."

"Don't blame me. I'm just an innocent bystander."

Gina snorted. "Innocent, my a—"

"Gina." Her mother gave her youngest a stern look as she passed around the third bowl.

The third was sweet and tangy, but it was the fourth that had everyone sighing and lobbying to send the bowl around for seconds. Teresa's basil marinara was the stuff of legend. No one even pretended not to recognize her secret recipe.

Mario groaned appreciatively as he cleaned his plate. "God, cos, this gets better every year. You gotta tell us how you do it."

Teresa smiled slyly, not bothering to deny the origin of the sauce. "I'll take the recipe to my grave."

"Nah, you'll turn the recipe over to your daughter who will carry on kicking Corregianni asses for another fifty years." Gina grinned as she said it, but Teresa went still.

"Actually..." Teresa reached blindly for her husband's hand and he gripped hers tightly. "I...that is, *we* have some news."

Her mother's gasp cut her off. "You're pregnant! Oh, Teresa!" She clasped her hands over her heart, tears already brimming in her eyes.

At the word *pregnant,* the table erupted. Chairs scraped back as the cousins leapt up, the wave of congratulations deafening as a round of haphazard hugging and backslapping began. Mia opened her mouth to add her felicitations, but then Chase's fingers brushed her wrist and she followed his nod to the shuttered look on Teresa's face.

Her sister looked like she wanted the floor to open up and swallow her. Hardly the look of a glowing mommy-to-be. Mia's stomach lurched sympathetically and the lingering taste of Teresa's peerless marinara soured on her tongue as her sister's lips formed the word, "No."

She repeated it, louder, but still going unheard by the celebrating familia.

"I'll get the champagne! Though none for you, Mama Teresa." Mario shoved back his chair, moving toward the kitchen and a look of panic crashed across Teresa's face.

"Wait!" Suddenly, sweet, I'd-rather-be-in-the-background Martin stood, raising his hands for quiet. He waved Mario back to his chair and cleared his throat in the restless, delighted hush that fell.

But before Martin could make his speech, whatever it would have been, Teresa spoke, her voice low and hoarse. "I'm not pregnant."

The enthusiasm at the table deflated like the air releasing from a balloon. Martin sat, reaching again for Teresa's hand and she snatched his up, clinging to it with a white-knuckled grip as she said, "But Martin and I have made a decision. You all know I haven't been able to...become pregnant on my own, and at this point it doesn't look likely—"

"Teresa..." her mother protested, but Gina hushed her.

Teresa swallowed, met her husband's supportive gaze and flashed a tentative smile. "We've decided to adopt."

A moment of startled silence met this announcement, but Nonna leaned forward and gave a small nod. "Good for you, bella."

Mia knew how badly Teresa had wanted to carry a child, to be a mother in every sense of the word, but she forced a bright smile, leeching all the pity from her eyes. "That's wonderful, Teresa."

Another, more cautious round of congratulations began, slowly gaining momentum. Mario stood to fetch the champagne—

Until her mother declared, "That's ridiculous, Teresa. Adoption isn't necessary."

Any celebratory sentiment at the table died a brutal death.

"The watch will fix your little baby-making problem, sweetheart," she went on. "You just have to have patience."

The watch I lost? Mia felt a stab of guilt. Had she somehow caused this with her carelessness? She had a sudden, fierce longing for the watch—more pure than any desire for it she'd ever had—but before she could give Chase the signal to scan her, Teresa lurched up out of her chair.

"*Damn* the watch, Mama!"

Shock froze Mia in place. And everyone else at the table, except for Nonna and Zia Anna who frantically crossed themselves.

Teresa just didn't say things like that. She was fairy tales and romance and magic and happily ever after to her core, and she *never* cursed, but now she was ranting against the family amulet like she'd been possessed by demons and they were pouring off her tongue.

"Everything is perfect thanks to the watch. Everyone is happy and healthy and gets everything they want because of a goddamn *watch*. But I'm not happy, Mama. I can't conceive. This is the only way I'm ever going to have a child and it would be nice if you could stop bragging about how wonderful Marley is *because of the watch* and how happy we all are *because of the watch* because I don't see how it is fucking fair that it is responsible for everything good and wonderful in the world but Grandpa and Uncle Freddy both died young and I'm not allowed to have the one thing I want more than anything in the world. I know this isn't how you pictured things. It isn't how I pictured them either, but couldn't you just shut up about the watch for five goddamn minutes and be happy for me?"

Tears were streaming down her face by the end of her speech. She choked back a sob and fled the room, the sound of her footsteps pounding up the stairs unnaturally loud in the silence she left behind.

"I didn't...you know that isn't..." There were tears in her mother's eyes as well, before she shoved back her chair and bolted for the kitchen.

Mia felt like a petrified tree, rooted in place but no longer alive, just a frozen husk of herself. Then Chase's warm hand closed over hers and she came back to herself. Suddenly everyone seemed to be in motion. Martin was rising to go after Teresa, Gina already on her way to the kitchen after their mother. Mia squeezed Chase's hand gratefully, then stood and spoke to Martin. "Do you mind if I try?" She nodded upstairs.

Martin hesitated—he knew as well as anyone that she and Teresa had never been particularly close—but something in her expression must have convinced him. He nodded his consent and accepted the scotch Tony pressed into his hand with the words, "Mama will come around."

Mia glanced back to see Chase circle the table and join their manly tableau, his charm on full display as he worked his hardest to distract Martin from his unease. She could've kissed him. So many men would've run like hell at the first hint of drama, but Chase was right in the middle of it, calming the waters. She knew she shouldn't come to rely on him, but right now, she was just so damn glad he was there, she couldn't make herself wish him gone.

Mia climbed the stairs and searched the second story before she remembered the attic access. Teresa sat, huddled at the top of the attic stairs, a ratty fifty-year-old stuffed rabbit she must've found among the dust up there clutched in her lap.

Chapter Eighteen
The Ties That Blind

"Are you going to say I told you so?" Teresa's voice wavered down the steps, but there was something fierce and bitter in the words that made Mia's chest ache.

She trudged to the top and perched on the step beside her sister, bumping Teresa's softer hip with her bony one. "About the watch?"

"The watch, magic, happy endings... Take your pick." Teresa spoke without looking up from the stuffed bunny in her lap, her long fingers slowly tracing the worn face.

Mia swallowed thickly, at a loss for the right thing to say. She'd never seen the point of the social stuff, but now she wanted to comfort her sister and didn't have the first idea how.

The moorings of her life seemed to be slipping loose and she was drifting. Teresa was a constant. She was a born dreamer and the last person on earth Mia had expected to renounce the magic they'd been immersed in since birth. She hadn't realized how much she relied on her sister's unfailing belief as a counterbalance to her own lack, until it wasn't there anymore, weighing down the other side of the scale.

She'd taken Teresa's role in her life for granted, blind to the value of the family belief system. She'd never acknowledged the good in Teresa's belief until it had gone bad. That very romanticism had festered into a toxin eating at her sister from the inside out, her desperation for a child creating something tight and bitter at her core.

She'd renounced magic, they suddenly had something in common, and now Mia wanted nothing more than to talk her back into believing. To have her sister back.

"Are you really miserable, Teresa?" she asked softly. "Aside from the baby stuff?"

"That's just it. There is no *aside from the baby stuff.* It's become all I am. Like my failure to have a child is my entire identity now."

All Mia could think about was the biological injustice of it. Teresa would be a wonderful parent. She was smart and loving and responsible. If anyone's DNA should live on, it should have been hers, but Mia doubted those words would comfort her sister, so she held her tongue, simply threading her fingers through Teresa's and resting their joined hands against her knee.

"I couldn't keep listening to everyone go on about how perfect everything is because of that stupid watch. Second only to God in the family mythology and sometimes even that ranking is in question. The sainted goddamn watch."

"Want me to bash it with a sledgehammer? Maybe drop it down the darkest well I can find?" Where it could already be for all she knew.

Teresa gave a short, bitter laugh that ended on a low sob. Her hand tightened sharply on Mia's. "I can't do it anymore, Mimi. I can't pretend I don't go home and cry every time Mama gushes about how Marley is so perfect."

"Oh Tessy..." she whispered, both of them falling back on their childhood nicknames for one another.

"I don't want to be this person. I hate that I'm so jealous I could scream. God knows it isn't healthy. I just... I can't live like this anymore, and neither can Martin." Her voice broke on her husband's name.

"Is he...?" She didn't know how to phrase it. Mia loved her brother-in-law. He'd been part of the family for sixteen years. But if he was blaming Teresa for their inability to have a child, she'd burn off his family jewels with hydrochloric acid.

"He's been amazing through all of this."

So no acid necessary. Good to know.

Teresa sniffled wetly. "He's the only thing keeping me sane. Just when I feel like I'm going to start screaming and never stop, he puts his arms around me and tells me I can fall apart and he'll hold the pieces, and all that awful, helpless anger just melts away for a while. But it never stays totally gone." She looked up, her red-rimmed eyes meeting Mia's. "I don't want to be angry anymore, Mia."

"You won't be. You'll adopt and it'll get better." *And I'll find the watch.* It couldn't hurt. "I'm sorry about Mama. This should have been a happy announcement."

Teresa's mouth twisted in a grimace. "I'm sorry too, but I'm not surprised. I'd been dreading telling her because I thought this might happen."

"How long have you been planning to adopt?"

"Years."

Mia gasped. Teresa had been planning this for years and none of them had suspected? How could they have been so blind?

"Daddy knew. I just... I couldn't tell Mama. We've actually had two false alarms. Two expecting mothers who decided at the last minute that they wanted to keep their daughters. Just like that. Poof. Adoption cancelled." She pushed on the button nose of the stuffed rabbit. "We'd already picked out names."

"God, Tessy..." Why hadn't she said anything?

"The agency we were going through recently told us we were bordering on too old to adopt an infant, so we decided to go the international route. We fly to China in three weeks to pick her up. If nothing more goes wrong."

"It won't. It will be perfect. Any child you adopt will be the luckiest kid on earth, Tessy."

Teresa gave a little cry and slumped over to tuck her head against Mia's neck, crying in earnest. Mia wrapped her arms around her big sister, the one who had always believed in happily-ever-afters, and crooned that everything would be okay, trying to make her believe again.

When after a half hour, Gina and her mother reappeared but Mia and Teresa still hadn't come back downstairs, Martin followed them up. The marinara contest had been declared a draw for the first year on record and the party had begun to break up, Corregiannis departing in twos and threes.

The awkwardness in the air made Chase itch. Made him feel like he had to move, had to act, had to *do*. Left to his own devices, he would have immediately gone to the beach for some night surfing, even if the waves were crap. But he couldn't leave Mia, so instead he found himself in her grandmother's kitchen, asking her mother if he could help wash the dishes.

Angelina Corregianni looked up and smiled weakly, elbow deep in bubbles, her eyes red but dry. "I never turn down a man with a dishtowel."

He came to stand at her side, picking up the towel hanging from a hook and accepting the first dripping bowl. For a while they just worked in silence—soap, scrub, rinse, dry—the repetition of the chore soothing in its own way. Chase was fixed on his task. It took him a moment to realize Mia's mother was watching him.

"You're a good boy," she said softly, turning her eyes back to the bubbles in the sink. "You must think I'm terrible."

She was a mother. He couldn't take those for granted. "I think you want your children to be happy."

"I do."

He almost didn't say it. He wasn't an advice giver or a problem solver, but... "Lots of people are happy adopting."

"Oh I know. Please don't think I'm anti-adoption. It's a wonderful thing. I just never thought it would be necessary. Not for anyone in our family. Especially not my Teresa." There was a wealth of truth in the way she said it. *My Teresa.* Her favorite.

Chase was a talker, but this time he let the silence do his talking for him. Bowls were stacked neatly on the counter and they'd moved on to pots when Mrs. Corregianni spoke again.

"Mia seems fond of you."

Did she? He didn't know what they were doing anymore. Was this business or pleasure? He wanted to kiss her again, but something that felt a helluva lot like fear held him back. He had no idea what he should say to her mother, or even what he wanted to say, so he said nothing.

Mrs. Corregianni gave a soft huff—half exasperation, half confusion. "But then, it can be so hard to tell with Mia. She's always seen things her own way. Even when she was a tiny thing."

Chase silently accepted a pot and slowly wiped it dry.

"I remember a time when they were both little," Mrs. Corregianni went on. "Mia must have been about four and Teresa six or seven. We were walking in the park and we saw a young couple, obviously newly in love and oblivious to anything in the world but one another. They were cuddled together on a blanket with a picnic and neither Mia nor Teresa could stop staring at them. Mia was looking at them like a science experiment. She asked me why they were touching and kissing and I told her they were in love. Teresa sighed and told me that she couldn't wait to fall in love, but Mia just said, 'Why, Mama? Why does being in love make you want to kiss?' I thought it was a phase, but she never did stop asking why."

Another pot passed between them.

"I never really understood Mia, but Teresa was my dreamer. She was my little princess who always believed in true love and everything was supposed to be perfect for her. It was my job to make sure everything was perfect for her, wasn't it? To protect her belief in soulmates and happy endings?"

There was no such thing as a happy ending in life. Only a happy middle followed by reality stepping in to end things however it damn well pleased, but Chase couldn't say that to Mia's mom. Not when she was still raw from reality kicking her in the face. So he just dried another pot.

Mia stepped into the kitchen, emotionally drained but feeling closer to her sister than she ever had before, just in time to hear her mother say, "I never really understood Mia."

Chase was drying dishes for her mother, shoulder to shoulder in a companionable way she couldn't quite make sense of. How had Chase become a part of her family, already so accepted he'd earned confidences from her mother that Mia herself had never heard? She might have been jealous, if she'd had the emotional energy to spare for it. As it was, she just watched the scene through a distancing fog, as if it were a scene in a movie she didn't particularly care about.

"...Teresa was my dreamer. She was my little princess who always believed in true love and everything was supposed to be perfect for her. It was my job to make sure everything was perfect for her, wasn't it? To protect her belief in soulmates and happy endings?"

Mia sucked in a silent breath, surprising herself with how sharply she wanted to hear Chase say that yes, true love was possible. Why was it so important he say that? Why did she want so badly for him to believe it if she couldn't?

Mia held her breath, waiting to hear what he would say.

"She still believes in those things," Chase replied finally. "But sometimes our happy ending doesn't look the way we expect it to. Doesn't mean it won't be happy."

The piece of her heart that had hollowed out when Teresa screamed *damn the watch* filled up with something warm. Immediately followed by a sinking sense of dread.

I'm getting in way too deep. Chase was a slippery slope and she was already halfway down.

"Hey," Mia said with forced casualness from the doorway as if to say *See? I wasn't eavesdropping on your conversation at all.* "You ready to go, Chase?"

Chase glanced to her mother and she flapped a soapy hand at him. "Go on. I'll finish up here."

Chase nodded, set down the towel and hesitated a moment before turning and walking toward Mia. "Hey," he said in a voice just for her as he approached. "How're you doing?"

The question was a minefield she wasn't prepared to cross. "I'm fine."

He didn't move, but she felt him pull away from her all the same at her curt response. She regretted the non-answer instantly, but felt helpless to fix it. Social ineptitude strikes again.

The drive home was awkward and silent. She spent every mile trying to figure out what to say—something she'd never been very good at and never cared that she sucked at before. Chase was supposed to be the smooth-talker, so why was he so quiet? Was something wrong? She should ask him, shouldn't she? Or would that be invasive? Men didn't like to talk about their feelings, or so she'd been told. So asking him would be wrong, right? But was not asking him insensitive to his needs? The male of the species needed a damn instruction manual.

She hated this feeling of uncertainty. She didn't like not knowing the right answer.

Mia pulled into her parking lot and parked next to Chase's Subaru. He was out of the passenger side almost before the car had stopped moving. Mia flinched at how eager he was to get away from her, putting the car in park, turning off the ignition and unbuckling her seat belt.

The door at her side opened and Chase's hand appeared to help her out. *Always the gentleman.*

Mia slid her palm across his and let him tug her out of the car. He didn't release her, shifting his grip to clasp her hand more solidly in his as he started walking her toward her door. Glancing down at their linked hands, she couldn't help thinking of Teresa and Martin and the way they had clung to one another at the table as Teresa made her announcement, presenting a united front, the two of them against anyone who would threaten their happiness.

I want that, Mia realized.

She didn't just want to procreate. If she had, there was frozen sperm just waiting to be purchased. She wanted more. She wanted the husband, the man who could put all her pieces back together and stand beside her when everything was falling apart.

The fear hit again. Sharp and utterly terrifying. *Too deep.* She was getting in way too deep. Would she even be able to find her way out again? Especially if he wasn't there with her to fish her out. She was falling alone, fool enough to believe in the fantasy they'd constructed for her family and his friends.

He released her hand at the door, waiting as she unlocked it, and then turned to leave. Mia heard the words leave her mouth before she even realized she'd had the intention to speak, desperately forestalling his departure.

"Do you think I could have caused this? Mom and Teresa at odds, everything feeling wrong... Is it all because I lost the watch?"

He shoved his hands in his pockets. "Do you want me to try to find it?"

She noticed he hadn't answered her question. Mia held out her hand. "Please."

She tried to focus on wanting the watch, but as always she couldn't seem to stop thinking about all the *reasons* she wanted it. She wanted Teresa's happiness, a healthy baby for her sister to take home and love, and for her mother to apologize to her sister and accept that not every happy ending was a cookie-cutter of hers.

Chase released her, rubbing his hands together as he backed away. "Still nothing. Sorry."

"No, it's me. I should be the one apologizing."

He cocked his head to the side, and Mia had the powerful feeling he wanted to say something, but whatever flirty, charming, oh-so-Chase thing he was going to say was smothered by the weight of the space between them.

He rocked on his heels. "G'night, Mia. Six o'clock tomorrow evening, right? For the tests?"

Mia nodded. They'd agreed she could run her test on his ability the following evening after official work hours, but talking about it felt strangely formal. Like they were only business associates.

Were they really only business associates?

Chase feinted forward, as if he might lean in for a goodnight kiss, but instead he just caught her hand and gave it a squeeze before bounding down the steps and across the parking lot.

Mia watched him go, leaning against her door, once again filled with the subtle regret that lingered in the wake of a kiss that should have happened.

Chapter Nineteen
Commando Skydiving

"Try not to think."

Chase snorted at Mia's absent—and one hundred percent sincere—command, and swallowed back the plethora of biting come-backs that lingered on his tongue.

She probably wouldn't have heard him anyway.

Dr. Corregianni was in her element tonight, engrossed in her monitors, muttering to herself as she tapped keys on her computer and periodically issuing absent commands like "Don't move" and "Relax, dammit."

Tonight was about getting a baseline, she'd explained. She didn't want him engaging his gift just yet. First she had to see what his brain did when he wasn't using it. He'd let the tempting cracks about not using his brain much anyway slide by, feeling the perverse urge to punish her with his silence.

A week ago he would have been charmed by her total focus, laughing and teasing her about her ability to block out the rest of the world as she worked, but not tonight. No, tonight he was jealous of a damned screen. Pissed that she was so comfortable with him now she *could* block him out completely. He wanted to prod her, rile her, get a reaction.

Only the fact that he knew it was his own ornery mood rather than anything she'd done kept his tongue in check.

His mood hadn't been helped by the sucky waves this morning or the weather that had shifted so he'd nearly frozen his balls off in his wet suit.

Chase studied the line between her brows as she frowned over the computer screen, her nose practically smudging the

LCD. The room was about the size of a doctor's exam room and that's what she'd called it, but there was no exam table in sight—thank God—just the large black leather chair that resembled a massage chair where he sat, a desk with a battalion of computers and bleeping machines, and a poster on the ceiling of the universe with a yellow "You are Here" arrow pointing toward a tiny dot.

He was hooked up to a machine which she called a modified EEG—"*of my own design, patent pending*"—that could have doubled for a torture device with all its electrodes and suctioned sensors, but so far her claim that this would be painless had been largely true. The only pain had been the excruciating awkwardness that filled every silence between him and Mia.

He'd fucked up the spark.

The vivid, alive feeling he'd had when he was with her last week had deadened as soon as he told her about his past, everything sweet and easy and fun about them sullied by the sudden complexity, muddied by his issues. He watched her studying his neural activity. Could she see the mark the accident had left on his brain on that scan? Would her beloved science have told her even if he hadn't hacked open his chest and showed her the empty space where his heart used to be?

"Stay still," Mia muttered without looking up, making Chase realize he'd begun to squirm in the chair.

He forced his muscles to relax. It wasn't her fault things were weird between them. She hadn't changed. It was all him.

He'd never told anyone about what happened to his family before. People who knew him at the time already knew and with people he'd met since he just avoided any contact that would require him to share anything of himself.

Except Karma. He'd told his boss, but she was the kind of person you could drop a bomb like that on and she would just nod, accepting the information with a complete lack of emotional response that he'd found soothing. Safe.

Telling Mia hadn't felt safe. It had felt like sky-diving without a parachute. Naked. He'd been waiting for the ground to hit him ever since, bracing for impact.

He never should have told her. Never should have met her family or kissed her in the pantry so he remembered the exact taste and texture of her lips when he dropped her off on Thursday night and she looked at him with those wide why-don't-you-kiss-me eyes. He never should have let it get that real.

"Mia."

"Hm?" She didn't even glance in his direction, scribbling something on the pad at her elbow, oblivious as ever.

"Look at me."

Her gaze stayed locked on the monitors. "I am."

Irritation flared hotter. "I'm not just a neural scan, Mia."

"Hm?"

Frustration—with himself, with her, with the whole damn situation—welled up in an angry rush. He wanted to push her, to stoke her temper until it was a wall between them, needing the distance of a fight. He reached up and the sensor at his temple came free with a suctioned pop.

The computer blipped a high-pitched warning.

"What the..." Mia's frown of concentration morphed into one of equal parts irritation and confusion, but her eyes stayed locked on the screen as she frantically tapped at the keyboard. She checked the wires connecting the sensors to the computer, wiggled the mouse, thumped the side of the monitor and even half-crawled under the desk to check the power plugs before *finally* lifting her head to look at him.

Her gaze landed on the sensors dangling from his hand and then swiveled, seemingly in slow motion, to lock on his face. The glare she turned on him would have lit a lesser man on fire. Her mouth pressed into a line.

"Why did you do that?"

Because he was sick of playing guinea pig for the night. Because he wanted her to actually *see* him. But mostly because he was done being the only one off-center and he wanted to piss her off, get under her skin and fire her up. Make her throw up her hands like a true Corregianni. He loved her temper. It fascinated him. Her frustration was a living thing—passionate and intense. So uncontained for someone so buttoned up.

If he could just make her lose her cool, maybe he wouldn't feel so raw.

He wanted her eyes shooting sparks and he knew the perfect thing to say to accomplish just that. "*Because.*"

Mia's glare intensified to life-threatening levels. Hell hath no fury like a scientist thwarted.

Because. *Because.*

Mia had always thought the phrase *seeing red* was a stupid metaphor, but now crimson seemed to seep into the edges of her vision, blanking her periphery until all she saw was the surfer in front of her with challenge in his freakishly blue eyes.

She could have let slide the fact that he pulled off the sensors—the scan was complete, after all, and she'd already saved the data for further analysis. Besides, today was just the baseline. Easily repeated. She could have shrugged it off, if not for that *because* and the fact that he'd been in a pissy mood all day. These tests had been *his* idea. *He* was the one who'd devised the stupid bet and all but bullied her into taking part and now he was bitching about being here? He didn't have to respect her, but to disrespect the science... Mia had no words.

Or, to be precise, she had six.

"What the fuck is your problem?"

"There has to be a problem just because I'm not bending over backward to accommodate you? I thought you wanted to penetrate my layers of bullshit. What's wrong, Mia? Don't you like what you found?"

"If I'd known you were an asshole under all that charm, I would never have tried to look further," she snapped, even as realization shuddered through her brain like a rickety train barely keeping to the tracks. She *missed* his bullshit.

Chase may exist to make sure the world's supply of bullshit didn't run out, but she *liked* that about him. She liked how smooth and slick and polished he was. She envied him his ease. She'd been jealous of the way he'd charmed her family. The way he'd charmed her. The man could talk her into anything, and then he'd just stopped talking.

"Sorry to disappoint you, sweetheart." His tone was brutally unapologetic.

Why had he gone quiet? Mia's brain kept fixating on that one question. Always the same one: *Why?*

"Did I do something to piss you off?" she asked, mentally retracing the origin of his crankiness. Her mother had noticed something was wrong on the weekend... "Is this about my family? About the adoption drama? Because I'm sorry about that, but I did warn you that everything is a catastrophe in my family. Drama is mother's milk to them—"

"And God forbid you let yourself be one of them. You'd have to stop looking down on them for five minutes to do that."

Mia flinched, hating his words and how they stabbed so close to the truth. "That's ridiculous. I don't look down on them," she insisted, but the lie tasted like chalk on her tongue.

"No? How about patronize? Condescend. *Disdain.* Like any of those words better?" Chase yanked off more of the sensors with each sharp, percussive word.

Her face felt hot and she realized she was breathing quickly, gripping the edge of the desk with one hand. "You don't understand." The arrogance was a defense mechanism. A reaction to the feeling of isolation and alienation she'd felt her entire life. *Every action will have an equal and opposite reaction.* Newton's Laws in effect in her life.

Chase's reaction was to launch himself out of the test chair and lean over her, bracing one fist past hers on the desk so their arms crossed like an X. Mia focused on that X. She couldn't look at his face, so close and angry.

"You know what I understand, sweetheart? I *understand* you don't have the first fucking clue how lucky you are to have them."

The reminder of his loss stabbed into her brain like a white-hot poker and Mia felt a rush of shame, matched by an irrational anger—yes, he'd been through hell, but did that give him the right to bitch at her? "I do know—"

"No. You don't."

Mia forced herself to look into his eyes and instantly regretted it. She didn't want to see the icy seriousness in his bright blue eyes because it came with pain. Pain she felt helpless to ease. She wanted to know the right answer, the right thing to say, but her mind was scrubbed blank. Moisture gathered in her eyes, like she'd been staring too long into the sun. "Chase... I..."

"You *don't*," he repeated and shoved himself away from her. He was out of the room, the heavy slap of his footsteps retreating down the hall before Mia's brain jolted back into gear enough to realize he was leaving.

"Chase!"

She tripped over her desk chair in her haste, ricocheting off the far wall as she burst out of the exam room and raced after him down the hall. He hadn't stopped, but he hadn't accelerated either.

"Dammit, Chase. I'm sorry." She caught the muscle of his upper arm with both hands, forcing him to slow. "I didn't mean—"

She didn't know exactly what she was going to say. Words were crowding her tongue—of condolence about his family, futile attempts at understanding or chewing him out for shutting her out—but she never got a chance to stammer through them.

He spun fast, catching her unawares, and suddenly she was pinned hard against the wall, the heady warmth of his body holding her there as all ten of his fingers dove into her hair and his mouth crashed down on hers.

Her brain cells melted under the heat, fusing together into one giant, useless blob of gray matter.

The kiss was desperate. Longing. Filled with achy loss and the frantic need to lose himself in her. Mia fell into the emotion of it. Helpless to even consider resistance, she clung to him and kissed him back for all she was worth.

The sensations were electric. His luscious, beachy smell swamped her as his hands held her steady for the demands of his mouth. The brush of stubble against her cheeks was almost as exotically enticing as the taste of him, but it was the needy rush of it that did her in.

For once he wasn't hiding himself behind layers of fast talk and charm or a barrier of icy distance. He was *here*, overwhelming her, all but inside her, his soul bleeding into hers like osmosis in action. Her blood rushed hard and fast, making her body feel heavy but simultaneously impossibly light. As if her very cells had been excited, agitated to the point where solid matter became steam, the molecules frantic and light enough to float right off the ground. He was the only solid thing left in her dizzy, floating world.

Then he jerked back.

As quickly as it had begun, he put her away from him, staggering to brace himself on the opposite wall. Mia stayed plastered to the wall where he'd left her, her synapses too melted to command movement.

"I'm sorry," he said without looking at her. He shook his head sharply and said it again. "I'm sorry. I can't. It won't happen again."

"What?" It was the only semi-coherent thing she could think to say, but he didn't hear it. He was already gone, the door to the lab clicking closed behind him.

Mia sank to the floor and tucked her knees to her chest, wrapping her arms around them in an attempt to find some warmth in the hallway that suddenly felt arctic. Her fingertips hovered over her lips. What had just happened? And why did she feel so hollow at the thought that it might never happen again?

Chapter Twenty
Groveling for Beginners

Chase stood on the sidewalk in front of the Lathrop Institute for the second time in as many weeks, wondering if he was going to be thrown out on his ass for daring to bring Dr. Mia Corregianni lunch. This time, lunch came with an apology. And strings.

Provided she let him in the door.

He hadn't exactly been Mr. Smooth last night. He yelled at her, bailed on her, practically mauled her in the hallway, then freaked out because it was all too much, too fast, and ran like hell. Not exactly his finest hour.

He hadn't slept. Chase tended to avoid self-analysis whenever possible, and after tossing and turning until three, he'd woken up, grabbed his board and headed to the beach. It was too ass-bitingly cold to surf—even feeling his most masochistic—so he'd sat down to let the icy sand freeze his butt as the black waves smashed against each other, creating frothy white tips.

Unlike most nights, his troubles hadn't left him at the shore. The truth had followed him there. The unflattering truth that he'd pursued Mia for their fake relationship because he hadn't thought either of them would really be caught by it. The fake relationship had seemed safe, and she had seemed safely emotionless. Almost robotic.

But she wasn't an automaton. She was real, and suddenly their relationship was too real. He'd shown her pieces of himself he hadn't let any other woman see and even though telling her about his past had freaked him the fuck out, he still liked her. He liked the way she tried to pierce through his evasions and wouldn't just get swallowed in his usual bullshit. He liked the way her family had wrapped around him and even liked the fact that she was so prickly and uneasy with them because it gave him a job to do, smoothing her way with them. But mostly he just liked her, the way she made him feel when he was with her. She woke him up and made him want to tackle every challenge she threw at him, like he hadn't in years.

Last night he'd liked her too much. Needed her too much. Wanted her so damn badly he'd been mindless with it.

And it had scared the shit out of him.

This morning, as the sun had begun to paint the waves, his shame over running out on Mia had been matched by a new shame. He'd treaded water for six years. Too chicken shit after being rolled by a bitch of a wave to try the next set. He'd dropped out, dropped back and waited.

His parents, his brother, Katie. They'd be so disappointed in him.

He needed to get back in there. Give life another chance to roll him hard and smash him against the coral because if he didn't, he might as well have died with them.

He couldn't do it without Mia. She was his catalyst. And she was probably justifiably pissed at him.

So here he stood, hat—and Chinese food—in hand, ready to implement Project Grovel. If he hadn't been barred from the building.

Fifteen minutes later, Nasrin opened the door to the lab for him and blocked the entry, giving him a look that would have been friendlier if she'd caught him shooting puppies.

"What do you want?"

He lifted the take-out bag and smiled winningly. "I come bearing egg rolls. There's enough here for you and Stephanie too."

The bag smelled like the waiting room to heaven, but she didn't budge. "Dr. C's been distracted all day. I don't suppose you have anything to do with that?"

"Isn't she always distracted?"

"Distracted *by* her work, not *from* her work," Nasrin explained, like he was one step above Cro-Magnon man on the evolutionary scale and it was barely worth her time to clarify. "And *not* in the dopey good way she was distracted last Thursday."

Chase couldn't help his grin. They'd gone out last Thursday night. "She was distracted in a dopey good way?"

Nasrin folded her arms, amping up her death glare until it almost reached Mia's level of proficiency. "We know you were coming over after hours yesterday and this morning she's upset. What did you do?"

Chase lost the grin and met her eyes squarely. "No offense, Nasrin, but that's between Mia and me. But I will tell you that I'm bringing both fortune cookies and apologies, neither of which I can deliver if you don't let me in."

"I'm letting you in," Nasrin informed him, still without budging, "but we love Dr. C and if you hurt her, I think it's only fair to warn you that we have access to all kinds of nasty flesh-eating chemicals and no moral compunction against using them to pickle your gonads."

Chase winced. "Duly noted."

Nasrin swung the door open all the way. "She's in her office."

Chase made his way through the cubicles toward Mia's office, feeling equal parts amused and intimidated when Stephanie looked up from her computer and cracked her knuckles as he passed. Then Mia was calling out an absent, "Come in" and he forgot all about her assistants as nervousness choked him. He hadn't been this worried about talking to a girl since he was thirteen.

Mia looked up from her computer almost instantly when he entered, surprising him with the fact that he didn't have to pry her away from it. Her gaze grew wary when she saw him hovering in her doorway.

"Chase. What can I do for you?" she asked, cautious and reserved.

"You can have lunch with me for a start. I'm sorry about last night. About the last few days. I've been...off."

Her dark eyebrows arched. "But you're better now?"

"I could be. I have a...proposition for you."

He'd planned to ease her into it, bring it up after he'd fed her when she might be feeling more charitable thanks to the quasi-orgasmic Mongolian Beef, but he couldn't stand to wait.

Mia looked down at her desk. "I don't know, Chase. Our last proposition is getting complicated enough."

"I'm hoping this will simplify things." He cleared his throat. "I was wondering if you'd like to go out with me. On a real date. One that isn't about showing off for my friends or your family. Just you and me. Us. To see where this goes. If you want." *Very eloquent, Chase. Show her that trademark charm.*

Mia frowned. "But last night..."

"I freaked out," he admitted. "And I'm not gonna say I won't ever freak again because I might, but I only freaked out because I really like you, Mia."

Her frown grew more ferocious even as color rose to her cheeks. "You like me," she repeated, as if confirming the unexpected results of an experiment.

"I do. And you like me too," he said, trying for his stand-by cockiness.

She rewarded him with a flicker of a smile before her fierce frown returned. "Okay."

"Okay?"

She glowered at him, tense and rigid and repressive. Miss Prim in full effect. "Yes, I will go out with you. When?"

"Tonight? About seven?"

"Fine." She puckered her lips.

Chase couldn't resist. He leaned across her desk and dropped a kiss on them. It was quick, a sneak attack, and when he drew back she blinked and frowned at him again.

"What was that for?"

He grinned. "I'm going to teach you to be impulsive. I'm going to make that cool, scientific heart of yours race."

And in the process he was going to remember what a racing heart felt like himself.

Her eyes narrowed. "That sounds like a threat."

"That's a promise."

"So who's this Peter guy?"

Chase timed his question during her backswing, but Mia didn't flinch. She thunked her putter against the fluorescent green golf ball with the perfect amount of force at the perfect trajectory to send it up the ramp, through the windmill, and around the spiral down to the hole, thwacking against Chase's real-men-choose-pink golf ball and sending it rolling farther from the hole.

"You tried to distract me," she accused, inordinately smug that he'd failed.

"I suppose I should have warned you," he said without remorse. "I cheat."

"Isn't the purpose of cheating to win?" She was kicking his butt. Three strokes ahead after only four and a half holes.

"I'm lulling you into a false sense of superiority." He approached his ball and gave it a tap. The hot pink ball dribbled slowly toward the hole, only to stop two inches short. "Do you feel lulled?"

Mia snorted. "Extremely." She sank her ball with one perfectly executed stroke.

Chase sank his, then bent to fetch them both and led the way to the sixth hole. "If I'd known you were going to be so smug about being a putt-putt savant, I would have tried First Date Plan B."

"Which was?"

"Bowling."

Mia glanced down at the pencil skirt and heels her assistants had picked out for her romantic dinner date. "Those were the choices? Mini-golf and bowling? I should have dressed for gym class. And for the record, I hated gym class."

"You're having fun. Admit it."

Mia adjusted her glasses to give herself a chance to smother her smile. She *was* having fun. More than she could remember ever having on a date. She'd half expected things to be awkward, especially after the strangeness between them recently, but easy, too-charming-to-live Chase was back in full force. Though there was something different tonight. The charm didn't seem like a façade. He was still playful, but there was a newfound sincerity to him now.

"Besides," he went on as she placed her ball on the sixth tee, "I figured mini-golf and bowling would be right up your alley. All velocities and angles and friction and drag. It was the most scientific pastime I could think of."

She lined up her shot and drew back her putter.

"Besides sex, of course."

She froze with her club drawn back. Her face flaming, she shot him a quelling look.

He grinned, completely un-quelled. "By the way, that little waggle you do as you're lining up your shot is insanely hot."

She looked down at her ball, barely seeing it. "I do not waggle."

"Oh, you waggle. Trust me."

She forced her eyes to focus on the ball.

"So Peter...?"

"My ex." His name returned the conversation to comfortable ground. Mia executed a flawless hole in one. "Talking about him won't rattle me, so you can just accept your defeat now."

"'Never give up. Never surrender'."

Mia snorted. "Did you just quote *Galaxy Quest* at me?"

"Did you just recognize a *Galaxy Quest* quote? I'm shocked. I thought you were all work and no play."

"Hey, I play." Though admittedly, she wasn't much of a player when left to her own devices. Her *Galaxy Quest* savvy came more from Gina's addiction to all things Alan Rickman than her own playful inclinations.

"With Peter?"

Honesty forced her to admit, "No. But Peter was even more work and less play than me."

"How long were you two together?"

She shrugged, stepping away from the tee so he could line up his own shot. "Eight or nine years."

Chase nearly spiked himself with his putter. "Seriously? You were with a guy for nine years and talking about him doesn't rattle you even a tiny bit?"

"We were compatible—both professionally and personally. What we wanted lined up neatly. Then he got an offer for a position in Edinburgh and we parted ways. No fuss. No drama."

"No drama. So you never loved him?"

Mia blinked, startled by the blunt question, delivered in his typically casual manner. "Not the way my family talks about love, no."

"And there was no other great love? No one besides Peter?"

"I never really had time for relationships. My work came first. If you want to talk about love, I love my work."

"Huh."

He sank his ball, falling another stroke behind and Mia trailed him to the next hole before curiosity got the better of her. "What does *huh* mean?"

"I just had you pegged as being like me. I saw the lengths you went to trying to isolate yourself and keep those who love you at arm's length—your family, even those research assistants of yours."

"I don't do that," Mia protested, but the words hit a bit too close to home, stinging more than she wanted to admit.

"I saw myself in you. Figured you were burned by love. Gun-shy after being shot in the face by life." He stepped back to give her access to the tee. "But your family is one marital success story after another and now you tell me you've never had the shit kicked out of you by a guy. I guess I just can't understand how someone who has only ever seen the good side of love can be so terrified of it."

"Why does it have to be fear?" she challenged. "Why can't it just be reserve? Caution?" Or a complete lack of skill in the area of interpersonal matters.

"Could be. If that's what you want to call it. But how does a woman grow up cautious in your family? Because, yes, you look too much like your father to have been switched at birth, but I can't think of any other explanation."

"Well if you find one, will you clue me in? Because I'll be damned if I know." She accidentally smacked herself in the shin with her club, wincing. "I'm awful at all that romantic nonsense. It's not how I'm wired. The faulty Corregianni. Don't you think I've heard that my entire life? All skepticism, no trust. If it seems too good to be true, it must be. I don't isolate myself, they isolate me. That odd girl Mia. Why does she have to poke into everything? Why can't she take anything at face value?"

She swung wildly and the green ball caromed off the edge and flew onto the next hole.

"Crap. Now you have distracted me."

"And here I thought ricocheting off that hole was part of your ingenious strategy."

Mia smiled in spite of herself, sobering as Chase waved to the teenagers on the hole she'd bounced onto and fetched the ball back, dropping it within inches of the hole. "That's cheating."

He grinned. "I did warn you."

Mia watched him line up his own shot, admiring the bunch of muscles across his shoulders and the way his blazer rode up as he bent for the shot, revealing his bounce-a-quarter-off-it ass in his faded jeans. "Do you know how Gina met her husband?" she asked conversationally.

He shook his head without taking his eye off the pink ball. "Don't think I caught that story."

"On the very first day she had the watch, she went to a jewelry store, just to stand out front, wearing the watch and looking through the window at the engagement rings. She started thinking about the man she wanted to marry, this man who'd only ever existed in her daydreams. So she's planning their perfect life together, when who should stroll by but Tony. He never walked that street on his way to work, but that day he took a detour. He takes one look at her face and says she looks like the kind of girl who needs a ring on her finger. Next thing you know, he asks her if she'll go inside with him and let him buy her one, right then, just to keep warm until he could work up the gumption to propose to her."

"Cute story."

"So cute," she agreed. "But it could never have happened to me. I would have hated the cheesy line. I would have looked for the catch. I would have told Tony where he could shove that engagement ring because I don't believe in Prince Charming, but not Gina. No, Gina just fell into her husband's arms and hasn't left since. Gina is a true Correggianni."

"So are you," Chase insisted. "Who says all Correggiannis have to be believers?"

Mia snorted. "My entire family says."

"Maybe." Chase took another shot. "How are things at Casa Correggianni these days? Still in a furor over the adoption?"

She wrinkled her nose. "Things are still at DefCon One between Mama and Teresa. I think even my mother knows she's being an idiot at this point, but getting her to stand down will probably take a United Nations resolution."

Chase opened his mouth to reply, but the ringing of his cell phone cut him off. "Sorry. I thought I'd turned it off."

"No, it's fine." Mia moved a few feet away to give him privacy, grateful for the interruption. Somewhere between holes seven and nine, things had gotten serious and she wanted the fun back.

Though by the look on Chase's face, the phone call was not going to resurrect the fun. By the time he closed his phone, his expression was as dark as she'd ever seen it.

"Everything okay?"

"No. That was my property maintenance company. Apparently there's a problem at my brother's house."

"Do you need to go now?"

He grimaced, his entire body tense. "Yeah. I should."

"Do you want me to come with you?" She didn't know what made her ask, but she knew as soon as she saw some of the tension in his shoulders relax that it had been the right thing to say.

"Yeah. Yeah, I'd like that."

She picked up her golf ball and began weaving through the remaining holes to the exit. Turning back when she realized he wasn't following. "Chase?"

He shook himself and started after her. "I'm coming."

Chapter Twenty-One
Househunters: Supernatural

Opening the front door to his brother's house was a shock. Not because memories rushed back to swamp him or anything melodramatic like that, but because he'd never really given a thought to what six years of neglect would look like.

It was like a scene out of *Great Expectations*. Dusty sheets covered the furniture that hadn't been sent to Goodwill, visible only by the moonlight that filtered through the slats of the window blinds since the electricity was disconnected. Chase found himself looking around for Miss Havisham in her wedding dress.

For the second time in as many days, he felt ashamed of the way he'd handled—or rather completely avoided handling—his loss. If there was a right and wrong way to grieve, he'd picked the wrong way.

Then Mia's hand slipped into his, her slim fingers cold as always, and the weight of his guilt lifted slightly. This was not the way he'd envisioned the evening ending. Watching Mia in her best naughty librarian get-up taking a stance and waggling her hips at every tee, he'd been playing putt-putt half hard and mentally mapping his personal trajectory toward her bed every time she calculated the angle on another shot.

And now they were at the last place he wanted to be and his libido might as well have taken a vacation to Peru. Best laid plans for getting laid...

He pushed open the door all the way and they stepped into the foyer. "Hello?"

A middle-aged man, his girth splitting the seams of his Levi's and the bright green polo shirt with Luxor Management embroidered on the pocket, hurried out of the kitchen area to greet them. "Mr. Chase? I'm Gary Valdez with Luxor."

"It's Mr. Hunter, but just Chase is fine."

Valdez consulted his clipboard and gave a self-deprecating laugh. "Whoops! Guess that's a comma, isn't it?" He rushed on, energetic to a degree that Chase found grating. "Sorry to bother you at night, Mr. Hunter, and I can assure you that Luxor does not make a practice of intruding upon the owners' evenings, but during our initial inspection of the property we came across a few items that qualify as safety hazards and it is Luxor policy to address those issues without delay."

"I gave my permission for you to do whatever you need to do."

"Of course, Mr. Hunter, but in the cases of repairs costing more than two thousand dollars, our contract requires that we consult with the property owner."

Chase's hand tightened on Mia's. She remained silent and steady at his side. "Two thousand dollars?"

Valdez grimaced, an exaggerated pantomime of sympathy that further shredded Chase's nerves. "It's the furnace, I'm afraid. We turned it back on yesterday to begin the process of returning the house to a livable state and today the neighbors reported smelling smoke coming from the house. We were unable to locate the smoke upon examination, but we shut off the electricity again and disconnected the furnace as a precautionary measure. Unfortunately, our technician has just informed us, due to the extreme disrepair..."

Chase tuned him out.

He'd heard all he needed to and couldn't focus on chitchat and bullshit at the moment. To his left was Toby's living room. He'd had his last real Christmas in that room. Toby and Nicole had just bought the house. They'd been so proud, so excited to host their first major holiday. So excited Toby had gotten a tree that was too big for the room. He'd tipped it at an angle into the corner so the angel at the top wouldn't brain itself on the ceiling, but it had been glorious, every inch decorated and bristling with lights.

Katie'd come over after spending Christmas morning with her folks an hour north. She'd curled up next to him on the love seat, everyone he loved in one room.

Then two months later, everyone he loved was gone.

Mia's hand felt icy in his, but the room was unbearably hot, stuffy as hell. Valdez chattered away, oblivious.

He couldn't be here. He just couldn't do it.

"Excuse me."

Chase didn't wait for a reaction. He slipped out the front door, not bothering to shove it all the way shut behind him, and leaned against one of the pillars on the front porch. He took a deep breath and the cool night air instantly cleared his head. Inside he could hear Mia dealing with Valdez, smoothing over his abrupt departure.

He shoved his hands deep into his pockets and wandered away from the voices, down the walk to where he'd parked his car at the curb.

A new furnace. They didn't come cheap and he was already taking all the work Karma threw his way. Working so he wouldn't have to sell. Still doing everything he could not to move on.

Chase pulled out his cell and dialed his boss. She picked up on the second ring, even though it was well past business hours.

"Chase."

"Hey, boss. Don't suppose you have any big-ticket clients lying around who need some knick-knack found?"

"I'm loving this workaholic leaf you've turned over, Chase, but you've already cleared half of Ciara's backlog and all the finds I had pending for you except Dr. Corregianni." There was a slight pause, then, "How much do you need?"

"I'm not asking for charity."

"And I'm not offering any, but a loan is another matter. What's going on, Chase?"

"It's nothing. I'll handle it." Her waiting silence prompted him to add, "I need a new furnace. It's smoking up my house and the neighbors are complaining."

"I see. Can you smell the smoke?"

"What?"

"Sometimes, to the untrained eye, a ghost infestation can manifest as mist or smoke. One of the symptoms of Wyatt Haines's haunting was a sabotaged furnace, I believe. Could you have a spirit problem?"

Chase's heart tightened into a hard knot. Had Toby and Nicole been hanging around all these years? Waiting for some kind of closure? "It's my brother's old house."

"Ah. I'm sorry. Would you like me to send Jo over to check if you have...lingering energy?"

Energy. Not spirits. Not restless dead souls haunting the house they'd once loved. He could handle it if he thought of it as energy. "I can't afford her." The ghost exterminator was fucking expensive.

"Pro bono," Karma cut him off, her tone sharpening when he suggested paying. "I'll send her right over."

"I'd appreciate it, but I was really calling about extra work."

She hesitated. "I might be able to find something for you to do. What's your degree in again? Architecture?"

"You know I didn't complete my degree." But for the first time, the idea of going back to school and finishing up didn't make his stomach revolt.

"Ah. Of course. Well, my latest secretary just quit. There's always filing to be done if you'd like to pick up some extra hours."

Filing papers or filing for bankruptcy...

"I'll take it."

Karma snorted. "My God, you are desperate. Come by tomorrow and I'll keep you busy." There was another momentary pause. "How are things going with Dr. Corregianni? Any luck with her watch?"

Mia chose that moment to step out of the house, pausing on the porch to shake Valdez's hand. She didn't smile, but her cool competence seemed to put the effusive property manager at ease. It certainly soothed Chase.

"We're still trying. Have any of the other finders had any luck? She's running out of time here."

"Nothing yet. Ciara's been pulled into another federal investigation so it might be a while before it gets to the top of her queue."

Chase cursed softly. He'd already visited all the pawn shops in the area—on the off chance Mia's watch had ended up in one of them, but there were no gold watches of the size she described. He'd wanted to find it—by magic or logic. Wanted to be her hero, though she seemed to care more about his brain scans than the missing watch most days.

"How is Dr. Corregianni handling its absence?"

"Pretty well, all things considered. She's running some tests on my ability, trying to figure out how I do what I do."

"Is she?" Karma's languid voice was suddenly very interested. "Tell her I might have some contacts who would be interested in funding an official study if she's so inclined."

"I'll do that."

Valdez retreated to the SUV he'd parked in the driveway and Mia started down the walk toward Chase, her face comfortingly expressionless, showing no reaction to the fact that he'd freaked out and fled.

"Give Mia my best," Karma said casually. "Good night, Chase."

He mumbled a response and pocketed his cell phone. There was no point in wondering how Karma had known he was with Mia. His boss's instincts could be eerie, though she claimed she didn't share the psychic abilities of her consultants.

As Valdez peeled out, waving out the window, Mia rested a hip against the hood of Chase's car at his side.

"Enthusiastic guy," Chase said, feeling uncharacteristically tongue-tied. "I had no idea furnaces were such a turn-on."

"He is energetic." Mia made a face, clearly sharing his opinion of the obnoxious property manager. "Once he figured out he couldn't install the new furnace tonight anyway, even if you made a choice, he agreed to email you in the morning with estimates on various models and information on the tax rebates that apply for the energy-efficient ones."

"Thank you." Some first date. He jerked his chin toward the house. "I know how to show a girl a good time, huh? What woman can resist the old broken-furnace line?"

"Am I complaining? It's not like you haven't done anything to help me."

"At this rate we'll need a CPA to balance the books between us. See who owes who what."

"You don't have to do that," she said softly. "Crack jokes and be witty all the time. Not with me. I get that this sucks for you."

He shrugged off her comment, feeling the inches between them like a glacial abyss. "I should stick around. Karma's sending one of the ghost girls to check for haunting issues—apparently furnaces are a symptom—but I can call you a cab if you want. Or why don't you take my car?"

He dug into his pocket for his keys, but Mia's cool hand closed over his wrist, stopping him. Her brown eyes were piercing. "I'll stay. Unless you don't want me to."

Something thick parked itself in his throat. Instead of speaking, he looped an arm around her shoulders and tugged her against his side. She looped her arms around his waist, burrowing close. Her icy fingers brushed his skin and he jumped, then held her tighter. "Jesus, you're freezing."

"Poor circulation."

He caught her hands, focusing on chaffing them to warm her. Neither of them suggested waiting inside the house. He wasn't ready to go back in and Mia wasn't pushing.

She tucked her cheek against his chest. Even though she was the one leaning against him, he felt like she was the pillar holding him up. She may be slim nearly to the point of frailty, but she never bent. Her will was iron, firm and straight, propping him up when he would have wavered.

"So ghosts, huh?" Her tone was arch, clearly not talking about his specific ghosts, but the existence of spirits in general.

"Did your scientific brain just implode?" he teased.

"My scientific brain will wait until it has a chance to evaluate the evidence."

The evidence arrived moments later on a Harley.

Jo Banks, Karmic's premier ghost exterminator, climbed off her hog, yanked off her helmet to reveal her spiked blond-with-black-tips hair and flashed them a cheeky grin. "Somebody call Ghostbusters?"

Chase had only met Jo a handful of times, but he'd always enjoyed her mouthy sense of humor at the Karmic Consultants Christmas party. She certainly hadn't mellowed since she hooked up with billionaire hotel-magnate Wyatt Haines. If anything, she'd become an even more unfiltered, unabashed version of herself. Her smile was just as wicked, but it came quicker now.

Mia frowned at the tall, stacked punkette the entire time Chase was briefing Jo on the situation, evidently not sure what to make of her. She kept frowning long after Jo had disappeared into the house, leaving strict instructions that they stay out here "lest things get wiggy."

"She's..."

"Not what you expected?"

"No. But I'd love to scan her brain."

Chase snorted, recognizing Mia's brand of compliment in the wistful comment. "Karma says she knows some people who may want to fund an official study on our talents, if you're game."

A look that was equal parts lustful hunger and greed suffused Mia's face. "Seriously? Did you just offer me funding?"

"I take it that's a big deal?"

"Researchers spend half our lives begging for money to do our work. To have someone *offer...*"

He grinned lecherously. "Do I get a finder's fee?"

He hadn't planned on kissing her. It wasn't a conscious intention, but before he knew what he was doing, his lips were on hers, gently, slowly, a comfortable, familiar kiss unlike any they'd shared before.

The sweet hello of a kiss made him realize how strange their relationship was—like the scales balancing intimacy and chemistry were wobbling wildly back and forth but never finding true center. Until now. This kiss was equilibrium.

Mia rose up on her toes, kissing him back without urgency, and he settled in to enjoy the lazy conversation of it.

When she finally pulled back, neither of them were out of breath, but his heart was thumping erratically. Chase looked up at the house.

"Tonight was the first time I went inside since the accident."

Mia arched in his arms to study his face. Chase didn't look at her. He didn't want to know what she saw. Instead he focused on the house.

"What was he like, your brother?"

Memories dusted themselves off and rose up. "He was honest, straightforward, really direct. You would've liked him." He gave a soft huffing laugh. "But he couldn't lie for shit. One time, when he was supposed to be watching me, we snuck into a neighbor's yard to do flips on their trampoline. Mom hated tramps and had made us swear we would never go near it, convinced we would break our necks..." He trailed off, the memory startlingly sharp.

"What happened?"

"I did a triple flip and broke my arm." He shoved up his sleeve, pointing to a small white scar on his forearm. "The bone punched right through. Toby puked all over the trampoline when he saw it. We ran home and by the time we got there I was about ready to pass out."

"Shock."

"Yeah, but I still had this great story about ninjas invading our yard and my arm getting broken defending our turf and all sorts of random bullshit I was sure my mom would buy. But Toby was a straight arrow. He called her, confessed everything and even offered to clean the trampoline. That was Toby."

Once he'd started, the stories spilled out. Stories about his brother, about his parents, about Katie. He talked himself hoarse, wandering through memories he wasn't even sure were wholly true anymore—too tempered by the fact of grief to hold the bite of reality. Mia listened and he just talked.

He hadn't done that either. Avoiding the memories inside the house and inside himself, he hadn't let himself grieve or move on. He'd just frozen in place trying to keep it from being true, stuck in denial. Was that the first stage of grief? The second? Whichever it was, he'd never gotten beyond it. Six years of stasis.

Then Mia happened.

He trailed off as Jo marched out of the house, dusting off her hands.

"Well?" he called out as her long strides ate up the walk.

"Zilch," Jo called back. "Nada. Big fat nothing. You're clean, Hunter. Not a single ghostie in residence and not even the lingering energy that there ever was one. Clean as a whistle." She paused, frowning. "If whistles are really clean with all those people spitting all over them. Sounds unsanitary."

Chase didn't care about whistles. He was too busy being relieved his brother wasn't trapped as a ghost in the house, in stasis as surely as Chase had been for the last six years.

Mia stepped away from him as Jo straddled her Harley.

"Ms. Banks? I was wondering if I might run some tests on you. On your brain, specifically."

Jo snorted. "Honey, do I look like a lab rat to you?"

Mia opened her mouth to reply, but whatever she would have said was drowned out by the cough of the Harley firing up. Jo secured her helmet and roared into the night, off to wreak havoc on her billionaire boyfriend's life, no doubt.

Mia spun back toward him, all but stomping her feet in frustration. "Damn."

"Don't worry. She'll do it if Karma asks her to."

"She makes a good point. About the whistles. The human mouth is a cesspool of bacteria."

"Is it any wonder I can't help wanting to kiss you when you talk about cesspools in peoples' mouths?" He opened the car door. "Come on. Let's get you home."

He closed the door after her and rounded the hood, taking one last look back at the house. Maybe he'd call Brody in the morning. Let him set up a meeting with a realtor. Maybe it was time.

Chase slid into the car beside Mia.

No more stasis.

Chapter Twenty-Two
Father Knows Best

"Mama?" Mia let herself in through the kitchen. Her call echoed back through the house, the complete silence convincing her the house was empty.

Crap. She'd hoped to catch her mother at home. Teresa had called again this morning, in tears because their mother had apparently scheduled a series of appointments with various fertility specialists—making her stance on the adoption very clear even though she and Teresa still weren't speaking.

Mia was the person least likely to be nominated as family diplomat, but she'd found herself agreeing to act as Teresa's ambassador to their mother just to stop her sister's sobs. She'd taken a late lunch and driven over to her parents' place, rehearsing the piece of her mind she planned on giving her mother the entire way. She'd worked herself into as much of a state of righteous indignation as she'd ever felt, perfectly aware that she was using Teresa's situation as an excuse to pick a long overdue fight with her mother.

Now the empty house taunted her.

"Mimi?"

Or maybe not so empty, but the voice that called from the den was a hesitant baritone, not her mother's strident alto.

She wandered past the infamous pantry to the one room that hadn't been touched when her parents renovated and tucked her head inside her dad's man cave. "Hi, Daddy."

Franklin Delano Corregianni sat in the battered recliner her mother wouldn't allow in any other room of the house, surrounded by wood paneling and books on all sides. A twelve-inch television was on in one corner, but he had his back to the basketball game replaying on it. He was a wiry man with thinning hair and a face that would always be called *distinctive* before handsome, but just seeing his unflappable calm had always soothed something uneasy in Mia. It did the same today, her anger retreating as her father waved her into the room.

"Is something wrong?"

Not surprising he would think so. Mia never left work during the day. Even on the weekends, she was more likely to be in the lab than anywhere else. A trait which now seemed myopic rather than dedicated.

"I was hoping to catch Mom at home."

"She's at one of her lunches. Save the Owls? Or maybe Thursday is Feed Africa." He shrugged. Both of her parents had retired a couple years ago, but while her father had buried himself in all the books he'd never had time to read, her mother had vowed to leave no charity volunteerless. It would have been noble if Mia hadn't suspected she mostly went for the gossip.

"She's probably telling the entire neighborhood how Teresa's insulted her by deciding to adopt."

He tipped his head to the side slowly. "Your mother wants you girls to be happy."

"But only if what we do matches her definition of what will make us happy."

"Mia." The scold was soft, but all the more effective for the lack of emphasis.

She flushed, ashamed of the negative words, but refusing to haul them back. Her gaze flicked to the stylish straight-backed chair stationed so the arm brushed her father's recliner. It was the only thing in the room that wasn't her father's style. Her mother's chair in her father's room. They were so different, they should have been incompatible, but that chair spoke to how they'd accepted one another's differences. If only her mother could be so accepting of her children...

"Mama thinks adoption is wonderful for everyone else in the world. Why can't she be happy for Teresa?"

Her father closed the hardback on his lap—something about the fall of the Roman Empire—and nodded her toward the overstuffed love seat. The cracked leather creaked as she perched on it.

"Your mother doesn't want to believe Teresa has given up."

"Adopting isn't 'giving up' and even if Teresa has decided not to throw any more energy at trying to conceive a biological child, it isn't Mama's choice."

"No, but it is hard for her to accept all the same. Give her time."

"She's upsetting Teresa. I don't see why we have to give Mama time when it's *Teresa's* life we're talking about."

"Is it?"

Mia felt a flash of anger, so unusual in her father's presence that it gave her pause. "This isn't about me or my relationship with Mama." She sighed, her eyes flicking back to the empty straight-backed chair. "How do you do it? You're so different..." Like she and Chase. Polar opposites in so many ways.

"We don't try to change one another. If you love someone, you accept them."

Mia snorted. "I think Mama might have a different definition."

"Perhaps. But she isn't the only one."

"What's that supposed to mean?"

"Didn't you come here determined to make her change?"

"Change her mind," she protested. "Not change who she is."

"Is that so very different?"

"Of course it is."

"If your mother doesn't have the right to tell Teresa she's wrong, how do you have the right to tell your mother the same thing?"

"This isn't a philosophy question, Daddy."

"Isn't it?" Then he flicked his fingers, dismissively, a silent *never mind*. "Your mother may always struggle to understand you, Mia. But she loves you. And your sister. Your mama...she's always reacted with her heart first and her head second. Right now her heart hurts because one of her girls is having to make a compromise your mama doesn't want her to have to make. She's handling it badly, but as soon as she sees Teresa's baby—wherever it comes from—she'll have a change of heart."

"And in the meantime?"

He shrugged. "Teresa is stronger than she looks. Not as strong as you, but she can handle this."

Mia blinked, startled. Her father thought she was strong? Stronger than Teresa? "I should get back to work."

He nodded, reaching for the book he'd set aside without another word. She stood, but paused on her way out of the room, crossing to her father and dropping a kiss onto his cheek. "Thanks, Daddy."

He patted her hand and she slipped out of the room. Nothing had been resolved, nothing changed, but she felt lighter in spite of the lack of concrete results.

She was halfway down the front walk when her phone rang. Mia scrambled for it, feeling a moment of panic that something had gone horribly wrong at the lab on the one day she'd taken an afternoon off. Not that there was anything *to* go wrong. There were no test subjects coming in today and only data analysis and sample testing to be done. That knowledge notwithstanding, she couldn't help the surge of irrational fear that the Lathrop building had exploded without her there monitoring its continued existence.

The call wasn't from her office, but from her little sister. She swiped a thumb to connect it, transferring to her Bluetooth as she climbed into her car.

"Hey Gina."

"Is it the apocalypse?"

Mia frowned. "Excuse me?"

"I called your office line first and you weren't there. I'm just wondering if I should be on the lookout for Four Horsemen."

"Cute. I was at Mom and Dad's. Teresa asked me if I could talk some sense into Mama."

Gina made a sympathetic noise. "How'd that go? I tried again yesterday but she's really digging in her heels. Did you have any luck?"

"She wasn't there. I ended up talking to Daddy instead."

"Probably for the best. How is Mr. Bennett today?"

"Who?"

"Just another of those cultural references you claim to be so savvy about. Never mind. Forget Dad. How's *Chase*?"

Mia had no idea how to answer that question. For all that she studied how the human brain reacted to emotional stimuli, she was starting to realize she didn't know the first thing about being in a relationship that was based on anything more than professional compatibility. A real relationship, not a cardboard facsimile of a bond. This thing with Chase was already more intimate than any relationship she'd had before. And she had no idea how to process that fact.

"Mia? You still there?"

"We went on a date last night," Mia blurted, incapable of thinking of anything more profound to say. "His furnace broke down."

"Is that some kind of clever euphemism I'm supposed to understand? Because I haven't slept a full night in two months and I'm a little slow with the innuendos these days."

"No, his actual furnace. In his house. It broke. So we had to cut our date short so he could meet with his property guy." And the experience had somehow been a thousand times more intimate than a date could have been.

"Oh, bummer. Furnaces are expensive as hell. Did you at least sex him out of his funk afterward?"

"*Gina.* Jeez." Mia swallowed thickly, her hands at ten and two as she tried to focus on the road and not the rather graphic images of her *sexing Chase out of his funk* that her hindbrain had provided. "We haven't...you know...yet."

"Playing hard to get, huh? Good for you. Make him work for it."

"I'm not playing," Mia protested, then admitted, "I don't know *how* to play hard to get."

"So what's the problem? You're obviously into him. He's insanely into you." Gina lowered her voice, "Don't tell me he's got ED?"

"Boundaries, Gina, for the love of God."

"Well, does he? Because there's a pill for that."

"As far as I know there is nothing wrong with his apparatus."

Gina's snort echoed in the interior of the car. "*Please* call it his 'apparatus' next time you're talking dirty to him. I beg you."

Mia's face flamed. "*Gina.*" Talking dirty, just another thing at which she was utterly inept.

She wasn't embarrassed by sex. It was a natural function, a biological imperative—scientifically pure. But her own lack of expertise in the area of copulation was daunting. Mortifying, even.

Not that she hadn't gotten busy, to borrow one of Gina's euphemisms, with Peter. Their intercourse had always been satisfactory, but the thought that her performance would be sub-par when compared with Chase's doubtless vast experience... Mia could not stomach the idea of being below average.

Her sister was talking, but Mia didn't bother to tune into the words, just waiting for a pause and asking, "How do you know if you excel at intercourse?"

A choking sound came through the speakers. "Christ, Mia. Warn a girl when you're about to ask something like that. I almost snorted OJ out my nose."

"It's a pertinent question to the topic at hand."

"Oh honey. Have you ever noticed that your vocab goes into uber-scientific mode when you're nervous?"

"I am...concerned. About the outcome of our copulation."

"The outcome? Like an orgasm? Mia, please tell me you've had an orgasm."

"I have." Mia pulled into the parking lot of the Lathrop Institute and turned off the engine, leaving the electrical system on to maintain the car's Bluetooth and folding her hands in her lap to keep from fidgeting. "My concern is that my performance, while practiced, will be less skillful than that to which he is accustomed and he will be disappointed."

Her real concern was that he would dump her for being crappy in bed, but she couldn't say that to her little sister.

She could *do* sex, but it wasn't the kind of interaction people wrote sonnets about. Not the way she did it. She was too cerebral to be effectively physical. She couldn't lose herself in sensation because she was always analyzing the biofeedback provided by her senses. Smart and sexual just didn't go together.

And it didn't help that she hadn't done it in a while. She just wanted so badly to please Chase. Sex would mean something with him. She was invested—far more than she'd ever anticipated being.

"Sweetie, you're gonna be great. Just try not to give yourself a complex about it."

Too late. "While I appreciate the sentiment, Gina, I'm not asking for a pep talk. Unless you have practical advice or techniques you would like to share."

"Hey, don't underestimate the importance of confidence. Being into it is about the sexiest thing a person can do."

An image of Chase flashed through her mind. His abnormal good looks and wry twinkling eyes. "I don't think being into it is going to be an issue." If only she could expect that *he* would be into it. She wasn't exactly pin-up material. She had a good body with efficient limbs that did what she told them, but studies had shown men preferred curves which she patently lacked. "I'm seeing him tonight for another round of neural scans. Maybe we should just get it over with. Like ripping off a Band-Aid."

"Sweetie, please don't broach the topic with him that way."

"Well how am I supposed to broach it? This is not helping, Gina. Unless you have more explicit instructions, I don't see how—"

"Okay," Gina said, taking on a businesslike tone, "I'm going to share with you my guaranteed, make-his-eyes-roll-back-in-his-head blow job trick."

"Oh, thank God. Hold on, let me get something to take notes." Mia dove into the glove box, pulling out an old oil change receipt and flipping it over as she rummaged for a writing utensil.

Gina laughed. "While you're getting a pen, try to practice step one: *Relax.* He's lucky to have you, Mia. If he gets to. You don't have to sleep with him if you don't want to."

Mia clicked her pen, holding it poised. "Okay. I'm ready. Shoot."

Gina giggled. "I'll give you a thousand dollars to say that when you're on your knees about to employ my trick."

"Gina."

"Sorry. Couldn't help it. Are you really taking notes?"

"I want to get this right."

"Okay. Step one, relax and don't forget to breathe."

Mia scribbled furiously. "Breathe. Check."

Chapter Twenty-Three
Inspirational Science

"Comfortable?"

Chase's eyebrows flew up at Mia's drill sergeant-like bark and he suppressed a grin. They were back in the exam room and he was back in the chair, but this time, as Mia slapped sensor after sensor onto his cranium, the tension in the room was decidedly hot, as opposed to the arctic chill of last time.

He was relaxed, actually. Surprisingly comfortable considering the train wreck of their last date and the financial ax hanging over his head. It was Mia who was jumpy as hell.

He'd arrived at seven o'clock sharp, ready for the next round of tests. When he'd gone in for a hello kiss at the door, she'd jerked like he'd tazed her, turned bright red and stared at the floor. She hadn't looked up since. Which would have worried him except upon closer inspection, he realized it wasn't the floor she was staring at. It was his crotch. With anyone else he would have thought she was checking out his package, but from the expression on Mia's face, it was more likely she was trying to see if she could castrate him with lasers shot from her eyes.

But all things considered... "Yeah, I'm comfortable."

"Good." She bustled around the room, fussing with her instruments, the unnecessary excess of movement uncharacteristic enough to be disturbing.

"Is everything okay?"

Her eyes finally snapped to his, gleaming bright and aggressive. "Of course. Are you ready to begin?"

He could have called her on the lie—she only got that combative gleam when she was feeling defensive—but she obviously didn't want to address whatever was bothering her, so he just held out his hand, palm up, and said, "Ready when you are."

They'd agreed to start with him trying to find the watch as she recorded his neural activity, killing two birds with one stone if he could get a successful read. If he couldn't get a lock on it, she would bring in her research assistants in the next session to hide things from one another which he might have a better chance of locating. She seemed convinced there would be a neurological reaction associated with success and had even mentioned the possibility that she could stimulate a successful read if she could identify the neural network responsible. Chase was inclined to think the lack of success had little to do with him—he was just the tool. It wasn't the compass's fault the hiker got lost.

Mia rolled her desk chair next to his, perched on the edge of it and placed her icy fingers across his palm. He wrapped his fingers around hers, giving a little squeeze. She frowned, twisting in her chair to face the monitors.

"Begin."

"Remember to focus on the watch and why you want it."

She nodded jerkily. Chase opened up the part of his mind that held his ability and the deafening static of Mia's mimosa-tanged intangibles crashed into his brain. Her incredibly *graphic* intangibles.

Her lips wrapped around his cock, sucking, drawing. His hands tight in her hair, urging her on, shoving himself deeper.

Chase nearly convulsed under the wave of eroticism that burst into his brain and erupted through his body. He was instantly hard, his breath coming fast, and even his damn eyelashes felt singed by the carnal heat pouring from Mia's mind into his. *"Jesus fucking damn, Mia."*

Mia dropped his hand, swiveling toward the monitors, her eyes alit with a hungry intensity that seemed to be purely intellectual—just proving how deceiving the surface could be for Dr. Mia Corregianni. "Your heart rate accelerated substantially,"

Mia marveled, talking to herself even though the words were ostensibly directed at him.

Chase bit back the urge to growl *Ya think?* while trying to get his body back under control.

"Did you find it?"

He shook his head, still trying to get the blood to divert back to his brain.

She cursed without heat, then tapped one of the monitors and began chattering about elevated activity in cortexes and other gibberish he didn't have a prayer of understanding. When he could breathe again without panting, he cleared his throat, more than a little surprised when her gaze immediately jumped off the monitor to meet his.

"How did that feel to you?" she asked, fingers poised above a keyboard to make notes on his answers. "Was that a normal failed find attempt?"

"*No.* Jesus, Mia." He wiped a hand across his face. "The transference is getting worse. I told you before that it feels different with you and now, it's like it's louder and *deeper* somehow. I don't know how else to say it. It's like I can see everything in your thoughts *except* what you want me to find. Normally, it's just static in the background, but with you, fuck, I don't know. It's like I've got a direct link right into your id or something."

"My id?"

"That's the sex part of the brain, isn't it?"

She frowned. "It's a psychological term, not a neurological one. Soft science." She waved her fingers in a woo-woo gesture clearly meant to degrade psychologists everywhere.

Whatever kind of science they were doing, it sure as hell wasn't *soft.* "Well, I'm tapped into something. And that something is horny as hell and loud as fuck."

"This is only happening with me? You've had other successful finds recently that did not result in an *id* connection?" She said *id* with mild distaste, clearly having missed the part of the conversation when he'd confessed to having a direct link to her fucking libido.

"Plenty of other finds. Every day. And you're the only one this happens with. Maybe you should scan your own brain while you're checking mine."

Mia blinked, instantly intrigued. "You're suggesting your touch stimulates a neurological response in your subject as well. Fascinating. I *should* test the findee's brain to ascertain whether the psychic connection could indeed have a symbiotic element. Excellent suggestion."

She didn't seem even mildly fazed by the fact that he'd read her sexiest thoughts. Something occurred to him. "Mia, were you *trying* to think about sex?"

She flushed. "Of course not. I was visualizing the watch."

"So you weren't in any way thinking of blow jobs?"

Her face grew redder still. "I wasn't *trying* to think about them. But you know how it is, your subconscious stores memories of conversations throughout the day and combines them to form original thought. Genesis. Inspiration."

Chase blinked. He'd always found oral sex inspirational. Nice to know she shared the sentiment. "You were talking about blow jobs today?" he asked, unable to mask his interest. Mia just kept getting more and more intriguing.

Her fair skin was roughly the shade of a cherry tomato now. "I don't see how that's relevant to the experiment."

It was relevant to his hard-on.

Was that why she'd been staring at his crotch? Because she was visualizing *that*?

They'd been taking things slow, sexually. Not for lack of chemistry, but because he'd been trying to be respectful. Mia wasn't a one-night stand.

And okay, yes, he was a little chicken shit. He hadn't been with anyone who mattered in years. Mia was gonna matter. He wanted to do things right between them and he wasn't even sure he remembered what *right* felt like. He'd been spending too much time on *right now* in the last six years. But if Mia's blow job fantasy was anything to go by, *right* and *right now* were about to collide.

She tipped her head to the side, her gaze distant as she analyzed something only she could see. "I think I like that you can see into my thoughts. Yes, my reaction definitely appears to be positive. Interesting."

"You don't find it...invasive?"

She considered that for a moment. "No. It's...welcome. I'm not, ahem, that is to say, I don't excel at intimacy, and this seems to be a beneficial short-cut in that regard." She cleared her throat, blushing furiously. "Shall we try again?"

Chase flexed his hand, extending it palm up. God help him. "Yeah. Let's do this."

Mia slipped her fingers into Chase's, trying to clear her thoughts of the carnal images that had been plaguing her all afternoon. But of course, in the act of trying *not* to think about something, she was directing her thoughts back to the very subject she was trying to purge.

The watch. Think about the watch.

Mia pictured the watch. It was gold. It was a magical menace. But an annoyingly effective one. It had somehow, even in its disappearance, managed to find a man for Mia. It was a startling thought. The idea that perhaps the watch had somehow managed to lose itself in order to guide her to her match. The argument seemed to imply that her inability to find the watch centered not around her own issues with the watch, but rather around the fact that she and Chase had not committed themselves fully to the relationship.

Consummated it.

Images rose to the front of her mind. *Mia straddling Chase, rising above him in the chair, his hands gripping her hips.*

"Mia!" Chase's strangled shout called her out of the fantasy.

She blushed. "Okay, that time I was thinking about sex. But only a little and only toward the end."

He bent forward, elbows propped on his knees, rubbing a hand hard across his face. "You're trying to kill me, aren't you?"

"It isn't conscious," Mia protested. She couldn't seem to control the drift of her thoughts where he was concerned. Though perhaps it was just the allure of the unknown. The combination of her nerves and his sex appeal were making it impossible to concentrate, but if they got it out of the way... *Rip that Band-Aid off.*

She nodded once to herself. "We need to have sex."

Chase's head snapped up so fast it had to have hurt his neck. "Pardon?"

Mia smiled. Such good manners. Even when she verbally cold-cocked him. "The sex stuff is obviously distracting me and detracting from the experiment. It's only logical to remove that variable by consummating this." She paused, a horrible thought rising up. "Unless you don't wish to."

"Oh I wish to." His voice was a growl.

Mia felt heat rushing through her body and looked away from the blaze in his eyes. "Excellent." She cleared her throat nervously. "Would you like to be on top or shall I?"

Chase made a choked sound.

Mia pressed on without looking at him. "I prefer the clitoral stimulation being on top provides, myself, but find many positions pleasurable and am quite willing to explore your preferences as well. Though I feel I should make it clear that I am not interested in other parties joining us, the giving or receiving of pain during sex acts, nor any sort of 'play' involving waste matter."

"Why don't we start with the classics?" Chase suggested, his voice sounding strangled enough that Mia forced herself to look at him. His face was flushed, his teeth snagged on his lower lip like he was holding something in, but his eyes were twinkling wickedly. Those eyes said he knew what he was doing. She pressed her thighs together against a sudden flare of warmth.

"That sounds quite satisfactory." She tried to peek a glance at his apparatus, but he was still bent forward, blocking her view and preventing her from applying Gina's trick just yet. "There's a couch, more of a day bed I suppose, in the room off my office where I frequently sleep. We can make use of it now, if that is acceptable to you."

He was already stripping off the sensors, with single-minded efficiency. "Lead the way."

Chase trailed her down the hall to her office and through the connecting door without touching her. A low hum vibrated just beneath her skin and her stomach was vaguely queasy. She couldn't tell whether the physiological reactions should be attributed to anticipation or nerves, but she was fairly sure it was the latter. She was beginning to regret her suggestion. Not that she didn't want to have sex with Chase. She certainly did. But things were so much easier when he took the lead. All she managed to do when she took the helm was suck all the spontaneity out of experiences. He was good at making her feel like a woman, rather than just a scientist, but he seemed content to let her be a scientist with regard to sex. That thought was more disconcerting than she had thought it would be.

She flipped on the fluorescent lights and waved a hand to the dormitory-style twin bed with its well-worn navy duvet, piled high with a mismatched collection of pillows. "There it is."

His hands were on her shoulders, gently turning her to face him. "Mia, are you sure—"

"Yes, yes," she cut him off abruptly. She didn't want him questioning her right now. Her nerves were shot enough without struggling to explain herself. When his brow furrowed, she launched herself at him and mashed her mouth against his.

It wasn't a romantic kiss. Or even a passionate one. It was clumsy and desperate and could have evolved to painful, but thankfully Chase took control. He caught her jaw between his thumb and forefinger and gentled the kiss, murmuring, "Easy now," against her lips in a husky drawl that ignited a waiting spark in her core.

Things progressed nicely from there. The first few articles of clothing were removed without any undue awkwardness. Thanks to the ingenious design benefits of button-down shirts and skirts with easily reached side-zippers, they didn't even have to stop kissing—a strategy of which Mia wholeheartedly approved. She kept her eyes squeezed shut and made sure she was making appreciative *mm* noises to encourage him to continue even as half of her mind was cataloguing and evaluating the experience. If this encounter was anything to go by, he was excessively proficient at bed sports, his hands deftly stimulating a physiological reaction wherever they touched.

"Stop thinking so hard," he murmured as he broke their latest kiss, his fingers skimming up her back to the clasp of her bra.

She shivered, all her erogenous zones—and several she hadn't been aware could be erogenous—sitting up and saying howdy, but she couldn't seem to open her eyes.

"Mia. Sweetheart."

Her name was coaxing on the lips that pressed to the side of her neck, even as his hands coaxed her bra straps down her arms.

Maybe she should have gotten drunk. Alcohol would have relaxed her, convinced her she could really do this, given her the foolhardy confidence to believe she wasn't totally out of her league with Chase Hunter.

"Hey." Gentle hands cupped her shoulders and gave her a light shake. "Get out of your head."

Easy for him to say.

"You can look, you know." She could hear the smile in his voice. "You might like it. Unless you're scared I'll have some unspeakable genetic abnormality and you won't be able to go through with it."

Oh great. Now she *had* to look. She opened her eyes just as he was reaching for the button on his jeans. He shucked the denim, the bright fluorescents somehow making his golden skin gleam while she looked pasty at best. He was the kind of attractive that ruined the bell curve for the rest of the population. Mia glanced down at her white flesh, automatically covering herself. The no-nonsense white cotton panties did little to enhance her meager sex appeal. She should have had Gina take her shopping for one of those bustiers to make something appealing out of her distinctly unimpressive bust. It wasn't like she had overwhelming skill to compensate for her physical shortcomings.

Down to his boxers—which at least were tented so perhaps he wasn't totally disappointed by her body—Chase frowned and reached for the hands shielding her from his view. Mia shied away, the backs of her legs bumping up against the bed.

"Mia, sweetheart, you look perfect." He flashed a rakish smile. "Mouthwatering."

He reached for her again.

"I'm probably going to suck at this," she blurted. She felt better as soon as she told him. Honesty was *always* the best policy. "I'm out of practice and studies have shown men prefer women with more," she waved at her flat chest, "flesh. You just...you might wish to adjust your expectations accordingly."

Chase grinned and slowly closed the distance she'd put between them, looking deliciously animalistic prowling toward her. "One," he slid one finger beneath her chin, "it's like riding a bike. Two," a second finger joined the first, tipping her chin back as his head lowered by fractions, "I *like* your flesh. And most importantly, three," his lips brushed hers ever so softly as his other hand slid smoothly down the curve of her spine, "for once in your life..." another fluttering kiss, "turn off your brain and just feel." He caught her hands, placing her palms flat on his warm, smooth chest. "Feel me, Mia. I'm not an experiment. I'm not a subject. I'm more than a collection of interesting molecules." His arms and words wrapped around her, easing her back onto the bed. "Let yourself see me. Be with me, Mia." His lips seared the shell of her ear and she arched her neck to give him better access. Heat flooded her senses. "*Burn* with me."

Chapter Twenty-Four
Chemistry: Not Just a Class

Chase slid his hands over the smooth lines of Mia's body. He couldn't let up. He wanted her here, in the moment with him, as much a slave to her physical needs as she had made him. If he stopped touching her for even a moment, her brain would re-engage, and as much as he loved when Mia over-thought everything, right now he wanted her over-feeling.

Kissing the delicate stretch of her neck, he slid his hands toward the slight curve of her breasts—and bumped into her hands, trying to cover herself. "Mia." Her name held a scold and a smile as he tugged her hands away and shackled them above her head in one of his. "No hiding. Your body is perfect," he murmured, his mouth close enough to her ear for his breath to caress the sensitive ridge. His palm found her nipple, rolling the sensitive button in a circle. She fit easily in his hand. The hard ridge of her ribs, the gentle softness of her breast, the firm point of her nipple—she was sleek elegance in every texture.

He couldn't find fault in her coltish lines. Her body suited her so perfectly—no excess, all sleek efficiency. Mia was all business from head to toe, but he knew how to turn her business to pleasure.

Chase nipped and licked his way down her throat, across the pronounced ridge of her clavicle, and guided her breast to his lips, tonguing the plum-colored point of her nipple until she squirmed and shifted her legs restlessly.

Chase sucked hard, drawing her into his mouth, and Mia arched like a bow under his hands. "I have...a trick..." she murmured breathlessly.

"Mmm?" he hummed against her flesh and she shivered. He worked his way down her body, nibbling at the indent of her waist and the dip next to her hip bones.

"It's a blow job thingy..." she panted.

His brain short circuited for a moment as blood rushed toward his cock in Pavlovian response to the words *blow job*, but he mumbled, "Later," against the skin of her thigh as he peeled her panties down to her ankles. He had her barely putting together coherent sentences. He was determined to keep her mindless—and make her more so.

"I'm told it's—oh my—very effective."

"Sounds great." He flicked his tongue over her clit and Mia released a ragged keening sound. "How's that feel?"

"Ungh," Mia groaned incoherently, spearing her fingers through his hair and pulling him back to her core. He smiled against her skin, and bent to take his sweet time, showing her every trick in his playbook. He found a rhythm and a pressure she liked and milked it, driving her up past the point of thought, taking his cues from the pitch of her breathy moans and startled cries.

She broke hard, shuddering roughly against his tongue, her thigh muscles clenching tight around his shoulders. Chase hummed his approval against her flesh and she went off again, a second tight orgasm ripping through her. As she came down again, she regained the ability to speak, her incoherent cries resolving into a steady chant of "Oh-god-oh-god-oh-god."

With that litany as accompaniment and encouragement, he crawled up her body, shucked off his boxers, and rolled on the condom he'd grabbed from his wallet earlier. He braced himself above her with straight arms on either side of her shoulders.

Mia's eyelids fluttered open. She looked up at him, overwhelmed and flushed and so perfectly, dizzily *his*. Her glasses tilted askew on her nose, but he didn't fix them. He liked the slanting lenses almost as much as the dazed gleam in her eyes—evidence of his conquest.

"You ready for this?" She better fucking be, because his control had about forty seconds before it snapped completely. His cock felt like Satan's fireplace poker—hot and hard and painful as hell. He told it that it didn't have much longer to wait.

She frowned up at him, trying to concentrate. God, he loved that frown. "What are you waiting for? Is there something wrong with your apparatus?"

"Damn, I love it when you go all science-y on me," he growled. He drove into her in a single firm thrust.

Mia gasped and her eyes rolled back, her hands clutching restlessly at his back. "*More.*"

Yes, ma'am.

Someone had set him on fire. Even the soles of his feet were burning, but Chase was determined to make this last. He drew out and plunged home again, then again. Mia's breathy pants resolved into syllables, words that slowly penetrated his brain.

"Oxytocin...endorphins...phenylethylamine...dopamine...ser otonin... *Chase.*"

She climaxed around him as his name joined the list spilling from her lips. Chase thrust once more, releasing himself inside her hot channel, and for one skull-splitting moment everything was perfect.

Too perfect.

Terrifyingly perfect.

Perfection meant loss could be right around the corner.

Chase rolled off her, pulling her with him and tucking her against his chest. She fit his arms like a key in a lock, cuddled close, and he held on for dear life. This slim, too-serious woman could break him like a twig if he let her, but it was too late to walk away now.

Just sex, he told himself. Just physical release. He could handle it, as long as he ignored the niggling suspicion that Mia Corregianni was already inside his soul.

She stretched beside him, making a low satisfied sound in her throat. "Figures you'd be good at coitus."

He snorted. "Thank you. What was all that phenyl-whatsit stuff?"

"Was that out loud?" She hid her face against his chest, then took advantage of the position to begin nibbling a path south.

"Out loud. And kinda hot. That big brain of yours is such a turn-on. This list?"

He felt her lips curve against his skin. "Chemicals released in the human body during intercourse."

He grinned, irrationally smug that his name had made the list. "I knew sex with you would be an education, Mia."

"You want an education?" She slid down his body. "I have this trick..."

Chapter Twenty-Five
Occam's Leash

"I need more sex tricks."

"Mia?" Gina snorted out a laugh. "Hello to you too."

"I don't have time for pleasantries. I need more data. He'll be here any minute." Or at least he should be.

Mia paced in her living room, pausing periodically to peer out into the rain for Chase. He was late. He'd never been late before. Though he did seem to be the type to be late. Maybe he'd been trying to make a good impression, faking punctuality these last couple weeks and tardiness was what she could expect now that the cow had given him the milk, so to speak.

"So I take it last night went well?"

"When I did the tongue-swirl thingy, his animalistic hindbrain overpowered the language center of his medulla oblongata and he lost the power of speech."

"That's great! I think."

"This was ill-advised. He's going to expect that level of sexual proficiency from now on. I need more tricks." Mia paced back to the couch, back to the window. Back and forth. Over and over. She was the Energizer Bunny of nervous wrecks, proving a body in motion would stay in motion.

She couldn't seem to settle into her own skin.

Last night, after they'd consummated things, he'd been the definition of consideration. He'd walked her out to her car, holding her hand, kissing her goodbye in the parking lot, and watching her drive away before getting into his own car. There'd been a moment, right before she closed the car door, when she could feel him waiting. It would have been so easy to invite him back to her place, but then she'd started wondering why he hadn't invited her to his place, why they'd never even *been* to his place, since he clearly didn't live in his brother's old house, and uncertainty had risen up and swallowed her impulse to invite him over to continue the copulation in the comfort of her own bed.

Where did they stand now, exactly? The sex had seemed like a logical and inevitable step, but now she couldn't help but wonder if she had somehow fouled her data. And unfortunately, she couldn't just pretend nothing had happened. She felt as though something had shifted inside her, deep down, on the cellular level, and she couldn't be certain the change wasn't visible.

Pacing was a very inefficient use of her time. How was it she always seemed to find herself dithering and pacing and wasting her mental energy when it came to Chase? If he hadn't told her to reserve Wednesday night for a date, she would still be at the office. There were scans to be analyzed, samples to be processed, and the files for tomorrow's volunteers to organize. She could be productive, but she was here. Pacing.

And begging her sister to teach her more coital secrets.

"Sex isn't a skill, sweetie. Well, not just a skill. Just, you know, experiment. You're good at that. Find what feels good for the two of you."

"I would need electrodes attached to the pleasure centers of his brain and a monitor of his vital stats to gauge the relative impact of various maneuvers."

"Or you could just ask him what he likes."

Mia let her silence speak for her.

"Or not. Look, honey—"

"I don't like feeling like this."

"Being into him?"

"I'm sorry. You're right. My statement was imprecise. I don't like this feeling of uncertainty. I never felt so unsettled in my sexual relations with Peter."

"I know you may not want to hear this, but I'm delighted he's thrown you for a loop. That feeling of uncertainty means you *care*, Meems."

"I don't want to be the one who cares more. Psychology and sociology may be soft sciences, but the research clearly states that the person in an interpersonal relationship with the most affection for the other is more inclined to be taken advantage of and manipulated by their emotions."

Gina snorted. "I somehow doubt you'll let yourself be manipulated by your emotions. Good sex can't have changed you that much."

"He's late, Gina. Clearly he's using our first post-coital date as a power play. I'm unaware of the sociological retaliation required to rebalance the scales and make a play to return to alpha status in the relationship."

"Sweetie, I don't think you were the alpha in that relationship to begin with."

"What else would I be? Obviously the coital relationship has changed things. In any pack, even one with a base unit of two—"

"Honey, hold up. You're going all science nerd on me again. What I got from that was that Chase is late and you're freaking out. Want a distraction? I have big family gossip."

"I can't think about Teresa right now."

"It isn't Teresa. It's Jamie."

Mia pictured the soft-spoken, petite, curvy brunette who was her cousin on her mother's side. Distraction achieved. "What's wrong with Jamie?"

"Why do you assume something's wrong? Couldn't it be good gossip?"

"Gossip is statistically more likely to be negative in nature."

"I intend to argue that later."

"Because you currently cannot argue it because your news is negative."

"I will cede that point."

"So what's wrong with Jamie?" Mia liked her cousin. Unusually shy for a member of the Corregianni horde, Jamie had always had a smile for Mia, even if she rarely strung two words together. As the watch's protector only last year, she was also the clan newlywed.

"She's staying at Aunt Marie's. Apparently she found suspicious charges on Danny's credit card—hotels, plane tickets, jewelers..."

"Identity theft. Digital information is never entirely safe—"

"Danny's having an affair, Mia. Jamie says he's been acting weird—secretive, working late—and when she confronted him about the charges, he said he hadn't made them, but Jamie could tell he was lying and the credit card company actually lets you see the signature on the receipts online—how cool is that? I mean it sucks for Jamie, obviously, because the handwriting matches."

"Adultery." The word knocked the wind out of Mia. They'd never had even a hint of infidelity in the family in the past, but now that she'd lost the watch...

It was spreading. First Teresa, now Jamie. Who was next? Gina? Would something happen to sweet Marley?

Her heart pounding in her ears, she barely heard Gina talking, rambling about how the aunts were sure it was a misunderstanding, but Joey, Nicky and Mario were planning a leg-breaking mission. Only the thought of their mothers' hysterics had kept them from already landing in jail on assault charges.

Oh God. Just what she needed. Her brothers and cousins in jail.

Mia had to find the watch. She couldn't be selfish and drag her feet just because she wanted more time with Chase. The clock was ticking down. The anniversary party was in a matter of days. Her family's happy façade was cracking. She'd always believed the Corregianni familial euphoria was just a silly veneer, but to see it tarnished made her chest ache like she'd been kicked by a mule.

No more fooling around. She had to find it. Even if it meant bringing in Gina to do the find with Chase.

"Gina, there's something I need to tell you. Something big."

"What is it? You know you can tell me anything, Mia."

At that instant, Chase's car finally pulled into the parking lot. A sign from the universe that now was not the time to tell Gina the truth? Did she believe in signs from the universe now? The headlights cut off and Mia's heart kicked into double time, the watch taking a back seat to the panic of seeing her new sexual partner again. "Oh God, he's here. Later. I'll tell you later. I've gotta go." She disconnected the call and tossed her phone on the couch without looking.

Only the rain stopped her from running out to meet him, though she had no idea what she would have said. Instead, she watched him climb out, the rain immediately darkening his blond curls. Even drenched the man was abnormally gorgeous. He bent back into the car, the denim of his jeans stretching lovingly over his gorgeous gluteus as he retrieved something from the front seat. It looked like a wadded-up beach towel, but he cradled it to his chest, hunched over to protect it from the rain as he ran across the parking lot and up her steps.

She threw open the front door as he reached the top. He didn't slow as he ran into the foyer. Grinning fiercely, he shook droplets of water from his hair as Mia secured the door behind him. When she turned back to him, his lips were there to meet her with a quick, startling kiss, his damp hair chilling her forehead.

He drew back and she frowned repressively, side-stepping around him and wiping away the dampness from her face. "You're all wet."

He shrugged. "I'll dry and so will you. You won't convince me you didn't like the greeting."

"I just don't see the purpose—"

"Kisses aren't supposed to have purposes, but that one did. I could see you thinking too hard. Gotta get you out of your head." The towel wiggled and Chase adjusted his grip, his grin broadening. "Speaking of things to get you thinking with your heart…"

"You can't think with your heart. It has a very specific purpose—to pump blood. Everything else is just fancy. In fact, studies have shown that emotion is a neural function. Look at how loss of memory can impact emotional relationships."

"So you don't want to see your present?"

Mia eyed the towel. "I don't trust you when you come bearing presents. Especially presents that move."

A tiny brown nose poked out from a hole in the towel, sniffing and squirming.

"Is it a rat?"

Chase snorted. "Jesus, no, I didn't bring you a rat. I did a few pro-bono lost dog finds today."

"And you kept one? Doesn't that defeat the purpose?"

"One of the family's other dogs had just had puppies and this little guy seemed to want to come with me, so they gave him to me as a thank you."

"Why did you bring him here?"

"I couldn't leave him alone on his first night." The black nose was followed by a white and reddish-brown muzzle. "And technically my lease doesn't allow pets."

"Are you going to keep it at your brother's house? Nice yard."

"The new owners might object."

"New owners?"

"I put it on the market today."

"You did?" That was huge. Mia felt something lurch heavily in her chest. "Chase…"

He shrugged, his gaze drifting around the room aimlessly, refusing to meet hers. "It seemed like time."

She couldn't think of what to say. To tell him she was proud of him seemed unbearably patronizing. To congratulate him would be inconsiderate of what he was giving up. She'd never been good with words, so Mia didn't bother with them. She just reached out and awkwardly squeezed his arm.

Miraculously, this seemed the right thing to do. His eyes suddenly met hers and something shifted in his tight smile. Something soft and lovely that made her chest feel like it was slowly being warmed from the inside out.

Then the towel gave a little yip and the connection was broken.

She frowned at the bundle of rag and dog. "Is it one of those yappy dogs?"

"No. It's a Miniature Australian Shepherd. Apparently they don't bark much. Already housebroken, I promise. The breeder said they're smart and highly trainable. Energetic, but they love to please and they form strong attachments with people. I thought you could use someone to teach you how that works."

"I don't want a dog." She'd never had one. She wouldn't know what to do with it.

"How do you know that if you've never had one?"

Damn the man for reading her mind. "It's messy. I can't ignore it at home when I stay overnight at the lab. It isn't practical."

"So you take him to the lab with you. It's not like you have chemicals lying around he can get into."

"It'll be a nuisance."

"You love him. Say, *Thank you, Chase, I love him.*"

Then the towel shifted and the wriggling, squirming, theoretical puppy became a pair of big brown eyes framed with long, curved puppy- lashes.

"It's a him?"

"How is it you always seem to be able to talk me into the most impractical things?"

"I'm tenacious." Chase watched the white and red puppy scramble over his stretched-out legs and pounce on the squeaky toy. When it squealed, the pup yelped in surprise, flipping all the way over the ball and twisting up from his back to renew his attack.

Mia didn't smile, intent on the dog.

He'd been right about this. He didn't care to examine why it had been so important to him that she accept the dog, why it had felt like such a risk, showing up with the puppy, asking her to accept the pair of them, but she'd barely argued and once the puppy clapped his big gooey eyes on her, she was done.

Chase had brought in the puppy supplies he'd stashed in the car, the toy among them, and they'd spent their "date" acclimating young Occam to his new home. It was getting late, already past eleven, but inertia kept Chase in place, unable to say good night or make a move toward the bedroom. Mia lay on her stomach on the living room carpet, watching the puppy with frowning fixation.

"If you don't want him, I can always take him home with me—"

"No," she snapped, shooting him a death glare. "No stealing my dog, you bastard."

Chase couldn't help but smile at the way she'd nearly ripped his head off. Already he was *her* dog. "So 'Occam'? I take it that's a science thing."

Mia nodded without taking her eyes off the dog. "Occam's Razor. All other factors being equal, the simplest explanation is the correct one. It's imprecise—largely to establish prevailing beliefs in the scientific community, but without those prevailing beliefs we would have nothing to refute and argue about, so a necessary simplification."

"Are you saying you see your dog as a necessary simplification?"

He'd been trying to goad her, but Mia's smile was sly as her eyes flicked sideways to him. "Occam's Razor cuts through all the bullshit that doesn't matter and gets to the heart of things."

The puppy rolled onto his back and twisted his neck to look at them upside down, his tongue hanging out the side of his mouth. Chase snorted, irrationally flattered by the name choice. "All hail, the mighty Bullshit Avenger."

"Would you really take him home? Even though your lease says you can't have pets?"

"Do you honestly think I can't talk my super into letting me keep a dog?"

She shrugged, her expression darkening. "I haven't met your super. Maybe he possesses superhuman powers of bullshit-resistance."

There was an edge to her sarcasm. He studied her as she was occupied by dissecting the dog's behavior with her eyes. Was she really bothered that he hadn't taken her to his place yet?

"It's not that great an apartment, Mia. You aren't missing much."

She looked daggers at him. "You're presuming that I'm upset about that. I'm not."

Oh, she was pissed all right. "It's not a home or anything. Just a place to store my boards when I'm not surfing. Does the fact that I've seen your house really mean anything to you?"

"You've seen my lab."

And her lab was her real home. "Good point. I'll show you my place anytime you want, but if you want to do the emotional bonding thing, we should probably go to the beach. That's more my home than any other place."

"I don't like the beach."

"Everyone likes the beach."

"Well, I don't."

Chase tipped his head to the side, mimicking Occam. "Are you trying to pick a fight with me?"

Her lips closed tight, making him itch to tease them open. "I just think it behooves us to acknowledge our long-term incompatibility."

"Because you don't like the beach." Skepticism saturated every word.

"Because we're too different in too many ways."

"So when you say compatible, you mean identical."

"Shared values are the cornerstone of lasting relationships."

"Did Peter teach you that?"

"You wouldn't feel the need to bring Peter up all the time if you weren't threatened by his superior compatibility with me." She snatched up the ball and began rolling it toward the dog, who yipped and pounced, sending it spinning back to her.

"I'm not threatened because the last thing you need is your clone in bed with you. People with opposite perspectives bring out the best in us."

"And have the most ability to cause us pain for things we can't change about ourselves. Just look at my family."

"All the more reason to find someone who could bridge the gap."

"You mean side with them. No, thank you."

"So you'd rather have sterile safety than someone who makes your heart race?"

"Racing hearts are fine in the short term. In the long term, you should consult a physician because something is seriously wrong."

"I'd rather take that risk than be bored to death."

She snorted and glowered at him. "You? You don't like risking your heart any more than I do. We're both masters of avoiding romantic entanglements."

"There. See? We have something in common. Compatibility achieved."

She grabbed Occam's ball and threw it at Chase's face. The puppy darted after it in a frenzy at the idea of fetch. "I don't know why I talk to you," she grumbled.

Chase caught the ball one-handed and then rolled it across the floor so the pup could leap after it. "You talk to me because I'm the only one who doesn't let you be right all the time."

"Your arguments are illogical."

"And it keeps you on your toes."

"It's annoying." But there was no heat to lend credibility to the words.

Chase eyed Mia, sprawled as she was across the floor. Her jeans were snug, but ridiculously unflattering. Mom jeans. Clearly bought in a hurry at a bargain bin rather than by a woman who appreciated shopping. Her hair was tugged back tight and unrelenting and her glasses were jammed back on her nose—he'd never seen her poke or fuss at them, as if they were too intimidated by her potential ire to dare slide out of place.

Mia was no sultry, sloe-eyed goddess. She was rigid and wound tight as a spring, disdainful of non-intellectual pursuits and baffled by the softer sides of humanity, but all of that was what made her Mia, which made her somehow sexier than any easy, obvious sexpot.

She was perfect for a fling. She'd never demand more of him than he could emotionally give because she had so little to give herself. But it wasn't only the safety that appealed to him. It was Mia.

He adjusted the fit of his pants and cleared his throat roughly, wondering how she'd react if she knew how much her intent frowns and glowers turned him on.

"I guess we'll just have to wait until we find the watch to confirm that I'm your One True Love," he joked, needing the lightness of the words.

Mia groaned and flopped face down. "If we ever find it," she moaned, her words muffled by the carpet. They'd tried earlier in the evening and all he'd gotten was the usual mimosa flood— weighted heavily with guilt about credit-card theft and broken legs, from what he'd pieced together.

"We'll find it. We have a few more days before the party and you can turn it over to the next in line with no one the wiser."

"I wish I had your idiotic optimism."

Chase snorted. "Thank you."

She waved a dismissive hand, not raising her head. "You know what I mean. You're a believer. I don't do that."

"No?" Occam darted into the kitchen and Chase rolled to his feet to collect him and bring him back to the living room, sitting back down within touching distance of Mia. She'd twisted around to sit on the floor with her back against the couch. His arm brushed her as he stretched his legs out beside hers. "You didn't try to pass off another watch as The Watch when you could have."

"That doesn't signify," she protested. "Someone might have recognized the fake."

"You kept it in your safe. Not in some random drawer or the bottom of a dumpster. So clearly you believe in that mumbo jumbo on some level."

"It's an antique."

"You thought it might have caused your sister's infertility problems."

"Low blow."

"But true. You can admit it has value, Mia. It's obvious you believe it does, even if its power is a bit harder to buy into."

"I don't see that it matters, now that it's missing." She burrowed her fingers into the scruff of Occam's neck and the puppy sighed blissfully, collapsing into her lap to be adored. "Fat lot of good keeping it in the safe did."

"You haven't thought of anyone else who could have gotten it out of there? Anyone else who had access? It couldn't have just evaporated. Maybe a family member borrowed it?"

"No one has the combination."

"No one you gave it to, for any reason?"

"What reason could there be?" She yawned and slumped down lower, her head dropping naturally onto his shoulder. With one hand, she continued to stroke the soft fur of the puppy, even though he had fallen into the instant sleep of the young. "The only things I keep in there are flash drive back-ups of my research."

Chase picked up her free hand, tangling their fingers together. "Want me to try to find it one more time?"

"Sure." Her voice was lazy and warm—and didn't hold even a shred of hope that this time it would work. "Maybe we should try it with you distracting me, since concentrating isn't working. Like hypnosis. Tell me again about surfing..."

He'd try anything. Chase began a soft, soothing litany about the perfect set—the flash of the sun off the water, the strain of his muscles as he paddled to catch the right wave, the way his body knew exactly what to do, exactly where to find that perfect balance as he snapped up to stand and instinct took over.

He kept the words calm and constant, opening up the link.

For a brief flash of a moment he saw the watch, more crisply than he'd ever felt it through her, but before the cord could snap taut with its familiar metallic twang, the image grew fuzzy, blurring with warmth and a soft contentment, swamped by the intangibles again, but this time without the angst and stress and longing that usually tinged them. Tonight it was happiness bleeding through her skin into his. A soul-deep desire for this moment to stretch out—savoring the firm swell of his shoulder muscle beneath her ear, the silk of fur under her fingers, and the sense that there was no experiment to rush off to, no work that couldn't wait, just this moment, this feeling, and the two of them.

Chase opened his eyes as he dropped the link, his chest tight with something hot and not entirely comfortable.

"Any luck?" Mia asked, blinking sleepily.

"Not tonight."

They lapsed into silence. Restlessness jumped in his bones. Time stretched as Mia snuggled against his side, on the verge of falling asleep herself. So trusting. So dependent. He jittered his legs, suddenly needing to go home more than he needed to get Mia into bed. "I should go. You're beat."

She made a vaguely affirmative humming noise, clearly barely hanging onto consciousness with her head still pillowed on his shoulder. "Thank you for Occam," she murmured.

He cleared his throat roughly. "No problem. I thought you'd be a dog person."

"Peter liked cats, but they smell terrible," she mumbled. There was a long silence then a resigned sigh. "We'll tell Gina. She'll find it."

Chase wasn't going to try to figure out that sequence of logic. She was out. He twisted awkwardly until he could lift Mia without disturbing her and settled her onto the couch, tucking the puppy into her arms and pulling a threadbare fleece over the pair of them. He carefully removed her glasses, setting them on the end table. She frowned in her sleep, but didn't open her eyes. "G'night, Mia."

She grumbled something that might have been a reply and burrowed deeper into the couch. Chase knew he should just walk away, but he brushed a hand across her brow, needing to touch her one more time before he could leave. He swallowed around something heavy swelling in his throat and turned away to let himself out. *Escape.* That's what it felt like when the door closed behind him. A near miss. But what he was missing, he didn't want to know.

Chapter Twenty-Six
Dr. Strangelove

Mia ignored the scans on her computer, distracted by the tiny growls coming from her feet where Occam was taking out his puppy vengeance on a rawhide chew. She was supposed to be studying the brain scans, looking for signs of love in the neural mapping in front of her, but she hadn't been able to focus all day—a fact that should have irritated her but somehow failed to.

"Dr. C?"

Stephanie stood in the doorway, the all-too-careful expression on her face screaming that she'd been trying to get Mia's attention for more than a few seconds.

"Yes, Stephanie?"

"Did you, um, did you get that email with the scans Nasrin and I did? Cuz usually you reply right away with confirmation, but we've sent them a few times and you didn't..."

Mia flushed, embarrassed to find herself distracted from her work. She hurriedly pulled up her mail program and saw the emails waiting for her, in triplicate. "There they are now," she said hurriedly. "Must be a glitch in the server."

Stephanie smiled, obviously relieved by the excuse and the reassurance that Mia wasn't dead—which would previously have been the only reason she wouldn't have given her utmost attention to her work.

"Do you want me to call IT and file an error report?"

"No, no. I'll take care of it. Why don't you and Nasrin, uh..." Crap. What could she have them do? She never felt so inept at running her team. What was it Chase had said about sex interfering with her results? This obviously wasn't what he'd meant. "Carry on with your...work."

Stephanie nodded, hesitating in the doorway. "Is Chase coming for lunch again today?"

Mia frowned. "No."

"Oh." Stephanie still didn't budge from the doorway.

"Was there something else, Stephanie?"

Stephanie beamed, clearly taking that as an invitation to step back into the room. "Nasrin and I were just thinking...well, that is, we just wanted to say that we really like Chase. He seems like a good guy and he takes care of you and we just wanted you to know that we like him. And he's superhot, which Nasrin says shouldn't matter but we both know totally does. So good for you, Dr. C."

"Is this you giving us your blessing?"

"Well, yeah. Sort of. How many times are you gonna find a guy who will rig a bet with you so that *you* win and get what you want? Men can be selfish pricks, but—"

"Wait. What do you mean? The Science versus Magic challenge? He rigged it?"

"Sort of, I mean, he threw it. We, um, we kind of cheated and told him where to find it, but he let you win anyway. Not that science wouldn't have won anyway," Stephanie went on hurriedly, "just that, you know, we had stacked the deck and he threw it just to see you smile. How sweet is that?"

"That's...something." She just had no idea what. Why had he done it? What had he hoped to gain? A smile? Seriously? She'd gotten to experiment on him...and that had eventually led to sex in her overnight room, but he couldn't have known in advance that he would get laid from it. Could he?

Mia was barely aware of Stephanie bouncing out of her office and back to her own cubicle. The scans in front of her might as well have been invisible for all she saw of them. She couldn't stop wondering what the hell Chase could possibly have meant by throwing the challenge.

What kind of person cheated so he would be sure to lose? It wasn't logical. People did not act outside of their own perceived self-interest, so what was his angle? Though wasn't that what she was studying? The defiance of obvious self-interest in the pursuit of the emotional satisfaction of love? But Chase didn't love her. He couldn't. It was too soon, wasn't it?

But was there a time limit? How did love even form? What changed in a person between lust and that something more?

When did attraction become a warm kernel of happiness deep in your soul, wrapped around the mere thought of one person, the idea of him? When had Chase started meaning so much to her? Was it Occam? The support he gave her with her family? The need he had shown for her in dealing with the memory of his own? When had chemistry become...

Mia went still, every molecule in her body holding as if waiting for a conductor to wave his baton and send them into a symphony.

She was in love with Chase.

Cymbals crashed, violins swelled, trumpets sounded—a silent explosion of realization. The scans on her screen suddenly snapped into focus. Scans of people in love.

"Stephanie! Nasrin!"

Her chair crashed back, smacking into the wall and nearly taking her down with the rebound as she staggered hurriedly around the desk and burst out of her office. She loved him.

Occam yipped and danced around her feet, nearly tripping her. Her research assistants' heads popped into the corridor and Mia ran toward them.

"Scan my brain!"

This was it. The moment of realization. When love hit. The actual instant when brain chemistry was altered by emotion. She had to capture it.

"Dr. C?"

"Hurry! Scan me now! I love him!" She flung herself into the exam room and the chair Chase himself had occupied only days earlier. Frantically scrabbling with the sensors, she struggled to focus on the way she felt about Chase, rather than on the adrenaline rush of a potential scientific breakthrough. She had before pictures of her brain—having scanned herself as a baseline more than once. Now she would have after pictures. After love.

She couldn't think about the sex. She couldn't think excitement or lust or infatuation. Instead, she tried to center her mind on the warm, tingly feeling wrapped around her chest, combined with something deeper, something that lent a weight of permanence to the sensation. Comfort merged with giddy delight, all of it twined around him. This was it. What the poets wrote about. What songs were written about. It was Chase.

Mia slapped on the last of the sensors and hit the button to start the scan, sitting very still and thinking very hard. About the man she loved.

Chapter Twenty-Seven
The Moment of Truth

"There's an offer on the house."

Chase's stomach plummeted without warning. "Already?"

"It's a lowball offer," Brody clarified, and Chase was instantly comforted by the thought of rejecting it. "But the agent says there's definite room to deal."

Brody began rattling off numbers and terms and Chase zoned out, tilting the cell away from his ears so the words became indistinguishable, blending with the sound of the ocean.

The waves were good today, the sun shining. He hadn't checked in with Karma. He hadn't called Mia. He hadn't wanted to do anything but ride the waves. So he had. Until his skin was soft from absorbing water, his eyes teared from the constant glare of the sun and his scalp itched from the salt. He'd ignored all those minor discomforts and paddled out again and again, each ride to shore somehow failing to match his standards for the perfect cut, the perfect curl, leaving him unsatisfied and dragging his arms through the heavy water as he hauled his body and his board out for just one more.

Eventually hunger had gnawed a hole in his gut and he'd come ashore to grab his wallet from his glove compartment so he could buy a burrito from the taco truck down the street, only to see his cell flashing with a voicemail. For a moment he'd hoped it would be Mia, not even sure what he expected her to say, or Karma ragging on his ass, but it had been Brody, proving today had fallen right back into last month's routine.

Now, as he listened to Brody ramble about closing costs, replacement furnaces and inspection guarantees, he almost wished he hadn't returned the call. He wouldn't have to be making this decision if he'd just ignored his hunger and kept surfing. The break looked fucking perfect, curling and holding that sweet curve as it rushed toward the shore.

"Chase?" Brody's voice interrupted his contemplation of the surf. "What should I tell her?"

Tell her I'm not ready for this. It was too much, too fast. Mia, the house. Sure, he'd been the one punching the accelerator, but last night it was like he'd suddenly realized his brakes were out and he was racing out of control. He couldn't do this.

"Tell her no."

Brody didn't miss a beat. "How do you want to counter?"

"No counter. Just no."

"Chase. Man. You can't—"

"It's my house. I can do whatever the hell I want with it. Later, Brody." He flipped the phone shut before he had to listen to more of his friend's bitching and pitched it through the open door onto the passenger seat. Chase absently brushed the sand off the elbow of his wetsuit, watching the surf, jealous of everyone carving the waves. He slammed the door and grabbed his board, heading back for the break, needing the water more than he needed a burrito. Life could wait.

When the scan completed and Mia expanded her focus from her myopic concentration on the love sensation sending happy hormones through her bloodstream, she found Stephanie and Nasrin wedged in the doorway—Stephanie beaming like she'd just given birth to a unicorn and Nasrin gaping at her like she'd grown a second head.

"Chase?" Nasrin asked.

Feeling suddenly awkward and defensive, Mia shrugged with studied nonchalance as she began plucking off the sensors. "I love him." The words sounded strange this time. Uncomfortable. She had no idea how he felt. *It's all fun and games until someone is vulnerable to having her heart ripped open.*

Stephanie was oblivious to her misgivings, squealing and bouncing in the doorway, her ponytail bobbing wildly.

Mia flinched at the shrill sound and kept plucking off sensors. "I guess the watch works. Even when it's stolen."

Stephanie's shrieks cut off abruptly, her mouth snapping shut with an audible click.

Nasrin's eyes flicked sideways and up to her cohort. "Stolen?" There was a strange note to her voice and Mia belatedly remembered how fascinated her assistants had been by the supposed magic of the watch when she'd first taken custody of it almost a year ago.

Just a few days shy of a year ago. Maybe her family would forgive her for losing the watch if she had Chase. It might soften the blow to know that it had worked. And if not, at least she wouldn't be alone when she told them.

Provided he felt the same way she did. But he had to, didn't he? He'd been the one flirting and seducing from the start. She certainly hadn't encouraged him. He had to want her if he'd gone to so much effort to attract her.

"You mean your family's watch?" Nasrin asked, bringing Mia back to her surroundings. "The magic one?"

She nodded absently, spotting Occam in the corner twisting his neck to try to get a better angle to chew on a low cupboard door. "It was stolen out of my house safe. That's how I met Chase. I hired him to track it down. So even though I resisted the magic, the watch still managed to do the one thing determined to get me with the man I needed—by vanishing on me."

Her research assistants were suspiciously silent as she climbed out of the chair and bent over the computer, checking the data had been recorded from her first love scan. She was engrossed in the data within seconds and was surprised when she looked up—what must have been almost fifteen minutes later—to find Nasrin and Stephanie still huddled in the doorway, whispering furiously to one another.

"You have to tell her," Nasrin hissed.

"I never meant for it to go on this long," Stephanie whined quietly in reply.

Mia frowned—more annoyed by the fact that they were blocking her path to her office than actually curious about their discussion. "Is this about Chase rigging the bet? Because Stephanie told me already."

"It isn't that," Nasrin said instantly, shooting Stephanie a meaningful look. "Tell her."

"I..." Stephanie twisted her hands and avoided meeting Mia's gaze until Nasrin elbowed her hard enough to send her ricocheting into the doorframe. "I borrowed your watch," she blurted.

"You?"

Stephanie paled and the rest of the story poured out, the words running together in a jumbled rush. "I never meant to keep it or anything. I just wanted to take it to this guy who said he could make a duplicate of it if he saw the original. Who doesn't want a magic love-finding watch, right?"

Mia hadn't wanted it, and from the guilty glance Stephanie shot her, her assistants had known that, but Steph kept hurrying through the story, her pale complexion looking almost gray with her distress.

"It was last May, remember? When the computers went all wonky and we lost all those files on the server? You sent me to your house to get the back-up drive from your safe and there it was. The magic watch. You'd been talking all about how you weren't going to ever wear it and I swear I never even considered keeping it for a fraction of a second, but it was right there and I thought I'd just return it to the safe the next time you sent me to grab something and you'd never even miss it. But then you never sent me to get anything else and I couldn't figure out how else to give it back to you without telling you that I'd borrowed it without asking and I didn't know what to do so I told Nasrin—"

"Only after you'd kept it for three months!" Nasrin protested, clinging to any pretense of innocence.

"But she didn't have any ideas and short of breaking into your house..." Stephanie's frantic voice trailed off. "I'm sorry. It was stupid."

Her assistant looked like she was waiting to be fired, but Mia barely heard her confession. Her heart was thudding too hard at the prospect that she hadn't irrevocably lost the watch. "Where is it?"

Stephanie waved down the hall. "In my desk. I'm so sorry, Dr. C. I swear we didn't know you were looking for it or we never would have tried to keep it a secret—"

"Go get it." Blood rushed in her ears. Hope was trying to rise up, but it was weighed down by the ballast of her fear that somehow it wouldn't still be in Stephanie's desk. That somehow the damn thing would have slipped away from her again.

Stephanie nodded stiffly and rushed down the hall. In her absence, Nasrin took a half-step forward. "Dr. C, we never intended to lie to you. I cannot express how profoundly sorry I am for my part in the deception."

"Did Stephanie get her duplicate?" Mia asked, her mind circling, spiraling, and landing on random tidbits of the story, fitting the pieces together like a jigsaw puzzle. She'd forgotten sending Stephanie to get the back-up drive, but she remembered it now as sharply as if it had happened this morning. It made sense. And her assistants were among the few people she'd complained to about the mumbo-jumbo watch, the few people who could have suspected its unique value.

"The guy at the shop said he couldn't make one," Stephanie answered as she reappeared in the doorway. "It's one of a kind."

She held the watch up between them. It spun gently as it dangled on its golden chain, catching the light and throwing it back. Mia reached out and cradled the weight of the cold metal in her palm. Stephanie dropped the chain as if she couldn't let go of it fast enough and took a hasty step back.

Mia studied the little trinket that had caused her so much grief in the last few weeks. And brought her Chase. She expected to feel some jolt of recognition, maybe a tingle of magic, or perhaps for Chase to come bursting in with a bucket of take-out food the instant it touched her skin. Instead there was nothing. No glimmer, no flicker, no magic. It felt lighter than she remembered. Less substantial. Almost...wrong. But she shook away the fancy that it was anything other than what it had always been. An old watch.

She pressed the latch and it popped open, the springs faster and smoother than she remembered. Perhaps Stephanie's magician had fixed it somehow. The second hand continued to tick away, comfortingly constant. She snapped the case shut and folded her hand around it, taking her first deep breath in three weeks. Or perhaps all year.

She had the watch—with twenty-four hours to spare. She had a pair of assistants who were going to be working fanatically to suck up to her for the foreseeable future. And she had Chase.

Provided he wanted to be had.

Chapter Twenty-Eight
I Think I Love You

Chase sat in his Subaru in the parking lot of Mia's office and called himself a dozen different kinds of coward because he couldn't make himself go inside. She was in there. Her car was in the lot and the lights in her office were still blazing, even though it was after nine.

He'd surfed until he lost the sun, then dragged himself out of the water, his muscles feeling like stretched rubber and his brain curiously empty. He'd driven to Mia's office under the vague compulsion to settle things between them, but now that he was here, he had no idea what that meant. He didn't want to break up with her, he just couldn't figure out what he *did* want to do about her.

He ran his fingers along the pattern of cracks and lines in his steering wheel. He might have sat there stalling all night, but Mia emerged from the building—without a jacket in spite of the wind that had kicked up since sunset and holding Occam's leash. The dog darted toward the bushes with single-minded desperation to empty his bladder, then raced back to tangle himself around Mia's ankles.

But she wasn't paying attention to the dog. She'd spotted his car, and likely the silhouette of his body in the driver's seat beneath the light of the streetlamps that kept the lot brightly lit.

She started across the asphalt toward him, with Occam nearly tripping her with his joy at being walked. Her stride was straight, focused and determined. Chase had a sudden empathy for the dippy confused circles of the dog that spun around her ankles.

Then Mia was at his door and he had no choice but to open it. He straightened to stand beside the car. "Hey."

She frowned. "What were you doing?" Typical Mia. No tact, all direct intellect.

"Just thinking. You still working?"

"I had a breakthrough of sorts today." For some reason, that statement made her cheeks flush so brightly it was visible even in the low light of the lot. "And speaking of breakthroughs." She transferred Occam's leash to her left hand and dug her right into her pocket, drawing something out by a gold chain until it dangled between them.

Chase blinked uncomprehendingly at the gold blob spinning on the end of the chain for a moment before realization struck him between the eyes. "Is that the watch? *The* watch?"

"Turns out Stephanie and Nasrin 'borrowed' it to see if they could have it replicated. They meant to return it, but I never sent them back to the house to get anything else out of the safe."

"You said no one had access."

"I'd forgotten I gave them the code. It was only once, almost a year ago. They've had it since May."

The magic watch, so innocuous and average to the naked eye, swayed hypnotically. Chase couldn't look away. He never had found it. His first failure as a finder, but that wasn't what made him feel like an elephant was doing push-ups on his lungs. "Quite a breakthrough."

"It wasn't just that." The watch disappeared back into her pocket. "Come inside. I want to show you something."

She turned and began tugging Occam gently toward the door. Chase followed, pulled just as inexorably on his own invisible leash.

In her office, Mia unclipped Occam, who darted off to investigate an invisible intruder underneath a desk, growling his ferocious tiny growl, before emerging with a piece of string that might have been a shoelace in a former life. Mia waved

Chase toward the chair facing her desk as she rounded it to take her own. "Sit."

The command was directed at Chase, but Occam plunked his butt down, wagging enthusiastically enough to shimmy his entire body. Mia patted the puppy who went into paroxysms of delight at the attention as Chase sat. She gave the dog a chew to distract him and then turned the full force of her focus on Chase. The frown on her face was familiar. He wanted to kiss her until it melted into a smile, but he couldn't make himself move from the chair.

"I was distracted today." It was an accusation.

A pretty response stuck in his throat. The hinges on his charm had rusted shut tonight.

Mia's frown intensified at his lack of response. She carefully selected a printout from papers on her desk and slid it toward him. "This is my brain a month ago."

Chase nodded, pretending to study the page. It could have been Occam's brain for all he could tell.

Mia set another, slightly different printout next to it. "This is my brain this afternoon."

She waited, obviously expecting something, so Chase made a "hm" noise and tapped the papers with his index finger.

"I realize this doesn't mean anything to you," she snapped impatiently. "But it's all there." She waved a hand at the pages. "It's science."

He usually felt like he had a good grasp on what Mia was driving at, even when she was at her most obscure, but tonight he was lost. "Okay, I give up. What's all there?"

Her frown darkened until she looked mildly homicidal. "I'm in love with you."

Chase stopped breathing.

She'd said it. She'd come right out and said it. He hadn't thought she would. She'd seemed safe. Emotionally stunted. Work obsessed. Not that he'd pursued her because he'd known love would never enter the equation. He'd known they were leading up to this point, but hearing her say it made it real.

He couldn't breathe. He couldn't love her back. He just couldn't make himself do it. He wouldn't be able to handle needing her. His love life was a car accident on the side of the road. *Don't look. Just drive past.* If he didn't look, it wouldn't be his car accident. It would be safely distant. Mia would be safely distant. She wouldn't belong to him.

"Chase? Are you okay? You look like you might vomit."

Only Mia could sound blithely unoffended when her profession of love was met with an I-might-hurl face. He would have smiled, but he didn't have control of his facial muscles.

He'd been okay as long as she was freaked by love and running in the opposite direction, but as soon as she became confident, so damn *certain*, he lost his shit. He'd been talking her into loving him, but it had been an argument, not a reality. Reality changed things.

He could lose her. *She could die.*

Chase lurched up out of the chair and it crashed over backward. "I can't." He couldn't form any other words, so he repeated those. "I can't—" *take the idea of losing you.* "I can't—" *go through that again.* "I can't—" *let myself want anyone the way I want you.*

"Chase." She stood as well, frowning now in concern and confusion. He probably looked like a mental patient and he didn't feel far from it.

There wasn't enough oxygen in the room. He needed to get outside. Fresh air. He couldn't breathe.

Chase bolted.

He heard Mia behind him, calling after him, starting to follow, so he moved faster, running now.

She'd had a busy fucking day. Finding the watch, figuring out how to love a damaged bastard like him. What had he done all day? Surfed and turned down an offer on the house and run like hell.

But even as a small voice inside him cursed his own

cowardice, his body kept moving, running, fleeing. To the hallway, into the parking lot, in the car, down the freeway. Away. He had to get away.

Chapter Twenty-Nine
Mr. Right Comes Calling

Watching Chase run like she'd just declared herself radioactive was hardly how she'd envisioned this particular encounter ending.

Occam growled and pounced on her shoe. Mia knelt next to him, sliding his fur through her fingers. "That could have gone better," she confided. He panted up at her adoringly. At least one male in her life was free of emotional baggage.

She probably ought to feel heartbroken right now. She'd never actually done the whole professing-your-love schtick before and the goal certainly hadn't been to reduce the object of her affections to blithering hysteria and send him fleeing the premises. As rejections went, it was pretty unequivocal.

So why wasn't she the sobbing mess pop culture would insist she should be right now? Why did she feel...

She didn't know how she felt. Certainly not hurt. She still loved him. At least, she was fairly certain she still loved him. And not in any angsty, agonized way. The thought of him was pleasant. Warm.

Maybe she just didn't have a good handle on what love was. If she'd truly loved him, she'd be shattered right now, wouldn't she? She'd seen both of her sisters in the midst of heartbreak and she didn't feel even remotely as crushed as they'd been.

Compassion. That's what she felt. She understood why this was hard for him. Why he'd run.

He'd be back. She couldn't even worry about the possibility that he wouldn't return because deep down, she had a strange certainty that he would.

Faith.

Mia, who'd never believed in anything, had faith in Chase.

The weight of the watch bumped against her thigh through the thin material of her pocket. She drew the watch out, cupping it in her palm and searching the plain gold for some trace of the miraculous.

Could it really be imbued with some romantic power? Was it possible that this old timepiece could somehow be responsible for finding her the one man who was perfect for her, who also happened to be the last man she would have picked?

If she put it on now, would he come back?

She needed him. And not just as a date for the anniversary party tomorrow.

Mia straightened from her crouch on the floor and went to the small bathroom off her office. Looking herself in the eye, she raised the chain over her head and, for the first time in her life, put on the watch.

It rested against her sternum. Inanimate. Unimpressive. Nothing more than a collection of gears and superstition.

A heavy knock sounded on the main door to the lab.

"*Chase.*"

Mia ran down the hall, Occam bouncing at her heels. She stopped at the door to smooth her hair in a futile attempt at composure.

The man she was meant to be with was on the other side of the door. Chase had shown her magic. He'd taught her how to believe in happily-ever-afters and meant-to-bes.

She reached for the handle and opened the door, simultaneously opening herself to the future she was meant to have.

He stood in the doorway, smiling affectionately. The man she was fated to be with. "Hello, Mia." His voice was warm, wrapping lovingly around her name.

But it wasn't Chase.

He was taller than Chase. Older. More distinguished. Her perfect match.

"Peter."

Chapter Thirty
Karma Alarm

It was after ten when Chase arrived at Karmic Consultants, but the light was still on in Karma's office. The curse of his life: workaholic women.

Tonight he was glad the front door was unlocked and she was easy to find behind the massive expanse of her desk. His boss didn't bat an eye when he walked into her office without knocking.

"Chase."

He arched a brow, trying for cheeky smartass but doubtless failing. It was hard to be cheeky when you felt like shit. "Were you expecting me?"

She shrugged, as cool, calm and put together as always, though when he looked closer her eyes were ringed with shadows and her mouth was pursed tighter than usual. "I had a hunch you might make an appearance."

A hunch. Karma's hunches had achieved legendary status amongst the consultants in her employ, though she never openly admitted to any precognitive tendencies.

"You can take Mia Corregianni off the books. She found the watch."

One carefully plucked eyebrow rose. "*She* found the watch. Without your assistance?"

"Not for lack of trying."

"Ah."

Just that syllable. A concise woman, Karma. She didn't ask if there was another reason he was there. She let her silence ask for her.

Chase cleared his throat. "She'll probably still want to do that study. On people with psychic abilities."

Karma nodded. "I've been wanting to get a scientist's view on our little family and she seemed quite intent." One blood-red nail drew a circle on her desk. "I'm surprised she didn't hit you up for a series of tests while she had you at her disposal."

"You know she did."

Karma spread her palm flat on the desk and leveled her gaze at him. "Are you here for another assignment? I don't have anything for you at the moment."

"Actually, I thought I might take some time off. The waves are good this time of year in Fiji. Or maybe Bali." The intention hadn't even been formed before he began to speak, but as soon as the words were out of his mouth, he liked the idea. The way he felt now, this icy-hot blade spinning inside his intestines, he never felt this way when the ocean was blue and perfect around him and the sun was beating all thoughts out of his head.

The heavy thud of Karma's fist against her desk jarred him out of his vacation fantasy. "You're an idiot, Chase."

The outburst was so uncharacteristic, he gaped at her. "Karma? Are you feeling all right?"

She ignored the question, plowing on, irritation bright behind her dark eyes. "There are times when it is important to let people be idiots—you're a man and it's your prerogative—but I think you've overstayed your lease on idiocy. I try to be patient, but I'm in no mood to indulge you tonight. I'm tired and you're a moron."

Chase blinked, as surprised by her admission that she was tired as he was by her declaration of his idiocy.

"Were you using Mia Corregianni?"

"I didn't—"

"It's obvious you have some kind of relationship with her and now you're running off to Bali. Scared off your too-pretty-for-your-own-damn-good ass." Her chin jutted up, the gesture oddly aggressive considering her usual contained stillness. "Why?"

She waited, obviously expecting an answer, but words froze like jagged ice chips in his throat. He swallowed in an attempt to melt them.

"I've watched you cling to your isolation. It was your right to choose your own way of mourning and I tried to respect that even as I watched you dodge every hint of a real, human connection. If you avoided anything that might have given you a real life because you couldn't face the fact that the life you might have had was taken from you, that was your choice. And if you want to choose that now—fine." Her hands swept out, eloquent in their impatience. "Is that who you want to be, Chase? A lonely old bastard who lived a shadow of a life because he was too chicken-shit to take a second chance?"

Her words bludgeoned him, battered him.

"Are you really that afraid?"

"*Yes.*"

The word burst out, stopping Karma's rant in its tracks.

"Yes, I'm that scared. And saying it doesn't change it."

She leaned back in her chair, her ferocity muted by his admission. "If you want to go to Bali, go to Bali. But consider two things while you're drifting on the water." She held up a single slim finger. "By running from the hope of more, you may find you are doing for yourself what you are so afraid of fate doing for you—ripping everything that can make you happy out of your life."

He felt his muscles tense against the assault of the words. "And the second thing?"

Karma's smile was icy. "You aren't just punishing yourself. What kind of selfish bastard is so scared of his past he hurts the people who love him? The woman he loves?"

"I don't l—" He couldn't finish the sentence. He already loved her. It was too late to deny it.

Karma shrugged, the gesture dismissing him. "Just something to think about on your flight to Bali. Alone."

What would Mia think of Bali? What would it be like to see it through her eyes? Chase shook away the thought, dismissing it roughly, and left before Karma could give him any more tough love. He'd had all he could take for the night.

He walked out to his car, determined to go home, only to realize the only place he wanted to go was Mia's house. His apartment, his parents' house, even the beach, none of it called to him, but he wasn't ready to see her again. Wasn't quite ready to stop being an idiot yet. He didn't know if he ever would be.

Chapter Thirty-One
Eggs-cruciating

Mia sat at her kitchen table, studying the man making her breakfast. It was the wrong man.

The watch was an anvil against her breastbone, taunting her with the life she'd thought she wanted.

Peter was back. The golden fleece of teaching positions had been offered to him at a nearby university and he was in town to "consider his options". Part of that consideration apparently involved her. And a family.

He'd appeared at her lab the night before and proposed before he even took off his coat. Scotland had apparently given him a personality lobotomy because he had decided he wanted a house in the suburbs and children on the honor roll to go with his academic success. He'd already explained that Mia was the ideal mother because they'd more than demonstrated their intellectual and social compatibility.

It was eerie how much his arguments had echoed her own thoughts—right down to the words she would have chosen to make the same points—but all she could think was that her children wouldn't have the charm gene or even a remote genetic probability of inheriting blue eyes.

Neither of which should matter, since Chase had taken himself out of the picture. And yet...

Peter stood at her counter, scrambling eggs with precise flicks of his wrist and humming tunelessly to himself. The years had been kind to him. Men did age insultingly well. The silver threading his dark hair at his temples and laugh lines creasing the corners of his eyes made what had already been an austerely handsome face even more dignified and elegant. His long-fingered hands, hands that should have belonged to an artist, still snared her attention with carefully practiced gestures to emphasize his points as he enumerated all the reasons they were perfectly suited to one another.

His voice was still deep and he still spoke with the same lingering deliberation, though he'd picked up just the hint of Scotland in his speech, more an inflection than an actual accent. He'd also taken to calling her "love" which she found inexplicably irritating, even though she'd long since stopped being bothered by Chase's mildly sarcastic sweethearts and honeys.

Peter stood in her kitchen—brilliant, stable, eminently compatible and laying out a life for the two of them in her own words. He was Mr. Perfect—correction, *Dr.* Perfect. Even Occam seemed to agree, panting softly as he leaned his tiny head against Peter's ankle and gazed adoringly up at the source of bacon scraps.

And all she could think was how much she missed Chase. Drop-out, bullshit artist, surfer Chase.

Chase who had walked out without even a goodbye.

She'd put the watch on to lure her love back to her...and Peter had appeared. Chase had taught her to believe in the magic of the watch, to trust it, but if it was pointing her toward Peter...

Peter looked over his shoulder at her as he unerringly opened a cupboard to get out the plates, his eyes crinkling. "I see everything is just as I remembered."

Mia frowned. Obviously he wasn't just referring to the plates. The wordplay wasn't like him and she had to bite back the urge to tell him that she wasn't as he remembered. She'd changed. Chase had changed her.

For the better?

In the harsh light of morning, she wasn't sure. She'd been distracted yesterday. Sure, she loved Chase, but did love make her inefficient? A less productive member of society? To be a better scientist, did she need to be with someone she didn't care about in a passionate manner? Someone with whom she could leave all thoughts of him at her lab door?

Was the watch perhaps telling her that she wasn't actually designed for romantic love? That her life would be richer through contributions to the human race rather than emotional self-indulgence?

"Have you thought any more about what we talked about last night?" Peter didn't look away from his task as he poured the frothy eggs into the skillet.

Last night. His proposal.

He was a good man, a brilliant scientist and the embodiment of a leave-your-emotions-at-the-lab-door husband. He'd let her stall him on the proposal, but it seemed her reprieve was over.

"I have. I—" She broke off, rubbing the watch, stalling for time. "It's the family anniversary celebration today. Do you remember it?"

Peter gave a low, mocking laugh. "How could I forget? How is your family these days? Still making sure the local tarot card readers are fully employed?" His smile blazed with superiority. "Has your crazy aunt had any more dreams prophesying the Royals in the Super Bowl?"

"World Series."

They'd always rolled their eyes at her family's antics together, the two of them sharing a laugh about it, above the silliness of love and superstition, but now she wanted to smack him for saying exactly what she'd always said. Peter didn't understand her family. He didn't have the right to look down on them.

"We should elope," Peter continued, turning back to the burner. "None of your family there to make you crazy. A quick weekend in Niagara Falls—knock out the wedding and the honeymoon." He sent her an understanding smile. "I won't keep you away from your lab for longer than that."

That was what she wanted, wasn't it? Efficiency. A man who understood her priorities. So why was it so hard to just say yes?

Her cell phone rang, releasing a tidal wave of relief into her system that she had an excuse to put off answering Peter. She glanced at the caller ID.

"It's Gina. I'd better take it," she said to Peter, though at the moment she would have taken a call from a telemarketer and been grateful. She beat a retreat into the living room. Sliding her thumb across the screen, she lifted it to her ear. "Hey, Gina. What's up?"

"A miracle has occurred," her little sister announced with her usual flair for the dramatic.

"Don't tell me. Let me guess. Marley spoke and her first words were: I love Auntie Mia."

"Better. Mama and Teresa are speaking again."

Mia felt a flash of guilt that she'd temporarily forgotten her sister's troubles, chased by surprise that her dramatic family had resolved a drama without her interference. "How?"

"Apparently—hold onto your test tubes—Daddy intervened. He told Mama she was going to miss out on a relationship with her next grandbaby if she didn't get her head out of her ass and stop punishing Teresa for her choice."

Mia's hand closed around the watch against her chest, squeezing it tight. "When did this...?"

"Just last night. Mama and Daddy and Teresa and Martin hugged it out and now Mama is determined to help Teresa decorate the baby's room so everything is ready for her when they bring her home."

"Her? They know the gender already?"

"Their adoption liaison contacted them this morning. Baby Girl Lee is about to become Baby Girl Amata. Teresa says she doesn't want to get her hopes up, but she has a good feeling that this time it's gonna stick."

Mia couldn't find the words. It was all coming together. She'd put on the watch and everything worked out for her family. Like magic. Could she really deny that Peter's arrival was meant to be now?

Gina misinterpreted Mia's silence. "Hey, I'm sure she would have called you and told you herself, but they've got a million things to do, getting ready for the baby. She said she left a message on your office line. I tried that one first too—"

"Do you want bacon, love?" Peter's voice carried easily from the kitchen.

Mia half covered the mouthpiece of her phone. "No, thanks."

"Is that Chase?" Gina giggled. "I should have guessed you had company when you weren't at your office on a Saturday morning. Just don't get so caught up in him that you're late to the party today. You two are among the guests of honor this year."

"Actually..." Mia swallowed around a sudden lump in her throat. "Peter's back in town."

The silence was deafening as Gina processed that revelation. "Peter..."

"He's been offered a position at a university near here and, ah, he crashed on my couch while he considers..." Mia trailed off and the next words popped out of her mouth uninvited. "He proposed."

"Oh shit. I mean that's—ah—wow—" Gina coughed. "What about Chase?"

"You can't be surprised. Chase and I are hardly compatible. How could any man understand that my professional ambition is the driving force of my life if all he cares about is the next wave?" That was unfair. She knew he was more than that. Better than that. But his departure had stung. Maybe now she was turning into that mopey heartbroken wreck she'd expected to be last night. She'd thought he would come back...

"Just because Chase isn't a nerd, doesn't mean he's not perfect for you," Gina protested. "Honey, you should see how you are when you're with him. You're *alive*. How can you walk away from th—"

"Chase left, okay?" Mia fingered the watch, rubbing it like a genie might pop out and start granting her wishes. "He isn't in the picture anymore."

"Oh Mia, what—"

"I don't want to talk about it right now, Gina. I've got...breakfast. See you later?"

Gina grudgingly agreed to let the subject drop and hung up after a reminder not to be late to the anniversary celebration at noon—though there was much less enthusiasm in her sister's voice at the prospect that Mia might be arriving with her fellow professor on her arm.

Mia hovered in the living room, not ready to go back into the kitchen and face Peter. That was a bad sign, wasn't it? That she didn't want to see him because he wanted her to marry him?

"Mia? How about some pancakes, love? Shall I whip some up?"

She looked longingly at the front door, wondering how Peter would react if she ran out of it. He'd probably just wait for her to get back. Patient. Logical. Unperturbed.

She stroked the watch, the gold warming with her touch. Its magic was working. And making her miserable. But misery was fleeting. In the long run she'd be grateful she married Peter. When she and her offspring became the first mother-daughter team to be awarded the Nobel Prize, she'd thank Chase for leaving the path to her best future open.

She pivoted on her heel, chin up, decision made. She had to be smart, true to herself. She would marry Peter. It was the logical choice.

The doorbell rang and her stupid, hopeful heart skipped a beat. Occam yipped from the kitchen and the sound of his claws scrabbling against the hardwood preceded his mad dash toward the front door.

Mia held her breath. It wasn't necessarily *him*. Girl Scouts. It was probably Girl Scouts. They were always hawking their cookies this time of year, weren't they? She scooped up Occam so he wouldn't attack the ankles of any unsuspecting cookie-hawkers. She shifted his soft, squirmy weight against her hip and opened the door.

Chase Hunter stood on her doorstep, the morning sunlight painting him like a golden surf god—and emphasizing all the ways they were incompatible. He was gorgeous, dynamic, *distracting*…and her heart stuttered to a stop on the hope that he was back to stay.

"I'm sorry."

The bubble of hope popped, pricked by the needle of the right words from the wrong man. He was back. He was sorry. He was so unfairly beautiful and defensively charming.

And she had to send him away, because above all else, he was the wrong Mr. Right for her.

Chapter Thirty-Two
Morning-After Imposters

Chase was man enough to admit when he was being an idiot—even if it took his boss calling him one repeatedly and a sleepless night spent sitting in the abandoned living room of his brother's house for the truth to penetrate.

He loved Mia. He couldn't control that any more than he could control the universe that might take her away from him. Being with her was a risk and it might rip him to pieces in the long run—if anything happened to her, it *would*—but he couldn't live his life dodging all the things that made it living. He had an existence, it was time he got a life.

For anyone else he didn't think he could have done it, but for Mia he could risk it. *With* her he would, because she was just as freaked out as he was about their inability to control the universe. But together they could lose control.

If he could convince her to take another chance on him. He hadn't shown himself to be a good risk by bailing on her last night.

"I'm sorry," he said again when Mia didn't speak. "I shouldn't have bolted like that. I freaked out and I'm—"

"No." Occam wriggled frantically in Mia's arms, trying to get to Chase and she cuddled him higher, tucking his head under her chin to soothe him. "You were right to go."

"Wait. What? I was right?" Chase frowned. He hadn't seen that one coming. He'd expected to have to beg for forgiveness, anticipated diffusing indignation and hurt feelings, but he should have known Mia wouldn't take the expected path.

"We both needed space to think. I was being impulsive—"

"Hey, impulsive is good. I fully support impulsive. Though I'm not sure presenting me with readouts documenting your affections counts as an impulse."

He was having some impulses himself. Like the impulse to kiss her until she forgot logic. She looked gorgeous, wearing an oversized Cal Tech T-shirt that had obviously been slept in and a pair of boxer shorts. And the watch. It dangled from the chain around her neck and whenever Occam stopped squirming long enough to give her a free hand, her fingers would flutter to brush at it.

A straight, dark lock of her slippery hair escaped from the knot at her nape and he reached out to tuck it back. Mia flinched away, holding Occam up like a shield.

"Mia, love? Your eggs are getting cold."

Chase froze with his hand still suspended in the air between them. That was a man's voice. Coming from Mia's kitchen. A strange man. Making Mia eggs. Calling Mia "love".

Twelve hours. He'd left her only twelve hours ago.

Chase's gaze couldn't resist the long bare expanse of Mia's legs. Another man had seen those legs this morning. Perhaps even woken up tangled in them.

No. She wouldn't have.

"Mia?" He couldn't breathe. She'd said she loved him *last night*. In every conceivable scenario of loss, betrayal was not how he had ever imagined losing her.

She'd gone pale. With guilt? She met his eyes without flinching, but that didn't tell him much. Mia had never been the flinching type. She was unswervingly honest. Not that she wouldn't sleep with another man, but that she wouldn't lie about it afterward. He'd know. Any second now she'd open her mouth and he'd know.

"Peter is back."

"Peter." Her ex. Mr. Compatibility. The name was a sledgehammer in his gut. He shoved his hands into his pockets and the fingers of his right hand brushed against the metal band he'd put there this morning.

"I put on the watch last night and there he was." Suddenly Mia couldn't meet his gaze. Painfully honest Mia studied the railing, the doorframe, anything but him. "Fate, right? Magic. He's The One."

"Since when do you believe in magic?"

She finally looked at him. "Since I met you."

Something in that look rocked him. She hadn't slept with Peter. Chase was sure of it. Her heart was still his, he just had to make up all the ground he'd lost last night and reconvince her to think with her heart, rather than that enormous brain.

"Come here." He caught her around the waist and tugged her out onto the front step with him.

"Chase—I can't—"

He didn't give her a chance to gather a coherent protest. Scooping Occam out of her arms, with the puppy squirming wildly in an attempt to lick every inch of Chase's face, he deposited the dog inside and quickly pulled the door shut—cutting Mia off from the puppy she'd tried to use as a shield and the man she thought had come at the call of the watch.

"My eggs..." she complained when he faced her, putting himself between her and the door.

"I'll make you more eggs. I make amazing eggs." He couldn't cook to save his life, but how hard could boiling an egg be?

A reluctant smile almost curved her lips. "You're so full of shit."

"And you don't let me get away with any bullshit. Without you I'd just run rampant."

"Charming innocent bystanders out of their wits."

"Exactly. I need you, Mia."

"I just need... I need time to think."

"No. No thinking allowed. Feeling only."

"I can't make life decisions based only on emotion, Chase. That isn't who I am."

"Okay, fine, let's be logical. Diversity."

She blinked, visibly thrown by the word he'd thrown down like a gauntlet. "Excuse me?"

"Diversity. It's better for the species to blend your genetic code with one that's very different from your own, right?"

"On a strictly genetic level…"

"Hey, you wanted logic. Let's be brutally logical. You and Peter are too similar. Marrying him would be like marrying your cousin."

"Actually no, it wouldn't—"

"Whereas marrying me would be good for the species."

Mia gave a small breathy laugh then pursed her lips tight as if to hold in any other outbursts of good humor. "How long did it take you to come up with that argument?"

All night. "It's a work in progress. I've been practicing it ever since you started harping on compatibility."

"I do not harp."

He shifted closer, needing to touch her, but she sidled away.

She leaned against the railing with her hands behind her, gripping it. "My eggs are old."

It took Chase a moment to realize they weren't talking about breakfast any more.

"If I want to have a family, I need to do it now. Peter is ready for that. Are you? Can you honestly say that you want to ensure the diversity of the species with me when you couldn't even handle me expressing a little emotion to you last night?"

"Last night I was an idiot. It won't happen again."

"You can't guarantee that. And even if you manage to control your panic next time, I want to be with a man who doesn't react to settling down with a fight or flight reflex. I need someone who wants a future with me, not someone who may never want it and has to be dragged to maturity every step of the way."

"I knew the age difference thing would come up eventually."

"It isn't age. It's maturity."

"It's neither," he snapped. "It's fear. My fear, your fear. God knows we've got baggage to spare, but that doesn't have to stop us. I'm going to accept the offer on Toby's house. We can fix up my parents' place, move in there if you like it. There's a yard for Occam. I'm not running anymore. I was an idiot, but I'm in this now. I know what I want and it's you."

"Chase...the watch..."

He couldn't wait any longer. He had to get his hands on her. Chase crowded her against the railing, both hands cradling her face. She pressed her cheek into his touch, and a fragile hope rose with that gesture. Whatever she needed him to prove to her, he would do it.

"You love me, right?"

A rosy flush warmed her cheeks against his palms. "I thought I did, but what if—"

"No. You're the least uncertain person I know. You *knew* you loved me. It was science, sweetheart. Science doesn't lie." He gazed into her eyes—no evasion, no dodging the truth or running from what he wanted. What he needed. He poured every ounce of urgency he felt into his words. "I love you, Mia. I know I was an idiot last night and I know Peter may seem like the right guy for you on paper, but magic isn't just about trusting a watch. It's about trusting yourself. Your heart. Peter came when you put on the watch? Well, so did I. One of us is a coincidence, but which one does your heart tell you it is? Which one of us do you want to be The One? It's me, Mia. Let it be me."

"I want it to be you," she whispered. The steel in her spine melted a little.

Then he kissed her, and it melted a lot.

She released the railing behind her to grab on to him, pulling him into the kiss with startling force. She was hungry, eager, and without conscious intent on his part his gift woke up. He felt the barrier between himself and her desires fading to transparency, her intangibles bleeding into him like osmosis through every eager touch.

She wanted him. Only him. All of him. The images flashing into his brain were graphic, sweaty, *so damn hot* and had him hard in seconds. The lines between them blurred until he wasn't sure whether it was Mia's fantasies or his own that he was seeing. *Mia, flinging her glasses aside, standing in front of him wearing the watch. Wearing* only *the watch.* That metallic string snapped taut with a twang so harsh it was almost painful. He saw the Corregianni watch, saw it crystal clear, and it wasn't around Mia's neck.

He jerked his head up. His breath came hard and he couldn't make himself let her go, but she had to know. "Mia. I know where the watch is."

She frowned, tucking one hand between them to hold up the gold bauble at her breastbone. "It's right here."

"No, it isn't." He closed his hand over hers on the watch. "This one's a fake."

Chapter Thirty-Three
You Just Can't Trust a Warlock

The Prometheus Unbound Bookshop and Spell Emporium was the physical manifestation of every imaginable occult cliché. It was musty, shadowy, cluttered and stocked with everything from crystal balls to jars of what looked suspiciously like pickled bat wings.

Mia wouldn't have been surprised to find that instead of Muzak, they played one of those haunted house recordings of creaking doors, howling wind and organ dirges. Instead, the shop was eerily silent. She gripped Chase's hand, wholly out of her depth.

"Prometheus!" Chase shouted, when the bell over the door failed to bring anyone rushing to assist them. Apparently efficient customer service didn't fit the atmosphere.

The wait was anticlimactic after the way they'd rushed over here. She was due at the party in less than two hours, but not without the watch. The *real* watch.

Mia had fobbed Peter off with a rushed explanation that something had come up, thrown on some clothes and left him in her kitchen feeding Occam her cold eggs. She'd have to deal with his proposal soon, but with Chase standing right there, it would have been almost cruel to refuse him in that moment—though Peter was unlikely to be heartbroken. He was too much like her.

Mia plucked at the sleeve of her sweater, unsure whether it was nerves or the pre-bake temperatures in the shop that made her feel like she was suffocating. Chase had taken custody of the fake watch. She wasn't sure which had her more freaked out—the possibility that the creep who'd traded her heirloom for a dud might not return it, or the question of who the real watch would choose for her if he did. She knew she wanted Chase, but what if this real watch reinforced what the fake one had seemed to say? What if Peter was really the better choice? Could her heart overpower her head a second time?

The faintest rustle of the fabric concealing the doorway at the back of the shop was their only warning as Prometheus appeared.

"You bellowed?"

The shop's owner was a tall, lean, scarecrow of a man—tall enough he had to duck his head coming through the doorway and built with the awkward, angled elegance of Jimmy Stewart. He was tanned with white creases of smile lines beginning around his eyes and close-cropped prematurely white hair that made it impossible to guess his age. *Stand aside, Anderson Cooper.*

He was an unusually handsome man—eye-catching by virtue of his unique hard-boned beauty, but all of the physical trappings were just window dressing, a shell for the force of the personality within. It was his eyes—intense, magnetic, black-hole eyes that seemed to suck everything toward him like a vacuum. Mia took an involuntary step forward before Chase's hand on hers pulled her back.

"You have something that belongs to us." Chase raised his hand, letting the fake watch dangle from his fingers.

Prometheus's black whirlpool eyes flicked to the gleam of gold then away, betraying no recognition, but a sliver of a smile curled his lips. "Do I? How interesting."

"A girl came in here a few months back—"

"So many girls come in here," Prometheus purred. "How to keep them straight?"

"She had a watch like this one," Chase went on as if the shop owner had not interrupted. "A charmed watch, and she asked you to duplicate the love spell on it. You told her you couldn't and gave her back a watch—but the one you returned to her was a fake." He swung the watch like a pendulum. "This fake."

"You seem quite certain of that. That you deduced so much would be impressive. *If* I had stolen something." Prometheus's smile had broadened to a full-fledged grin. "Who are you? I make it a practice to know the names of people who accuse me of dirty deeds."

"Chase Hunter, Karmic Consultants."

"Ah. Of course. How nice to meet you, Chase Hunter, Karmic Consultants." The tall man rocked back on his heels, beaming now though the smile never touched the calculation in his eyes. "I should have guessed you were one of Karma's little pets. Fascinating woman, your employer."

"She's a puzzle wrapped in an enigma and all that shit. The watch? We'd like it back."

"Of course you would. Marvelous enchantment on it. So cleverly wrought." Prometheus cocked his head like a raptor considering his lunch. "I don't suppose you'd believe me if I said I only borrowed it so I could unlock the secret behind the enchantment and duplicate it for the lovelorn of the rest of the world. Altruistic purposes only. That's right up the Karmic Consultants alley, isn't it?"

"Duplicating it for profit, no doubt."

"A man has to make a living. Or do you only employ your psychic gifts for charity fundraisers?" His long fingers flicked out and for a moment there was a tantalizing flash of gold between them, vanishing and reappearing in a dizzying sleight-of-hand. "Capitalist do-gooders. How does that work exactly? I admit I find the concept of the Karmic Consultants intriguing. Hopelessly naive, but intriguing. It's much the same as what I do—helping people with paranormal maladies for profit—but your boss has built her business on virtue which seems to contradict itself nicely."

As he spoke, his fingers continued to weave patterns in the air and the gold—Mia's watch—continued to tease them with flickers of its presence in his deft hands.

"The watch," Chase prompted, his palm out flat.

Prometheus seemed not to hear. "I tried to hire Karma once. Did you know that? But she refused to work with someone whose ethics are as, shall we say, *gray* as mine. Pity." He made a fist and Mia heard the soft clink of metal on metal in his grip. "I'll give you the watch."

Relief sent dopamine rushing through her blood. "Thank—"

"Don't thank me yet. Nothing is free in this world."

"You *stole* it," Chase snapped. "Mia is the rightful owner."

"Ah, but possession is nine-tenths of the law and all that. How will you prove to a court that the one you hold is not the real watch? Do you think a judge will be impressed by your psychic talents? Come on, bargain with me. I'll give you a good deal."

Mia heard a clicking sound and realized it was Chase grinding his teeth. "What do you want?"

"Just a favor." Prometheus's fingers began to dance again, taunting them with glimpses of the watch. "One little favor. From Karma."

Chase shook his head. "I can't speak for her."

"Take it." Prometheus flung out his hand.

The watch flew at them so abruptly Chase dropped the fake and half-ducked to catch it with both hands before it could break his nose.

"One favor owed. Those are the terms."

Chase shook his head. "I didn't agree to that."

Prometheus smiled his Cheshire cat smile. "But you took the watch." He turned and headed to the back of the shop without looking back. "Tell your boss I'll be expecting her call. I'm not a good man to keep waiting. Who knows what kind of mischief I'll get into?"

The curtain rustled shut behind him, but Mia didn't fool herself that he wasn't still watching. The man was a spider, toying with the flies who'd flown into his web, and her animal hindbrain told her to get the hell out before the web ensnared them forever.

Chase apparently had the same idea, grabbing her hand again and all but dragging her out onto the sidewalk. He kept pulling until they reached her car and he more or less shoved her into the driver's seat, rushing around the hood and sliding in the passenger side.

Mia glanced at the clock as the car came to life. One hour and eleven minutes. Factoring in driving time, they should make it. Barely. She held out her hand. "Let me put it on."

"Karma's, first," Chase said, his voice sharp and commanding. "We have to make sure he didn't put a curse on it before it goes anywhere near your neck."

Mia put her foot down on the accelerator and drove, trying to ignore how sexy Chase was when he was in take-charge mode.

"Mia, how exquisite to see you." Karma met them at the door to her office, once again looking flawless in unwrinkled turquoise silk, as if the thought of being tired or impatient had never crossed her mind, let alone colored her behavior as it had with him last night.

Chase bore the slightly smug smile she directed at him with good grace, since he figured he deserved it. After she had gushed over Mia to her satisfaction, she stepped back and clasped her hands in front of her. "I take it this isn't a social visit."

"Afraid not." He'd never seen Karma have a social visit. It seemed strange to think that she might have a social life.

He took the watch, which he'd wrapped in a napkin from Mia's glovebox to avoid touching its surface any more than necessary, out of his pocket and handed it to her, quickly bringing her up to speed on the situation. She betrayed no reaction, taking it all in calmly, save an almost imperceptible flinch when he mentioned Prometheus's name the first time.

She gingerly unwrapped the watch, careful not to touch the metal. Chase didn't see anything unusual about it, but Karma must have. She glowered at the innocent gold disc. "He put

263

something on it. Doesn't look like a curse though..." Karma trailed off, muttering to herself as she rounded her desk and sat, bending over the watch until her nose almost touched it.

Chase caught Mia's hand. It was icy as ever and he tugged her against his side, gently chaffing her chilly fingers.

"Could he have deactivated the love charm?" Mia asked, speaking low to avoid disturbing Karma's concentration.

"I haven't a clue," he admitted. "I don't know enough about that sort of magic to know if that's even possible."

"If he did..."

"If he did, we'll just have to find another nineteenth-century Italian gypsy woman to recharm it. Karma probably has half a dozen of them on speed dial." He raised her hand to his mouth and brushed a kiss across her knuckles. "No worrying."

An electrical zap sounded, loud enough to carry across the room to them, and Karma jerked back, swearing.

"Karma?" Chase started toward her, Mia at his side, but Karma waved them back.

"I'm fine. It was nothing. Just a little hello from Prometheus."

"Is the watch...?" Mia trailed off, squeezing the circulation from his fingers with her grip on his hand.

"That was the only booby-trap on it and it was designed for me. He must have suspected you would bring it to me." She muttered something unflattering about Prometheus's ancestry under her breath then went on, scooping up the watch in her bare hands without incurring another shock, "I can't be one hundred percent certain, but I believe the charm is still intact."

Mia closed her eyes with a groaned, "Oh, thank God."

Karma rounded the desk and handed Mia the watch. "Wear it and good luck." Her eyes flicked to Chase as she said it, as if Mia was going to need the luck to handle him. He kept his mouth shut for once.

Until they were at the door and the devil prompted him to ask, "Are you going to give Prometheus his favor?" *Or shove it up his ass?*

Karma's mouth tightened and murder entered her eyes. "I don't honor bargains with thieves."

Chase hustled Mia out into the parking lot, leaving Karma to plot vengeance against the warlock.

"Who is he?" Mia asked, clutching the watch to her chest though she seemed to have no awareness of it in her hand.

"Prometheus? An innocent shopkeeper or a devious, unscrupulous warlock, depending who you ask."

"He's like a spider."

Chase tipped his head. "Not a bad analogy. What eats spiders? Lizards? I never saw Karma as terribly lizard-like. More of a puppeteer. Or an idle god. She has that omniscient thing going for her."

"Should we be worried? Do you think he'll come after us if she doesn't give him the favor?"

"I don't think he'll stir himself for mere mortals like you and I. If he goes after anyone, it'll be Karma. But in that fight, my money is on her."

"I don't know..." Mia muttered something that sounded like "black-hole eyes".

Chase didn't want her musing about any man's eyes but his. He covered the hand holding the watch with his. "You wouldn't be asking about Prometheus because you're afraid to put this on, would you?"

Chapter Thirty-Four
The Burden of Proof

Mia hadn't been conscious of clutching the watch until Chase's hand closed over hers and warm static tingles suddenly radiated from the surface. It *knew* him. Mia's heart lifted with optimism, but her head wasn't quite ready to give up the fight. Thirty-four years of habitual behavior didn't give up so easily.

"Why are you so eager for me to wear it?"

"Because I know I'm The One and the watch is going to tell you so."

His arrogance was annoyingly adorable. "Just because a piece of metal likes you, doesn't mean you're The One."

"Of course it does. You, me, faith and the watch—the ingredients of a long and happy life."

She glowered at him. "Did my mother tell you to say that?"

He grinned. "I think it was Nonna—or Zia Anna, I still can't tell them apart—but I couldn't agree with her more."

"That's such bullshit. When the watch seemed to be pointing toward Peter you told me not to believe in it. Now you say it's all we need?"

"That watch was a fake."

"You didn't know that!"

"But I knew it was wrong."

"That's ridiculous. You can't just discard whichever piece of evidence doesn't support your argument. It isn't scientific."

"I'm not a scientist. I'm a fool in love. We're allowed to rig the rules however we want to get the girl."

He was smiling as he kissed her. The curve of his lips against hers made the watch's tingles shoot from her palm to her lips and back again in a closed circuit of lust that was too warm and comforting for the name.

Lifting his head, he plucked the watch out of her loosened grip and gently turned her by her shoulders. The warm, tingly weight of the watch settled against her breastbone as he gently brushed aside the hairs escaping from her bun and fastened the clasp at the nape of her neck.

She'd expected her doubts to evaporate under a tide of certainty but nothing changed. The watch continued to radiate promising tingles but nothing more. She supposed she shouldn't be surprised. This was her love life after all and emotion never could stand up to the burden of proof. It took faith—something she'd never had until Chase, and something she had a feeling she would never have again without him.

She turned in his arms, studying his face—his gorgeous genetic anomaly of a symmetrical face—for any trace of doubt, of the fear that had crippled him less than twenty-four hours ago.

"I love you," she said, the words as sharp and aggressive as machine-gun fire. "And I want to get married. Right away. And have babies. While my eggs are viable. Does that scare you?" She was testing, pushing, prodding for weakness in his affections, trying to send him running. Better now than later. Now would be bad enough. Later was unthinkable.

Chase didn't bolt. He laughed. "Do you have a schedule in mind? Because I should probably have a copy of it." He dug into the front pocket of his jeans and pulled out a small circle of gold with a microscopic diamond. "I've been carrying this around all day. It was my mother's. My parents couldn't afford much when he bought it for her, but she refused to let him replace it when they got more money."

A lump formed in her throat. The ring was perfect—small enough that it wouldn't catch on things around the lab, but still powerfully significant because of its meaning to Chase. Like dark matter, visible only through the gravitational effect it had on objects around it.

His smile was gently teasing as he held the ring out to her. "I'll sweep you off your feet, Mia, but you've gotta give me the chance."

Damn. That was her one chance to be a romantic and get a sappy proposal and she'd screwed it up. Wasn't that just typical? "Pretend I didn't say anything," she said, trying to wipe away the mistake. "Pretend I'm a patient girl who is normal and waits for you to propose whenever you want to because it's more romantic that way."

Chase stepped closer and rested his forehead against hers, his blue eyes sparkling. "I don't want to pretend any of that. I just want you. Impatience, science addiction and all."

The kiss was electric. Exciting. It shouldn't have been. Now that the thrill of the chase was over and they knew they were going to end up together, it should have been boring, run-of-the-mill, but her toes curled and her heart pounded and she realized she would never get bored of this man's lips. *Or his hands...or his apparatus.*

When he finally raised his head, Mia let go only because they were in the middle of a parking lot and if things went on much longer they were going to get a citation for indecent exposure.

There was a perfectly good bed at her house. Unfortunately, it would have to wait. They had a party to get to. Just as soon as she collected her puppy and turned down a proposal.

"You realize this means you're a Corregianni now. You have to come to the anniversary party with me and you'll never have a peaceful, relaxing, quiet holiday again."

"Mia, darling, you've already got me. No need to tempt me with your family."

"It was a threat, not a temptation."

He shrugged, opening the car door for her. "One woman's threat is another man's happily-ever-after." He rounded the hood and climbed in beside her, leaning over to grab a quick kiss. "Be nice to me and I might let you scan my brain later."

She grinned against his mouth. "Define 'nice'."

Chase leaned back to put his seat belt on. "I see a long future of trading sexual favors for scientific experiments."

"You could just volunteer. Out of the goodness of your heart."

He laughed. "Where's the fun in that?"

Mia grinned. He had a point. And for a woman who'd never used the word *fun* to describe her life before, the foreseeable future looked pretty damn good.

She'd still win the Nobel Prize, but on the way, her life would be filled with joy and laughter and a steady supply of charming bullshit.

It didn't get better than that.

Chapter Thirty-Five
Rollercoasters & Romantics

The one hundred-twenty-first annual Corregianni anniversary party was in full swing by the time Chase and Mia arrived at Nonna's house. May first wasn't just the day Gianni and Anna Maria had gotten married. Because of its significance in the family, dozens of other Corregianni couples had chosen that day to tie the knot over the decades—including Mia's parents and both of her sisters.

Mia twisted the ring on her left hand with her thumb. She and Chase would not be joining the May first marriage cabal. There was no way they were waiting a whole year. With Chase holding her hand, Niagara Falls didn't sound like such a bad option.

Peter had taken her rejection remarkably well. He'd seemed more affected by the thought of losing Occam than her, but she tried not to take it personally. The dog *was* endearing to an addicting degree.

He was currently alternating between trying to drag Chase toward the exciting noise in the backyard by his leash and using it to tie a knot around Chase's ankles. The second time Chase nearly did a faceplant into the grass in order to avoid stepping on the dog, he dropped Mia's hand so he could use both of his to wrangle the energetic puppy.

"We'll work on *heel*."

"Good idea." Mia was smiling as they rounded the corner into the backyard.

Streamers arched between the trees and round tables almost disappeared beneath giant floral arrangements, each prominently displaying a card with a different couple's names scrolled across it in gold lettering. A buffet table looked ready to buckle under the weight of the food on display. The Corregiannis didn't celebrate in a small way.

"Is that a chocolate fountain?"

Before Mia could reply, a cheer went up as her family spotted them—and for the first time, she felt her smile widening and her heart lifting at the sound. The children descended on Occam and the older generations descended on Chase and Mia with Nonna and Zia Anna leading the charge. Their identical eyes lit on the watch, hanging prominently from the chain around her neck.

"She's wearing it!"

"I knew she'd come around."

"Always such a good girl."

"Do you see the ring?"

"Lovely ring. Classic."

"Not as lovely as mine, of course."

"Your Angelo did have wonderful taste."

Gina pushed her way to the front as Nonna and Zia Anna began to compare the wedding rings of everyone in earshot. Marley was asleep on her shoulder, immune to the Corregianni cacophony.

"I knew you'd pick Chase," she gushed, grabbing Mia in a one-armed hug. She started towing her toward the porch steps. "Come on. I have gossip. *Good* gossip."

"But Chase..."

"Is family now. No babysitting needed. Besides, he looks like he's in heaven. Come on."

Since Chase did indeed look like he was enjoying himself, Mia let Gina drag her up onto the porch where they had a view of the yard. Gina pointed toward the buffet. "Look."

Mia followed Gina's arm to where a couple were cuddled together in front of the cannoli. "Is that Jamie and Danny?"

Gina beamed. "It is. Turns out Danny was staying out late working overtime so he could surprise Jamie with a trip to Paris for their anniversary. All those charges she thought were so suspicious? They were presents for her. Total misunderstanding. And you thought there could never be positive gossip."

"I didn't say never. I said statistically rare."

"Okay, well, statistically whatever, they're happy. Teresa's happy. I'm happy. You're happy. Hell, even Mama's happy. You still think the watch is bogus?"

Did she?

Mia ran a thumb over the smooth gold surface, automatically seeking out Chase's face in the crowd of her family. He was talking to Mario, gesturing, laughing, but as if he felt Mia's gaze, his head turned, their eyes locked and he smiled, just for her. He said something to Mario, then he was weaving through her family, all the people she loved in the world, making his way to her side.

Mia vaguely heard Gina's arch "I think I see Tony looking for me." Then Chase was there, tucking her against him, her back to his front, and it was just the two of them, looking out over the wildly gesticulating hands and voices raised over one another.

"Enjoying your party?"

Mia almost corrected him, told him it wasn't hers, but this year it felt like it was. She was home in a way she'd never realized she could be. Had the watch done this?

She saw her mother and Teresa, obviously arguing but with only their usual levels of affectionate aggravation. Her father and Martin sat nearby, speaking quietly. Jamie hadn't left Danny's side. Marley had woken up and was being passed around like a party favor, as Nonna and Zia Anna spread mayhem wherever they wandered.

Her family. Not perfect, but hers.

She wrapped her fist around the watch. No, not magic. Relationships were rollercoasters with a thousand highs and lows. Forever didn't happen by magic—even if you had a magic pocket watch helping out. There were road blocks and stumbles, misunderstandings and flaring tempers. Especially flaring tempers where the Corregiannis were concerned. Mia had never seen those parts before because she was never looking. It had all seemed like a fairy tale idyll. She'd missed the bumps and bruises, but she'd missed the big picture too. She'd never seen the love smoothing them through the rough patches. She hadn't wanted to see. Until Chase.

You didn't need magic when you had love to spare, but it couldn't hurt. And that faith that it would all work out, that forever did happen and true love was real, maybe that helped a little too.

Chase closed his hand over hers on the watch. "Are you going to miss it? You never really got much of a chance to wear it."

"Are you kidding? Good riddance. I can't wait for it to be someone else's problem." She frowned, scanning the crowd. "Did they already announce whose turn it is next?"

"Actually it's your sweet, not-at-all-homicidally scary linebacker brother Joey."

Mia smiled. "Poor bastard. He doesn't know what he's in for."

Chase wrapped both arms around her waist, his cheek resting against her hair. "Should we warn him?"

Mia leaned back into his arms. "Nah. Some experiments you just have to do yourself."

Epilogue
The Clone Army

"We need a spare." Mia frowned fiercely at the smushed red face of their sleeping daughter. The nurse checking her vitals shot her a worried look, but Chase just grinned. Mia'd been glowering at the baby pretty much nonstop since the nurse first handed her over the day before. So much so that he'd already been pulled aside and shoved handfuls of post-partum depression pamphlets. Twice.

But the nurses on the maternity ward didn't know Mia, the woman who'd looked at him like she was plotting his execution when she first told him she loved him.

"Why? Is this one defective?" Chase reached out to stroke the impossibly smooth cheek of Carmina Hunter—they'd be calling her Karma for short. She was far from defective. No more perfect being had ever been created in the history of the earth. It was inflating and unbearably humbling at the same time. *We did this. We made her.*

Mia shot him her patented death glare. "There is nothing wrong with my daughter."

"So why the spare?"

Her gaze veered back to the baby and the stern glower returned. When she spoke, her voice was soft and rough, each word catching in her throat. "I love her too much and I've only known her a day. If anything ever happened to her, I'd just shatter into a million pieces and no one would ever be able to put me back together." She looked up, her eyes glistening with a rawness that only he ever got to see.

"We'll talk about it later," Chase promised. They'd argue about it later was more like it. Mia had not had an easy pregnancy. She'd been on bedrest the last three months and she still looked pale from the emergency C-section. Chase would be scheduling his vasectomy just as soon as he was sure she wouldn't castrate him with a carving knife for getting one. But that was a fight for another day. "I'll buy you a spare. I hear they're cheap in China."

The nurse made a small, shocked sound in her throat and scuttled from the room.

Mia just scowled at him. Her gaze flickered over his features and she sighed. "Damn. I'll need your DNA too."

Chase snorted out a laugh. "Is that your way of asking for my sperm? Cuz you know how hot I get when you go all science-y on me, but the doctors said no funny business for at least six weeks."

"I'll need your sperm too, obviously, but also your DNA. For cloning."

"Cloning," Chase repeated, forcing himself not to laugh. Mia was supposed to be resting and if she saw him laughing at her, she'd strain herself decking him.

"If anything happens to you, I'll have to clone you," Mia said, dead serious. "I can't be expected to live without you."

At that Chase did laugh, warmth tightening his chest. "You're such a sappy romantic." He bent and kissed his wife, the woman who had shown him how to throw his heart into the hands of the universe but who refused to allow fate any say over hers. His fierce, scientific Mia whom he didn't doubt would keep him and Carmina safe by dint of her will alone. "You're just going to have to take that risk like the rest of us. Have a little faith in my ability to live forever, sweetheart."

"You suck."

"I love you too," he murmured against her lips.

Chase looked at his wife and the tiny scrap of perfection in her arms. All the proof he needed that magic existed. Magic of the love variety.

Scientifically proven, pocket watch-approved.

About the Author

An Alaskan born and raised, Vivi Andrews still lives in the frozen north when she isn't indulging her travel addiction by bouncing around the globe. Whether at home or on the road, she's always at work on her next happily-ever-after. For more about her books or the exploits of a nomadic author, please visit her website at www.viviandrews.com, stop by her blog viviandrews.blogspot.com, or email vivi@viviandrews.com.

She could resist this bad boy...if he wasn't so darned good at it.

Superlovin'
© 2012 Vivi Andrews
A *Midnight Justice* story.

Darla Powers, a.k.a. DynaGirl, is the Jessica Rabbit of crime fighters, but that doesn't mean it's easy finding a date. When her latest ex opines she's not helpless enough to make him feel manly, she flies off to take out her romantic frustrations on a villain dumb enough to pick tonight to break into a secret government vault.

Lucien Wroth's father may be a famous supervillain, but Lucien doesn't see himself as a bad guy. Just one determined to free his baby sister from a supercriminal's clutches. He's this close to getting his hands on a vital set of schematics when one sultry superheroine catches him elbow-deep in a top-secret safe.

Darla is horrified when Lucien's pretty face—and bulging muscles—distract her enough to let him get away. No one escapes DynaGirl. But somewhere along the way to getting revenge for her public humiliation, she and Lucien become uneasy allies...resisting an all-too-easy attraction. Suddenly she suspects the perfect man for a good girl just might be a very bad boy.

Warning: This book contains heroes, villains, mind-games, epic battles, bustiers, leather, and an infamous "Women of the Cape" Maxim photo spread.

Available now in ebook from Samhain Publishing.

Real vampires do musicals.

Biting Oz
© *2012 Mary Hughes*
Biting Love, Book 5

Gunter Marie "Junior" Stieg is stuck selling sausage for her folks in small-town Meiers Corners. Until one day she's offered a way out—the chance to play pit orchestra for a musical headed for Broadway: *Oz, Wonderful Oz.*

But someone is threatening the show's young star. To save the production, Junior must join forces with the star's dark, secretive bodyguard, whose sapphire eyes and lyrical Welsh accent thrill her. And whose hard, muscular body sets fire to her passions.

Fierce as a warrior, enigmatic as a druid, Glynn Rhys-Jenkins has searched eight hundred years for a home. Junior's get-out-of-Dodge attitude burns him, but everything else about her inflames him, from her petite body and sharp mind to what she can do with her hip-length braid.

Then a sensuous, insidious evil threatens not only the show, but the very foundations of Meiers Corners. To fight it, Junior and Glynn must face the truth about themselves—and the true meaning of love and home.

Warning: Cue the music, click your heels together, make a wish and get ready for one steamy vampire romance. Contains biting, multiple climaxes, embarrassing innuendos, ka-click/ka-ching violence, sausage wars and—shudder—pistachio fluff.

Available now in ebook and print from Samhain Publishing.

It's all about the story...

Romance

HORROR

www.samhainpublishing.com

CPSIA information can be obtained
at www.ICGtesting.com
Printed in the USA
FFOW01n1234210414
4916FF